Joan Jonker was bor[n] [...] [...] tireless campaigner for the charity-run organisation Victims of Violence, and she lives in Southport with her son. She has two sons and two grandsons.

Joan Jonker is the author of *Victims of Violence*, and two other novels, *When One Door Closes* and *Home Is Where The Heart Is*, which are available from Headline. Her affectionate and humorous tales of Liverpool life have already won her many fans in her hometown and are sure to delight readers everywhere.

Man Of The House

Joan Jonker

HEADLINE

First published in 1992
by Print Origination (NW) Ltd

First published in hardback in 1994
by HEADLINE BOOK PUBLISHING

Reprinted in this edition in 1995
by HEADLINE BOOK PUBLISHING

15 17 19 20 18 16

ISBN 0 7472 4660 2

Typeset by CBS, Felixstowe, Suffolk

Printed and bound in Great Britain by
Mackays of Chatham PLC, Chatham, Kent

HEADLINE BOOK PUBLISHING
A division of Hodder Headline PLC
338 Euston Road, London NW1 3BH

To my family and many friends
for their encouragement,
and a special thanks to Mary Johnson
for her help and patience with my erratic apostrophes.

Chapter One

'Sod it! I'm sweatin' cobs an' gettin' nowhere!' Eileen muttered under her breath. She glared first at the donkey stone in her hand, then at the offending front door step that had resisted all her attempts to come up white. 'Waste of time, anyway! When the kids come chargin' in it'll be as black as the hobs of hell again!'

With a look of disgust on her face, Eileen threw the donkey stone into the hall before leaning against the wall. Rivulets of sweat were running down her face and she wiped them away with the corner of her pinny before folding her arms across her waist, where they disappeared from view beneath the mountainous bosom. Her attention was drawn to the house opposite and the man perched precariously on top of a rickety ladder nailing coloured bunting to the frame of the bedroom window.

'I 'ope that ladder's safe, Tommy!' Eileen bawled. 'I'd hate yer to fall an' break yer fishin' tackle!'

Hanging on to the window sill like grim death, Tommy Wilson peered over his shoulder. 'Missus wouldn't worry,' he grinned, 'save her having one of her headaches every night.'

'Yer don't mean to tell me she gets away with that old

1

trick?' A laugh rumbled in Eileen's tummy, and when it erupted every ounce of her eighteen-stone body shook. 'Tell 'er the bloody war's over now, and that includes skirmishes in the bedroom.'

Tommy lifted his hand to deliver one more blow with the hammer before answering. 'I'll tell her you said that, but I'll make sure I'm out of arms reach when I do! She packs a powerful punch does my Missus!'

'Yer'll 'ave to learn to put yer foot down then, won't yer!' Eileen watched as Tommy came down the ladder, testing each rung first before lowering his weight on to it. 'Either that, or learn to duck!'

Tommy chuckled, wondering if his wife had heard the exchange between him and their neighbour opposite. There'd be hell to pay if she had. Ada didn't always appreciate Eileen Gillmoss's jokes. But Tommy liked the big woman. At least she knew how to smile. Not like some he could mention who looked as though a smile would crack their faces.

Eileen waved back as Tommy moved indoors, then gazed up and down the street where people were rushing to finish the decorations in time for the street party due to start at four o'clock. She'd heard all the streets in the neighbourhood were being decorated, as people prepared to celebrate the end of the war in Europe.

The end of the war! Eileen screwed her eyes up tight. Even though she'd heard Winston Churchill on the wireless saying that Germany and Italy had surrendered, and hostilities in Europe had ceased, she couldn't believe it.

'Goin' asleep on yer feet, are yer?'

Eileen opened her eyes to see Cissie Maddox standing in front of her. She grinned sheepishly. 'I couldn't sleep if I tried, Cissie! I'm shakin' like a leaf with excitement.' She swept her arm wide to take in the coloured bunting stretching across the street from house to house, the Union Jacks of every size and shape swaying in the slight breeze, and pictures of the King and Queen, with the two Princesses, adorning the windows of nearly every house. 'Looks great, doesn't it? Makes yer feel real proud.'

'Everyone's done a good job,' Cissie admitted. She lived two doors down from Eileen, and they'd been neighbours for years. They'd had their differences over those years, mostly about the kids fighting, but all that was forgotten now. She was the same age as Eileen and matched her in size ounce for ounce. But Cissie took more care of her appearance, with hair neatly permed, a face that was seldom seen without make-up, and clothes that didn't look as though they'd come off a rag and bone cart.

'Have yer made the cakes and jellies?' Cissie's face was serious. 'We'll have to start bringin' the tables out soon.'

'Keep yer hair on, Cissie! Everything's under control,' Eileen's chubby cheeks moved upwards to cover her eyes as she grinned. 'No, I'm not goin' to tell lies today, I might put the mockers on meself! I haven't done nowt, Cissie! Me mam's made the cakes, jellies and blancmange. All I did was boil the water.'

'Thank God for that!' Cissie rolled her eyes expressively. 'At least we'll be able to eat the cakes.'

'Watch it now, Cissie! We've just got one war over, don't you an' me start another one!'

'Okay, we'll call a truce till tomorrow.' Cissie was silent for a moment, then sighed softly. 'We'll 'ave our fellers home soon.'

'Oooh, don't mention it, Cissie!' Eileen looked up to the skies. Her Bill had been a prisoner of war since 1940, and the only contact she'd had with him in all that time had been through heavily censored letters. 'Every time I think about it, I get that excited I 'ave to run to the lavvy! I'm not kiddin', I've been to the lavvy that many times today I've worn a groove in our back yard.'

Cissie touched Eileen's arm in a rare gesture of sympathy. Her husband was in the army too, but, thank God, he'd never been further than the Isle of Man. 'It's been a long time, and you've had a lot to put up with.'

'It was a case of 'aving to put up with it!' Tears were threatening and Eileen had no intention of making a fool of herself in front of Cissie Maddox. 'I'd better get in an' give me mam a hand.'

Seeing the signs, Cissie moved away. 'I'll give yer a knock when it's time to bring the table out. And don't you go luggin' that big table out on yer own, d'yer hear? Get one of the men to give yer a hand.'

Eileen had her foot on the front step. 'Our Billy should be 'ome in time to help. I've sent him up to the Sedgemoors to ask if Mary wants to bring the kids to the party.' She gave a deep chuckle. 'Can't see them havin' a street party round by them . . . they're too posh for anythin' so common.'

Eileen walked through to the kitchen where her mother, Maggie, was just taking a tray of fairy cakes out of the oven. 'Mmmm! They smell good, Mam!'

'That's the lot, thank God!' Maggie slipped the hot tray on to the wooden draining board. 'They should smell good, too! All our sugar and margarine ration has gone into them. And I'm warning you, if you don't keep the kids out of here there'll be none left for the party.'

'I wonder where the kids 'ave got to?' Eileen frowned. 'I haven't seen them for ages.'

'Probably wandering round, looking at the decorations.' Maggie was edging a knife expertly round the cakes to dislodge them from the tray before sliding them on to a plate. 'They've never seen anything like it before.'

'Aye, poor little buggers.' When Eileen nodded her layer of chins wobbled. 'They're too young to remember the street parties we used to have for Empire Day.'

Maggie ran her flour-caked hands down the front of her pinny. 'I'll have to sit down for half an hour before I get washed and changed, me feet are killing me. And a cup of tea would go down a treat.'

'Go an' sit down then, an' I'll make us a cuppa.' Eileen pushed her mother into the living room. 'Go on, do as yer told, unless yer want a fourpenny one.'

Mother and daughter sat in companionable silence facing each other across the table. The front door had been left open and a medley of sounds drifted in from the street, but both were lost in thought and oblivious to the racket outside. Eileen was studying her mother through lowered lids as she sipped on the piping hot tea. People said she took after her mother in looks, but, as Eileen mused now, her mother was only half her size. They might have looked alike years ago, but that was before Eileen started piling the weight on.

Eileen let out a soft sigh. The war years had certainly taken their toll on her mother. Her hair was now snowy white, and deep worry lines were etched on her forehead and under her eyes. She looked worn out, and Eileen blamed herself for it. When her dad had died fifteen years ago, it was she who persuaded her mother to come and live with her and Bill. Said it would be better than living in that big old house on her own. And the arrangement had worked fine until the war started and Bill had been called up. Eileen remembered how she'd jumped at the chance to work in the munitions factory when her mother had offered to mind the three children for her. Mainly it was because she wanted to do her bit for the war effort, but the money had certainly come in useful. They'd have been in queer street if they'd had to manage on Bill's army pay and the few bob her mother got in widow's pension. But no one had expected the war to last five years. So, in her sixties, when she should have been sitting back taking life easy, her mother had been saddled with three children to look after. Not that she'd ever complained. And when Eileen had offered to pack in work and look after her family, her mother wouldn't hear of it.

'I wonder how long it'll be before Bill gets home?' Maggie broke the silence. 'It could be only a matter of weeks.'

Eileen ran a finger round the rim of her cup. 'It's like a dream to me, Mam! To tell the God's honest truth, I'd got to the state where I thought I'd never see 'im again.'

'You'd better get used to the idea quick, my girl, and get yourself moving!' Maggie shook her head in despair as she eyed her daughter's limp, straggly, mousey-coloured hair, the smudges of dust streaked across the chubby face, and the washed-out dress under the washed-out pinny. The seams of the dress were all burst open, and Maggie would lay bets that there'd be a couple of pins holding the hem up. 'If Bill walked in now and saw you looking such a mess, he'd have a fit! And as for this . . . well! I just give up!' Maggie snorted in disgust at the chaotic state of the room. Clothes had been flung over the backs of chairs, and those that had missed their target were left to lie on the floor with the cast-off shoes, toys and newspapers. 'If I said this place looked like a pig sty, I'd be insulting the pigs!'

A lazy smile spread across Eileen's face. 'Don't be gettin' yer knickers in a twist, missus! I've got two days off work to celebrate the end of the war, an' I'm gonna do just that! I'm gonna celebrate like I've never bloody celebrated before.'

Maggie tutted. 'What have I told you about swearing? If Bill hears you, you won't half get it in the neck, I'm warning you!'

Despite her words, Maggie was having trouble keeping her face straight. She could never hold out long against her daughter's infectious humour. 'You know, I must have a screw loose, putting up with you all these years!' Maggie scraped her chair back. 'Come on, let's get ourselves tidied up.'

Eileen stretched across the table and clasped her mother's arm. 'Sit down a minute, Mam, I've got something to tell yer.'

Maggie was so used to having her leg pulled, she hesitated. But there was something about the set of Eileen's face that made her curious, so she sat down. 'Make it snappy, or we'll never be ready in time.'

'I was goin' to tell yer tonight, when we had more time. But I'll tell yer now, save yer walkin' round like a wet week.' Eileen licked her finger and rubbed it over a tea stain on the oilcloth covering the table. 'Remember when Mary and Harry got married and went to live in Orrell Park?' She looked up to see her mother's eyebrows raised in surprise. 'Just be patient, Mam! All will be revealed as I go along, but I've got to start at the beginning. I know I skitted Mary about goin' to live in a posh house, an' everythin', but deep down I was a bit jealous. Every time I went up there and saw how nice she kept the house, and then came back to this dump, it was like a slap in the gob.'

'You can't compare yourself with Mary!' Maggie said heatedly, quick to defend the daughter she'd watched struggle for the last five years. 'Mary didn't have three kids to look after, and go out and earn a living! She had a husband bringing in a good wage every week!'

'I know that, Mam! And I don't begrudge Mary a thing, honest I don't, 'cos she's me best mate! And it wasn't Harry's fault that the Forces wouldn't have him! But seein' their house, an' our Rene's posh house at the Old Roan, well it started me thinkin',' Eileen grinned into her mother's flushed face. 'D'yer know Cookson's shop in Walton Vale? Well, for the last three and a half years I've been puttin' five bob a week away in a club there. And yer know what, Mam? I've got me club card upstairs with forty pound ten shillings on it.'

'Go way!' Maggie gasped. 'Fancy you not letting on all this time.'

'I didn't tell yer at first 'cos I didn't think I could keep it up! Yer know what I'm like with money, it goes through me hands like water. And I didn't half miss that five bob every week in the beginning, I can tell yer! Many's the time I was tempted to use it, like when our Billy wanted new kecks and was walking round nearly bare arsed, or when the sole came off our Joan's shoes. Then I'd think of Mary's house, an' our Rene's, and I held out. Then after a while, when I could see

8

the money mounting up, I was determined to carry on, no matter what.' Eileen looked directly into her mother's eyes. 'Isn't that a nice surprise, Mam?'

'You can say that again!' Maggie was flabbergasted. 'What are you going to do with all that money?'

'Mr Cookson said he'll get me a dining room suite for here, an' something for the bedroom. It'll only be that Utility stuff they're makin' now, but Mr Cookson said it's very good.'

'I don't know what to say, love!' Maggie was so happy for her daughter she felt like crying. It was about time something nice happened in her life.

'There's more to come, Mam!' Eileen's eyes were lost in the folds of flesh that crept upwards when she laughed. 'I may as well give yer all the good news in one go, so as yer can get that worried look off yer gob an' enjoy yourself! I've got enough Sturla's cheques in me bag, an' clothing coupons, to rig us all out for Bill comin' home. That's me, you an' the kids. Oh, an' yer'll be pleased to know I've booked an appointment to 'ave me hair permed next week, when I'm on night shift.'

'Well, I never!' Maggie's head moved from side to side. 'I can't believe it! Here's me been worrying meself to death about Bill coming home to this mess. I had visions of him walking in, taking one look round and walking straight out again.'

'Mam, if he's missed me as much as I've missed him, he won't be interested in anywhere but the bedroom.' Eileen saw her mother's embarrassed blush and laughed. 'I know you think I'm a loose hussy, but I couldn't care less! If I have me own way, no one will see Bill for a week.'

Maggie tutted. 'You'd make the devil himself blush, you would! I don't know who you take after, but it's certainly not me!'

'Oh, aye! What did yer coal man look like?' Eileen roared. 'Or perhaps it's the milkman I take after!'

This time Maggie's chair was pushed back with a vengeance. 'You can please yourself, but I'm going to get ready for the party.' She left the room in a huff, but Eileen's long guffaws followed her up the stairs and by the time Maggie reached the landing she was doubled up with laughter. The last five years might have been hard going, but she wouldn't have swapped living with her eldest born for the grandest mansion in the world.

Chapter Two

Church bells, silent for so long, rang out their message of thanksgiving. The ships in the Mersey blew their sirens and bus and car drivers hooted their horns. It was a day for rejoicing and it seemed the whole population of Liverpool had turned out to celebrate as one big family. Main roads were packed tight with people who wanted to share their relief, joy and pride. Friends stopped to hug and kiss, their laughter mixed with tears. Complete strangers were shaken by the hand and embraced, and anyone wearing a service uniform was surrounded by a back-slapping crowd and hailed as a hero. Even those who had lost loved ones on the battle fields or in the blitz of nineteen forty-one, when so much of the city was destroyed, came out to celebrate the defeat of Hitler and Mussolini. The atmosphere was heady with emotion as people linked arms to sing 'The White Cliffs of Dover' and Vera Lynn's other much loved song, 'We'll Meet Again'. And long snake-like lines were formed as revellers danced the conga across busy main roads, bringing traffic to a standstill. Bus drivers were seen to leave their vehicles to join on to the end of these human chains. Timetables were thrown to the wind as legs kicked out to the accompaniment of 'Aye, aye, Conga!'

This was a day for the history books, and people up and down the country were determined to make it a memorable one.

In hundreds of side streets, neighbours were celebrating with parties of their own. But if a prize were to be given to the most noisy and boisterous, it would surely go to Bray Street. And it wasn't the children making the noise, either! They'd been stunned into silence at the sight of their kitchen tables being carried out to be added to a line which stretched down the centre of the cobbled street. And when the food appeared they were wide-eyed with amazement. They'd never seen so much food in their lives. The jellies were made from gelatine, the cakes with powdered egg and the blancmange with powdered milk, but to the kids it was like something from a fairy tale. With paper hats on their heads, they tucked in with gusto, afraid the mirage would disappear before their eyes. And while the children were feasting themselves, the grown-ups indulged in the beer and port wine they'd clubbed together to buy. So by the time the food had been demolished, the grown-ups were full of merriment and ready to let themselves go. The men removed some of the tables, Tommy Wilson was persuaded to bring his accordion out, and the party started in earnest.

'In the name of God, just look at the state of her!' Maggie was leaning against the wall watching the antics of her daughter. Wearing her best blue floral dress, and without a pinny for once, Maggie didn't know whether to laugh or cry. 'What would you do with her?'

'Don't be worrying,' Ada Wilson was holding her tummy, laughing at the sight of Eileen attempting a tango with Cissie

Maddox. Two eighteen-stone women tripping the light fantastic was a sight that brought tears to Ada's eyes. 'She's the life and soul of the party!'

'Is that what she is?' Maggie answered dryly. 'I think she's had a few too many drinks.'

At that moment Tommy Wilson broke into a Scottish reel and Cissie gave up. 'I've had it,' she gasped.

'Go on!' Eileen puffed. 'Yer can't take it!' She was out of breath, but being on her own didn't deter Eileen. With one hand on her head and the other on her ample hip, she broke into a jig. With an audience clapping and cheering her on, she lifted a leg and began twirling it around, showing the legs of her knickers which were minus the elastic.

It was at this moment that Mary and Harry Sedgemoor, with their two children, turned into the street. 'Oh, my God, I don't believe it!' Harry was giving two-year-old Tony a piggy back, and he held on tight to the child's hands as he roared with laughter. 'Do you see what I see, or are my eyes deceiving me?'

'Oooh, I wish we had a camera,' Mary chuckled. 'We could pull her leg soft over this.'

'Auntie Eileen!' Three-year-old Emma made a dash forward and Mary had to grab her quick. 'I want to see Auntie Eileen!' The little girl struggled to free herself so she could run to her favourite Auntie. 'Let go of me, Mummy, please!'

The music stopped, and as Eileen mopped the sweat from her brow she spotted her friends. 'Yer'll 'ave to bring the next turn on now, folks! Me mates have arrived.'

Moving through the crowds, Eileen held her arms wide. 'Where's my two little sweethearts, then?'

Emma reached her first and was clasped in a bear hug

when young Tony pulled on Eileen's skirt. 'Lift me up, Auntie Eileen,' he lisped. There hadn't been many pleasures in Eileen's life in the past five years, except for her three kids and her mother. But there were two that would always stay in her mind. And that was when Mary and Harry had asked her to be godmother, first to Emma, and then to Tony. And she loved the two children as though they were her own.

'Yer've missed all the eats!' Eileen looked over the heads of the children. 'I thought yer'd 'ave been here ages ago.'

'We would have been, but we had to stop and look at all the decorations,' Mary was still giggling over the sight of the big woman doing the Highland fling. 'Do I need to ask if you're enjoying yourself?'

Eileen grinned sheepishly. 'Well, what the hell, kid! The war's over and my feller will be home soon! Isn't that something to be happy about?'

Harry patted his pocket. 'I've got a camera in here, and the next time you give me cheek in work, I'm going to let everyone see your version of a Scottish reel.'

Harry was Eileen's boss in the munitions factory. But he was much more than that . . . he was a good mate. 'Blackmail, eh? Well, two can play at that game, old son!'

'I should be so lucky to have done something you can blackmail me with,' Harry began to shake with laughter. 'I noticed you've got your blue ones on today.'

'Go on with yer, yer cheeky bugger!' Eileen's hand went to her mouth. 'Oh, isn't Auntie Eileen naughty for swearin',' she looked down into two pairs of bright eyes, one vivid blue, the other a deep velvety brown. 'Shall we give Auntie Eileen a smack?'

'No!' chorused the two children. They loved this big

14

woman who always made them laugh. 'You're not naughty . . . is she, Mummy?'

Torn between teaching them right from wrong, Mary compromised, 'Auntie Eileen isn't naughty, but the words that come out of her mouth are sometimes very naughty. But we'll forgive her this time, shall we?'

'Let's go in and I'll make yez a cuppa.' Singing 'Roll Out The Barrel', and with a tiny hand clasped in each of hers, Eileen swayed through the crowd, which had quietened down without her to lead the singing. 'Make way folks! I'll just 'ave five minutes with me mates, then I'll be out again.'

'There yer go!' Eileen lifted the two children on to the couch. 'I'll scrounge yez some lemonade in a minute, but let me see to yer mam and dad first.' With a grin on her face and her eyes twinkling with happiness, Eileen turned to Harry. 'D'yer want tea, or something stronger? I've got a little drop of the hard stuff put away especially for you.'

'Go on, you twisted my arm,' Harry laughed. 'But I'll need more than a drop to catch up with you.'

'What yer want and what yer'll get are two different things, mate! Don't forget there's been a war on, an' luxuries are in short supply.' Eileen waddled towards the kitchen muttering under her breath so the children couldn't hear. 'I'll soon be gettin' somethin' that's been bloody well non-existent for the last five years! An' that's a man in me bed!' Eileen struck a match over a gas ring and put the battered kettle on. She knew Mary wouldn't touch whisky, so she'd make her a cuppa. From the kitchen cabinet she took two glasses and a half bottle of whisky which, after several sly drinks, was already half empty. Her eyes squinting, she measured two

equal amounts into the two glasses then slyly hid the bottle at
the back of the crockery in the cupboard. With a glass in each
hand she turned to the living room, but stopped at the door.
Emma was sitting on Mary's lap while young Tony stood
between Harry's knees. What a lovely-looking family they
are, Eileen thought. Mary, at twenty-five, was beautiful, with
her long, blonde, naturally curly hair, wide vivid blue eyes,
long dark eyelashes beneath perfectly shaped dark brows,
gleaming white teeth and skin as smooth as a baby's bottom.
With a figure as good as any film star, she was a real cracker.
And Emma was the spitting image of her. She was going to
be a beauty when she grew up.

Eileen's eyes went to Harry and Tony. There was nothing
of Mary in Tony, he was a tiny replica of his dad, with dark
hair and deep brown eyes. He even had a dimple in his chin,
like Harry. If he grew up to be as handsome as his dad, with
the same kind nature, he wouldn't go far wrong.

Eileen sniffed. There'd been times when the Sedgemoors'
marriage hadn't been all sweetness and light, but thank God
that was all behind them now.

'I've put the kettle on to make yer a cup of tea, kid!'
Eileen bustled in. 'The kettle won't be long.' She placed a
glass in front of Harry. 'Get that down yer, mate!'

Footsteps came running down the hall and Eileen groaned.
'The charge of the bloody Light Brigade! No peace for the
wicked.'

'Hi, Auntie Mary! Hi, Uncle Harry!' Eileen's two daughters
ran in, breathless. 'Can we take Emma and Tony out to the
party?' The two girls looked like twins, but there was two
years between them. Edna, the baby of the family, was ten,
but she was as tall as twelve-year-old Joan. And, Eileen was

16

fond of saying, she was a damn sight more forward and cheeky. Both as thin as rakes, they had their mother's mousey-coloured, straggly hair and hazel eyes. Today they'd been allowed to wear their best dresses, and, much to Eileen's surprise and relief, they'd managed to keep them clean.

'D'yer want to come and hear the music, Tony?' Joan coaxed, while Edna stood in front of Emma asking the same question. 'We'll look after them, Auntie Mary, promise!'

Mary looked across at Harry, and when he nodded she let Emma slip from her knee. 'No going out of the street, d'you hear?'

'Oh, for Christ's sake!' Eileen's eyes rolled to the ceiling. 'Will yer stop mamby-pambying them, kid! Anyone would think the wind was goin' to blow them away!' Emma and Tony were out of the door like a shot before their mother had time to change her mind, and Eileen grinned. 'Mind you, there's times I've wished for a gale force wind to blow my three away.'

'Where's Billy?' Mary asked. 'I haven't seen him around.'

Billy was Eileen's eldest and the apple of her eye. She'd deny she had a favourite, and she really did love all her kids, but Billy was special because he looked so much like his dad. 'He's gone down to Walton Vale to see some of his mates.' There was pride in Eileen's voice. 'He's fourteen in a few weeks, yer know. He'll be leavin' school in July an' gettin' himself a job.'

'He's a big lad for his age.' Harry finished off his whisky. 'He'd easy pass for sixteen.'

'Don't I know it! When he was younger I couldn't keep him in kecks because he wore the arse out of them. Now he's growin' so fast he's growin' out of them before he has a chance to wear them out.' A sly grin crossed Eileen's face. 'Not a word, but I've got him a pair of long kecks for when he starts work.'

'Not before time,' Harry told her. 'He's far too big for short trousers.'

'He's not goin' in long trousers till he starts work,' Eileen answered. 'He might look grown up, but he's still daft enough to go slidin' down the railway embankment and tearin' the arse out of his kecks.' Her eyes widened as she pushed her chair back. 'Oh, my God, I forgot I'd put the water on! There'll be no arse left in me kettle!'

The empty whisky bottle stood in the middle of the table and Eileen's face was flushed with the mixture of drink and excitement. Her glass clutched between her chubby hands and her dimpled elbows resting on the table, she grinned at her two best friends. She'd told them in great detail, and much pride, about the money she'd been saving in Cookson's shop, and what she intended spending it on. 'So, I won't know meself in a few weeks time.' Her words were slurred and she noticed the smile exchanged between Mary and Harry. 'Okay, wise guys! But yer'll be laughin' the other shide of yer faces in a couple of weeks. Yer'll 'ave to wipe yer feet before yer get over me doorstep, and yez'll 'ave to stand up 'cos no one's gonna be allowed to sit on me new furniture.'

Harry had no difficulty keeping his face straight. 'Mrs Gillmoss, you are as drunk as a lord.'

'An' you, Mr Sedgemoor, are bloody jealous!' Eileen tilted her head to drain the last drop of whisky. 'Anyway, I'm not drunk!' Mischief danced in her eyes. 'A bit tiddly, perhaps, but not legless . . . yet!'

There was deep affection on Mary's face for this big, loud-mouthed woman who was always there when you needed her. It was Eileen who had saved her sanity when things had seemed so bad Mary never thought she'd survive. 'Before you get all this posh furniture, are you going to decorate?'

'I'm goin' to 'ave a bloody good go, kid! I want this place lookin' like a palace for my Bill comin' home.'

'I'll give you a hand,' Harry was quick to offer. 'I'll scout around tomorrow and see if I can pick up some paper and paint. We could start at the weekend and between the two of us it shouldn't take too long to do the whole house.'

'That's my mate!' Eileen's face screwed up in a wink. 'With you to help, we'll get through this place like a dose of salts.'

'And me!' Mary wasn't going to be left out. It was always Eileen who had given, but now Mary saw a way of giving something in return. 'I'll get Doris next door to mind the children and I can give you a hand. I'm no good at paper hanging, but at least I can brush the floor and keep you going in cups of tea.'

Eileen stretched across the table and laid one hand on Mary's arm and the other on Harry's. She squeezed gently. 'Me two best mates!'

Chapter Three

'"Oh, I've got a loverly bunch o' coconuts, 'ere they are all standin' in a row",' Eileen sang at the top of her voice as she waddled down the hall, clapping her hands, her wide hips brushing the walls on either side. She was closely followed by Mary and Harry who were almost doubled up with laughter. '"Big ones, small ones, some as big as yer 'ead . . ."' Eileen stopped singing as she stepped from the dark hall into the bright daylight. A second later her loud laugh rang out. 'Ah, ay, kid! Wait till yer get an eyeful of this!'

'Why, what's up?' Mary's eyes followed Eileen's pointing finger to a table where Emma and Tony were sitting. Their eyes were the size of saucers as they spooned red jelly into their mouths while watching the antics of the grown-ups. Someone had put two cushions on Tony's chair, but even with the help of these his chin barely reached the top of the table, and most of the jelly was missing his mouth and landing on his blue and white romper suit.

'Ooh!' Mary growled through clenched teeth. 'Just look at the state of him!' She would have dashed forward but Eileen's hand restrained her.

'Knock it off, kid, it's supposed to be a party! Yer can't expect kids to look like angels all the time!' Eileen's head

21

jerked towards Harry. 'Is she always such a bloody fuss pot?'

Harry put his arm across Mary's shoulders and squeezed. 'Anything Mary does is okay with me.'

'Oh, my Gawd!' Eileen groaned. 'All this sloppy stuff is makin' me want to throw up!' Suddenly her fat arms grabbed Mary round the waist, lifted her off her feet and spun her round. 'Just you wait till my feller gets home, kid! We'll show yez 'ow to coochy coo.'

Harry's laugh accompanied Mary's blush. 'You'll be out of practice, won't you? If you want any advice, come to me.'

'Yer cheeky bugger!' Eileen lowered Mary to the ground. 'It might 'ave been a long time, but I've got a bloody good memory!' Her dig in the ribs almost sent Harry flying. 'I could teach you a thing or two, clever clogs!'

'For heavens sake don't encourage her!' Mary disentangled herself from Eileen's arms. 'I'm going to see to the children. You two can get on with it.'

'Whoops!' Eileen watched Mary walk away, thinking how pretty she looked in her white summer dress, her long blonde hair bouncing on her shoulders. Then the big woman turned to wink at Harry. 'Is your wife's mind really as pure as the driven snow?'

Harry tapped the side of his nose with a finger. 'Ah, now, that would be telling tales out of school.'

'Nanna!' Tony shrieked as he ducked under Mary's hand and slid from the chair. 'Here's Nanna and Granddad, Mummy.'

Mary turned to see Harry's mum and dad walking towards them. She watched with a smile on her face as Lizzie Sedgemoor scooped Tony up in her arms while her husband, George, waited for Emma to catch up with her brother then lifted her high in the air. Every time Mary saw them with the children she felt a deep sense of gratitude. Because although Emma wasn't their real granddaughter, she was treated exactly the same as Tony. Never, by word or deed, had they shown any favouritism. And one of these days, when she could pluck up the courage, she'd tell them how grateful she was.

'I've had jelly, Nanna.' Tony's sticky fingers were clutching her hair, but Lizzie Sedgemoor didn't care. She loved the bones of him, and Emma. And although at the time there'd been blue murder between her and Harry when he'd told her he was going to marry Mary Bradshaw even though she was expecting another man's child, Lizzie had never regretted having Mary for a daughter-in-law. She'd turned out to be a good wife to Harry, and as a mother she was second to none. Emma was a real little lady, well spoken and well behaved. But young Tony, now, was a very different kettle of fish. He was a little devil, always into mischief like Harry had been at his age.

'We thought you might be here.' George had to shout to make himself heard above the noise. 'There's a party in our street, but it's not a patch on this one.'

'That's because Eileen Gillmoss doesn't live in your street,' Harry answered, nodding his head to where Eileen was standing beside Tommy Wilson, her face doing contortions as she belted out the words of 'When Irish Eyes Are Smiling'. 'Eileen could have a party on her own!'

'Aye!' Lizzie grinned. 'You don't get many like her in a pound!' She kissed Tony before asking, 'Will you go to Daddy, sweetheart, while I go and sing with Auntie Eileen?'

'Well I'll be blowed!' George's mouth gaped in amazement. 'I haven't heard Lizzie sing in a month of

Sundays!' He sat down on a chair with Emma on his lap. 'Mind you, she had a fair singing voice when she was a girl.' Harry's mother was a well-built woman, but standing between Eileen and Cissie Maddox, their arms around each others shoulders, she looked quite slim. When they'd sung all the Irish songs they could think of, they started on the Scottish, their voices louder than the rest of the crowd put together.

Maggie was sitting next to George, with Tony on her knee. Tired with all the excitement, the little boy had lost the fight to keep his eyes open and was fast asleep in the crook of her arm. Maggie looked over at Mary who was sitting on one of the tables, her legs swinging in time to the music. 'Shall I put him on the couch for half an hour? He'll never be able to sleep properly with all this racket.'

'I'll take him from you.' Harry sprang to his feet. 'When he wakes up we'll have to make tracks home. We've left Mrs B. on her own long enough.'

'It's a pity Martha couldn't be here to see this,' George Sedgemoor said. 'I've never seen anything like it in all me born days.'

Harry took the sleeping child from Maggie and cradled him in his arms. 'Yeh, but it's not every day we win a war, is it, Dad?'

'No, you're right there, son!'

'Ooh, me head's splittin'!' Eileen propped her chin on her hands. But even though she felt lousy, her sense of humour didn't desert her. 'And I wish yer'd stop swayin' from side to side, Mam, yer makin' me feel sea sick.'

'Don't come looking to me for sympathy.' Maggie tried to look annoyed, but inside she couldn't stop laughing. How come this daughter of hers could turn everything into a joke? You could never stay angry with her for long because she always came up with something funny. 'Take a couple of aspirins and see if they help.'

'Ain't got none!' Eileen faced her mother across the table. The party was still going strong outside, but when the Sedgemoors had left, Eileen decided she'd had enough. Her throat was sore and every bone in her body ached from the dancing. 'It was some party though, Mam, wasn't it?'

'You can say that again!' Maggie said. 'And you certainly made the most of it, you made more noise than anybody.'

'Well, considerin' the size of me, I'd sound bloody funny with a little pip squeak voice, now wouldn't I?' Eileen laid her palms flat on the table and rested her head on them. 'I'll just calm down for a few minutes, then I'll go an' see what the kids are up to.'

'The two girls are playing in the street, so leave them for a while and have a rest.' Maggie intended getting the girls upstairs before their mother could see the state of their new dresses. They'd been crawling under the tables playing tag, and they were filthy. But if she washed them first thing in the morning, Eileen wouldn't know any different. What the eye don't see, the heart don't grieve, Maggie thought. 'Billy came back before, but you were too busy enjoying yourself to notice him. He wanted to go up to his mates again, and I said he could but to be back by nine o'clock.'

'Cooo-eee.' The sound brought Eileen's head up. 'Oh, Christ! It's our Rene!'

'Sshh, she'll hear you.' Maggie just had time to hiss before her younger daughter came in with her husband, Alan, and Victoria, their three-year-old daughter. It was hard to imagine that Rene was Eileen's sister, they were so different in every way. Rene was small and slim, with dark brown hair that was always set in the latest style, and attractive green eyes. She was always well dressed and well spoken. As Eileen would, and did say, she spoke as though she had a plum in her mouth.

'Hello, Mum.' Rene kissed her mother, then her eyes went to Eileen. 'You look a bit rough! Been out there enjoying yourself?'

'Yer could say that!' Eileen twisted in her chair. 'Hello, Alan! Yer won't mind if I don't stand up, will yer? Yer see, I'd fall flat on me face if I attempted to.'

'Hello, Auntie Eileen.' Victoria stood by Eileen's side, her young face wearing a serious expression. 'We didn't have a party in our road.'

'That's because yez live in a posh road, sweetheart.' Eileen grinned. 'It's only common folk like us what know 'ow to enjoy themselves.'

'Sit down and I'll make a pot of tea,' Maggie fussed. 'I can't offer you anything to eat because everything we had went towards the party.'

'That's all right, Mum, we've had something to eat.' Rene sat in the chair Maggie had vacated. 'Alan went in to work this morning, then we went to see his parents. We had a bite to eat there.'

The chair croaked in protest as Eileen swivelled round to where Alan was sitting. She was very fond of Alan. He was well educated, his parents lived in a nice house in the posh part of Allerton, but he wasn't a snob. Neither was he a coward. He'd been one of the first to join up, and because of his education he'd soon risen to the rank of Captain in the army. He was serving in the Middle East, under General Auchinleck, when he'd been wounded during the fighting, and his right arm had been so badly shattered he'd been shipped back to a hospital in England where his arm had been amputated. Everyone thought it would be the end of Alan's working life, but with much patience, and enduring a lot of pain, he'd proved them wrong. He'd had an artificial arm fitted, and the army had kept him on, giving him a desk job in the Ministry of Defence office in Liverpool. He was a handsome man, tall with blond hair, bright blue eyes and a ready smile.

'How's yer mum and dad, Alan?' Eileen hiccupped, and would have fallen off the chair if she hadn't grabbed the edge of the table. God, she felt terrible. The room was spinning round, and Alan with it. But she made a valiant effort. 'I bet they're over the moon, now the war's over.'

Alan could see Eileen's face was growing greener by the minute, and she was swaying dangerously on the chair. 'Mum and Dad are fine.' He winked across at Rene before saying softly, 'Why don't you go and lie down for half an hour? You'd feel much better after a rest.'

'Yes, come on, our kid!' Rene moved round the table and took hold of Eileen's arm. 'I'll give you a hand.'

Eileen was in no state to argue. Lumbering to her feet, and guided rather than supported by Rene, she staggered to the door. Holding on to the frame like grim death, she turned to Alan. 'I'm sorry about this, Alan.' The three hiccups came in quick succession and were followed by a sly grin. 'Right now I might not know me arse from me elbow, but somewhere in this drunken brain of mine, I do know this is the happiest day of me bloody life!'

27

* * *

'Well, thank God for that.' Maggie flopped down on one of the chairs by the table and gave out a long sigh. Joan and Edna had been in and she'd taken their new dresses off and put them in the sink to steep. Dressed in their school gymslips, they'd gone out to play again, taking Victoria with them. 'That's one load off me mind! If our Eileen had seen their new dresses, she'd have had a fit.'

'What beats me,' Rene said, 'is how anyone thinks the more they drink the more they should enjoy themselves! It's ridiculous to get in the state our Eileen's in!'

'She's the one who'll suffer, not us!' Maggie was quick to defend Eileen. She might criticise her daughter herself, but she wasn't having anyone else do it. 'Anyway, who can blame her? She's not seen her husband for five years, and doesn't know how he is except that he's in some prisoner of war camp in Germany!' Maggie shook her head. 'She's had to work hard for the last five years, has our Eileen! What with the kids to look after and going out to work! I don't know how she's kept up! And even if she has had too much to drink, I certainly don't begrudge her wanting to show how happy she is.'

'Mam, I don't begrudge our kid anythin'.' Rene's posh voice had gone, and her broad Liverpool accent back. 'Our Eileen is one in a million, an' I wouldn't 'ave her any different.' Her green eyes travelled to Alan. 'She was a pillar of strength when I needed her, and I'll never forget it.'

'Eileen's strength is her downfall,' Alan said quietly. 'Because she's always laughing and joking, everyone thinks she doesn't have a care in the world. She keeps her troubles to herself.'

Maggie made a fresh pot of tea, then, as they sat round the table, she told them of Eileen's secret savings. 'You could have knocked me over with a feather! You know what she's usually like with money, it comes in one hand and goes out the other!'

'Me and Alan have just been talking about the state of this place,' Rene said as she looked round the room. Apart from the old, scuffed furniture, there were rips in the wallpaper where the kids had been allowed to play toss the ball, there were dirty hand marks on the walls and woodwork, and the lino was torn in several places. 'She could do with throwing the whole lot out and starting from scratch.'

'That's just what she's going to do.' Maggie thrust her bust out proudly. 'Harry Sedgemoor's promised to give her a hand to decorate the whole house. I only hope they can get it all done before Bill comes home.'

'I'll come and give a hand,' Rene said quickly. 'I can paper quicker than our kid. Between the three of us, we'll get through the house in no time.'

'And Mary's coming,' Maggie told her. 'She can trim the paper and that'll save time.'

Alan was listening with frustration. It was at a time like this he cursed his disability. 'I'm sorry I can't offer to help,' he said quietly. 'But I can mind Victoria, and you could send Joan and Edna down. You'll get more done without the children under your feet.'

'Thank you, darling!' There was deep love in Rene's eyes. Only she knew what the war had cost her husband. A stranger seeing him sitting there now would think he was perfectly fit and well. It would only be after they'd been in his company for a while, they'd notice his right arm hanging useless by his side, a glove covering the artificial hand. 'That would be a big help, wouldn't it, Mam?'

Maggie grimaced. 'You don't know what you're letting yourself in for, son! Those two girls are holy terrors! Honestly, they'd make a saint swear!'

'Don't worry about me, I can cope,' Alan assured her. 'I'll put them in detention if they get out of hand.'

'You'd be better off putting yourself in detention and throwing away the key,' Maggie said dryly. 'I'd rather do a day's work down a coal mine than mind those two. So, while they're driving you to distraction, just remember that you were warned.'

Chapter Four

The bus drew up outside the munitions factory and as workers lined the aisle ready to get off, Eileen rubbed her sleeve over the steamed-up window and peered out. 'It's still there, Florrie,' she muttered to the woman sitting next to her. 'I thought it might 'ave disappeared over the last few days.'

Florrie stood up, glad the journey was over. Sitting next to Eileen Gillmoss had its compensations, but it also had its draw backs. You were always sure of a good laugh, but with the big woman taking up three quarters of the seat the journey was pure purgatory. The one cheek of her backside that had managed to stay on the seat was numb, and Florrie rubbed hard to bring back the circulation. 'I'll be glad when my feller's home and I can pack in work.'

'Yer not the only one, Florrie.' Eileen stepped from the bus and joined the afternoon shift workers making their way through the gate. She held her pass up for the security guard and gave him a wide grin. 'No need for gas masks today, Joe!'

'What?' Joe kept his face straight. 'I thought you had yours on!'

'Yer cheeky swine!' Eileen shook a fat fist. 'I've a good mind to come over there and sort you out.'

'Is that a threat or a promise?' Joe called after Eileen's retreating back. 'If it's a promise, I'll take you up on it.'

Eileen turned and walked back a few paces. Placing her bag on the ground, she squared her shoulders, thrusting her enormous bust out. With her hips swaying seductively, she patted her hair with one hand and did a very passable impersonation of Mae West. 'Why don't you come up and see me sometime, big boy, and I'll show you my etchings?'

For a few seconds Eileen shared Joe's laughter, then she hurried to clock on before making her way to the cloakroom. A smile still on her face, she pushed the door open. 'Did yez hear that . . .' The words died as Eileen noted the women who had been laughing and joking on the bus just a few minutes earlier were now standing quiet, a look of shocked horror on their faces. 'What's wrong?'

It was Maisie Phillips who answered. 'You know Isobel, who works in Mr Burton's office? Well we've just heard her husband's ship was blown up and there were no survivors.'

Eileen's mouth gaped. She'd thought the days of the dreaded telegram were over. 'But I thought there was no more fightin' now the war's over!' She gazed around the faces of the women. 'Are yez sure?'

'It happened the day before Germany surrendered,' Maisie told her. 'Isobel got a telegram on VE day.'

'Oh, my God! The poor kid!' The full implication hit Eileen. 'They only got married on his last leave, didn't they?'

Ethel Hignet came and stood beside Maisie, linking her arm. 'Yeah! They got married six months ago.'

'Bloody hell!' Eileen pinched the bridge of her nose, suddenly feeling very frightened. What would I do if they told me Bill was dead, she asked herself. The answer came quickly.

Stick me head in the bloody gas oven! After changing into their overalls and tying on their turbans, the women left the cloakroom to take over from the morning shift. The news about Isobel's husband had spread like wildfire, and the mind of every woman standing beside the conveyors in the shell inspection shop was on the pretty young woman who was now a widow after only six months of marriage. In fact, all she'd known of married life was the two weeks leave her husband had been given from his ship to get married.

Eileen looked across the conveyor and gave a pale smile to Jean Simpson who worked the other side of the machine. Jean had been put with Eileen when Mary had left to get married, and although that was over three years ago, Eileen still missed seeing Mary's pretty face opposite her. Not that Jean wasn't pretty, but she'd look a damn sight better if she didn't plaster her make-up on so thick. Sometimes Eileen thought she must have put it on with a trowel!

A smile crossed Eileen's face. She'd pulled Jean's leg unmercifully over the last three years about the American she was going out with. Told her he probably had a wife and six kids back in the States. His name was Ivan, he was a dentist, and in the three years he'd been stationed in the old Merton Hotel in Stanley Road, had risen to the rank of Major. Jean didn't half swank about him at first, until Eileen told her to belt up 'cos she was sick of hearing his name. Then she met him one day when he'd come to pick Jean up and was waiting outside the factory gates in a jeep. And he was so friendly it was impossible not to like him. He was very generous, always sending some luxury in for Eileen that you couldn't buy in the shops. But in spite of that, Eileen still harboured the thought that he had a wife back in the States and was only using Jean.

But two weeks ago Eileen had had her eye wiped and Jean the last laugh when she'd come into work flashing an 'I told you so' smile and a large diamond engagement ring on her finger.

'How are you fixed for Saturday?' Harry had sneaked up behind Eileen and grinned when she jumped.

'Christ, Harry! Yer frightened the livin' daylights out of me!' Eileen put a hand to her heart. 'I nearly jumped out of me skin!'

'Go on, you were miles away!' Harry leaned against the conveyor. 'I managed to get some wallpaper and paint, so we can make a start on Saturday if you like.'

'That was quick.' Eileen squinted at him. 'Where did yer manage to get the paper and paint from?'

'Would you worry where I got it from?' Harry grinned. 'Considering nearly everything you've bought through the war has either been black market or fallen off the back of a lorry.'

'Harry, I don't care where yer got it from as long as yer got it!' Eileen's eyes shifted from Harry to the moving conveyor then back again. 'Saturday suits me fine.'

'I've only got six rolls, enough for one room, so you'll have to scout around yourself if you want the whole house doing.' Harry straightened up. Twice every shift he did a check on the conveyors to make sure there were no problems, but today it seemed a pointless exercise. 'Daft to go on making shells when the war's over, isn't it?'

'I've been thinkin' that meself,' Eileen said. 'But I hope they go on makin' them for a while yet, 'cos I need the money.'

'Don't we all?' Harry sighed. 'But there's bound to be a lot of changes in the near future and I'm wondering where we'll all end up!'

Through lowered lids, Eileen surveyed the faces of the women round the canteen table. For over five years six of them had shared the same table, but it looked as though they'd soon be going their separate ways, never to see each other again. Jean Simpson would be getting married and making her home in the States. No chance of ever seeing her again! Eileen's eyes moved to Maisie Phillips. Maisie was small and thin with bleached hair. The lines of age were hidden under the thick make-up she wore, and nobody knew how old she really was. She'd been thirty-nine when she'd started work at the factory and according to her she was still thirty-nine. Eileen thought she'd lost ten years somewhere along the line because Maisie was fifty if she was a day. But Eileen would never find out because Maisie lived in Huyton and there was no chance of them bumping into each other at the shops.

'We're all very quiet,' Ethel Hignet's ill-fitting false teeth clicked into place. 'I bet we're all thinking the same thing . . . how long it's going to be before this place closes.' Ethel was a foot taller than her friend Maisie, and as thin as a rake. Eileen was always telling her that when she turned sideways you couldn't see her. She followed Maisie everywhere like a pet dog, and agreed with everything she said. Patting her black frizzy hair, she asked, 'Well, am I right?'

'We'd 'ave to be bloody thick not to know things aren't goin' to stay as they are for much longer,' Eileen growled, picking a long chip off her plate and dipping it in the baked beans. 'An' d'yer know what? I've been sick of the sight of yez for the last five years, but I won't 'alf miss yez.' She took a bite of the chip, ignored the red sauce that trickled down her chin and went on speaking with her mouth half full. 'It won't seem the same not seein' yer ugly faces every day.'

The women exchanged glances. They all felt the same, but never thought they'd hear such an admission coming from the lips of Eileen Gillmoss. She usually turned everything into a joke. Maisie studied her face thoughtfully. If it carried on like this they'd all be in tears. Better to take a leaf out of Eileen's book and make a joke of it. 'There's one thing I will miss,' Maisie said, 'and that's your table manners! Honest to God, I'd be ashamed to take you anywhere!'

Eileen made a fist of her hand and rested her layer of chins on it. This was more like it, she thought. I was beginning to feel morbid. Fluttering her eyelashes she put on what she called her posh voice. 'Har you by hany chance hinsinuating that I don't have hany manners, Mrs Phillips?' A grin creased Eileen's face. ''Cos if yer are, I'll give yer a slap in the gob that'll knock yer into the middle of next week.'

There were smiles round the table now as Maisie asked, 'You an' whose army?' She leaned forward and grinned into Eileen's face. 'Do us a favour and wipe your chin! You're worse than a flippin' baby!'

Eileen rubbed a hand across her chin then wiped it on her overall. 'I'd buy a bib, but they don't make them in my size.'

Maisie stood up, followed quickly by Ethel. 'It's time to get back.' She walked a few paces then turned. 'A tablecloth would do the trick.'

'Ha-ha, very funny.' Eileen was stumped for a second, then she shouted after Maisie, 'We don't 'ave tablecloths in our 'ouse! Would yer settle for a sheet?'

* * *

The house was quiet when Eileen let herself in, and she sighed with relief as she walked down the hall. She wasn't in the mood for the kids chattering and arguing . . . not tonight. She was tired, and after she'd had a cuppa she'd hit the hay.

It was dark in the living room, but the light in the kitchen was on and Eileen could see her mother pottering around. 'I thought yer'd be in bed by now, Mam!'

'I thought I'd wait up for you.' Maggie's face was flushed and Eileen sensed her mother was on pins over something. But it couldn't be anything bad because Eileen knew her mother well enough to know that if there was anything wrong she'd have been on the front step waiting.

'Go and sit down and I'll bring you a drink in,' Maggie fussed. 'I've got the kettle on, it won't be long.'

Eileen waited till they were both seated with a cup of tea in their hands, before saying, 'Whatever it is, Mam, spit it out!'

'Alan called in on his way home from work. He's been trying to get some news about the camp where Bill is, but he said things are chaotic at the moment because there's hundreds of camps and it's impossible to find out anything.' Maggie paused for breath. 'He said to tell you that the army are working flat out to get the prisoners home as soon as possible and he'd keep on trying to get some information for you. The minute he hears anything definite, he'll come down right away and let you know.'

Eileen felt a shiver run down her spine. It had been such a long time, but now the waiting was nearly over. 'Does Alan think he'll come straight home?'

Maggie shook her head. 'He didn't say, love! But with the

hundreds of thousands of prisoners, it's going to be a big job.'

'I've waited five years, Mam, I can wait a few more weeks. As long as I know he's safe, that's the main thing.'

'It'll give you a chance to get the house ship-shape.' Maggie wasn't going to tell her daughter that Alan had said some prisoners might be in a bad state. News filtering through to the War Office was that the British troops who had reached the camps were horrified by the conditions the prisoners had been kept in. But it would serve no purpose putting that sort of worry on Eileen's shoulders until they knew for sure how Bill was. 'You'll need a few weeks to get this place ready.'

'Well, I've made a start, Mam!' Eileen reached over and put her cup on the table that had one leg shorter than the others and wobbled at the slightest touch. 'I called in to Cookson's on me way to work, and Mr Cookson will 'ave me dining room suite in by a week on Monday. He showed me one he 'ad in the back of the shop, an' it's in a dark shiny wood. It's got a sideboard, table and four chairs, an' it's lovely, Mam! We won't know ourselves, we'll be that posh!'

Maggie raised her brows. 'How much?'

'Just over twenty pounds for the suite, and a couple of pounds for some lino.' The tiredness had left Eileen now and she felt on top of the world. 'It'll cost me a few quid for wallpaper and paint, then we need a new rug for 'ere to finish the room off. I reckon there'll be enough over to buy a new bed and some sheets and things. The old wardrobe and dressing table will 'ave to do for the time bein', but if I give them a good polish they should be all right.'

'I can't wait to see it all done.' Maggie lowered her head to hide a smile. 'You'll have to watch the kids, though, or they'll wreck the place in no time.'

'Mam, if they so much as lay a finger on anything, I'll kill 'em!' Eileen's body shook as her imagination took over. 'How about lockin' them in the box room until the minute Bill walks in the door? Or tyin' their hands and feet together an' puttin' a sock in their mouths?'

'You'll need to do something.' Maggie's lips formed a straight line. 'You've been far too soft with them, and now they think they can do anything and get away with it.'

'Not any more,' Eileen vowed. 'They'd better start learnin' how to behave or they'll have their dad to answer to! He won't put up with any of their shennanigans!'

'I just hope you haven't left it too late! They've run rings round you and me for the last five years, so you're not going to tame them that easy.'

'Stop yer worryin', missus, an' let's get to bed.' Eileen lumbered to her feet. 'I want to be up early tomorrow so I can go out scrounging for paper and paint.' She grinned cheekily. 'Who d'yer think I should honour with me presence first?'

Maggie fiddled with the ties at the back of her pinny. 'Just don't ask me to come with you, that's all!'

'Oh, yer poor little frightened thing!' Eileen switched the light off and looked back at the windows. 'It seems funny without the black-out curtains, doesn't it, Mam? I'd got quite attached to them.' She smacked her mother's backside. 'Up to bed with yer, it's way past yer bedtime.'

Chapter Five

The following two weeks were so hectic, Eileen didn't know whether she was coming or going. She would roll out of bed after a few hours sleep and after a quick bite to eat would have a scraper in her hand, or be holding the ladder steady while Harry painted the ceilings, or measured the walls for size before cutting out the strips of wallpaper. She and Harry were only able to do a few hours before setting off to work together, leaving Rene and Mary to carry on with the task of transforming Eileen's house.

Rene and Mary had found willing neighbours to mind the children, and every day they turned up and worked like Trojans. Rene was used to decorating because with Alan the way he was, she was the one who had to do all those sort of jobs at home. As quick as Mary pasted a piece of paper, Rene would run up the ladder and have the paper on the wall like a flash. And while they beavered away, Maggie kept the floors swept and had tea on the go all the time.

Eileen worried that the children were being neglected, but consoled herself with the thought that it wouldn't be for long and she'd make it up to them. She could be heard muttering as she scraped the walls, and her remarks brought smiles to the faces of those near her. 'There must be six bloody layers of paper on these walls! Either that, or I'll soon be able to see what next door's 'avin' for their tea.' A bit later, they'd hear, 'I want me bumps feelin', goin' through this!'

Eileen was allowed a respite on the Monday to have her hair permed. And when she came back, the straight straggly hair had been turned into a frizzy mop. She took one look in the mirror and groaned. 'I look like a bloody hedgehog that's had a fright!'

One day she had a letter from Bill. It had been sent from the camp in Germany and was very brief. In it, Bill told her that the German guards had fled the camp the day before the British troops arrived and that he would be home soon. If Eileen hadn't been so tired in mind and body, she might have asked herself why Bill didn't sound happier, or why he didn't say he was as eager to see her as she was to see him. But with so much going on, Eileen didn't take heed of the lack of emotion in the one-page letter. Her husband was alive and that was enough to send her spirits soaring.

On the Saturday afternoon, exactly two weeks from the time they'd started, five very relieved people stood back to admire their handiwork. Every room in the house, and the landing, hall and stairs, had been papered and painted. Light, flower sprigged paper matched up with white paintwork, and the house had never looked so bright. Even the kitchen had been given a coat of pale yellow paint, giving the effect of permanent sunshine.

'I don't know what to say.' Eileen could feel a lump forming in her throat. 'It doesn't look like the same house!' A tear trickled down her cheek and she hastily brushed it away.

'It looks lovely, an' I don't know 'ow to thank yez enough.'

'You're welcome, our kid!' Rene felt like crying herself. 'And I've got to say it's been well worth the effort.'

'Mary, if you'll run a mop over the floor in the living room, I'll put the lino down.' Harry was eager to see the job finished before they packed in for the day. 'Once the lino's laid, we can bring the furniture down.'

The new furniture had been delivered earlier in the week and Eileen had asked the men to carry it up to her bedroom. She wasn't taking any chances on it getting knocked around while so much work was going on. The old dining room suite had been put in the yard waiting for a scrap cart to come round, and the only thing left in the room was the well-worn couch. 'It's a pity about that.' Eileen nodded to the offending couch which stuck out like a sore thumb against the light wallpaper and white paint. 'It's goin' to spoil . . .' She turned to see Rene and Harry whispering together. 'What are you two whisperin' about?'

Rene blushed while Harry grinned. 'We were just making a date, d'you mind?'

'Eh, watch it!' Eileen laughed. 'He's married to my best mate!'

'Give us a hand to get the couch into the yard,' Harry said. 'I can't lay lino with that big thing in the way.'

'I wonder if Milly Knight in the corner shop would mind if I used her phone.' Rene avoided Eileen's eyes. 'I said I'd let Alan know what time I'd be home.'

'Milly's all right.' Eileen lifted one end of the couch. 'She won't mind a bit.'

'I'll make meself useful by putting the kettle on for hot

water for the floor,' Mary said. 'It'll need going over a few times, it's so dirty.'

Harry was just cutting the lino round the fireplace when Rene came back. 'Bloody 'ell, our kid!' Eileen roared. 'Where the 'ell 'ave you been? I was beginnin' to think yer'd run off with the coal man!'

Rene turned her head to wink at Harry. 'One hour,' she mouthed silently before answering Eileen. 'I've been having a chat to Milly.'

'It's all right for some people, isn't it!' Eileen's nerves were taut. Her house had been like a bomb site for the last two weeks, and there'd been times when she was sorry she'd started. But now she couldn't wait to see the curtains up and her new furniture in place. 'Does anyone know where the wire for the curtains is? I could be gettin' them ready to put up.'

'I'll see to the curtains!' Harry was on all fours pressing the lino neatly under the skirting board. 'You make yourself useful and brew up.'

'Bloody tea tanks, the lot of yez.' Eileen lumbered towards the kitchen. 'I suppose yez know yer've used all me tea ration up, an' I'll 'ave to go on the scrounge to Milly Knight.'

She came back into the room a minute later to find Rene, Mary and Harry in a huddle by the window, their heads together, whispering. 'What the 'ell is goin' on?' she demanded. 'Youse are up to somethin', an' I want to know what it is!'

'There's nothing going on, it's just your bad mind.' Harry took her arm and pulled her towards the door. 'Give us a hand to get the sideboard down. I can manage the rest on me own.'

'Hang on a minute, till I get me wind back.' Eileen let the end of the sideboard rest on the stairs, while Harry, on the bottom stair, supported the full weight of it. 'If I haven't lost any weight after all this, then all I can say is there ain't no justice.' Eileen was breathing heavily. 'Me heart's goin' fifteen to the dozen.'

'Only a few more stairs to go,' Harry coaxed. 'Just one last effort.'

'If this is what yer 'ave to go through to be posh, then me 'ouse can be like a muck midden for all I care.' Eileen heaved the end of the sideboard. 'Okay, Tarzan, let's go! But if yer rip me new wallpaper, I'll 'ave yer guts for garters.'

'They wouldn't go round your legs,' Harry gasped, walking backwards a few steps until Eileen was off the stairs. 'A clothes line would be more like it.'

'Yer cheeky bugger!' Eileen dropped on to the bottom stair, her face flushed with the exertion. 'Don't think because yer've done me 'ouse for me that it entitles yer to insult me.'

Rene and Mary, grinning like Cheshire cats, moved in to take over. 'We can manage it between us now.' Rene bent down and ruffled Eileen's hair. 'You should have let your Billy stay in to help lift the furniture! It's no job for a woman.'

'I can manage the table and chairs on me own,' Harry said. 'Why don't you take a breather? Walk up to the corner shop and have a natter with Milly. When you come back we'll have everything in place.'

'I wouldn't mind a breath of fresh air,' Eileen admitted. 'The sweat's pourin' off me.'

'Then poppy off,' Mary told her. 'It'll be a nice surprise for you when you get back.'

Eileen leaned her dimpled elbows on the counter of the corner shop. In the last half hour she'd been brought up-to-date with all the local gossip and her eyes were shining with amusement. 'Isn't it amazin' what can happen in two weeks?' Eileen watched as Milly served a customer with two ounces of tea before tearing a coupon out of the woman's ration book. 'I haven't 'alf missed our little jangles.'

Milly waited till the woman left the shop. 'I've kept the juiciest bit of gossip till the last.' She hitched her well-corseted bust up. 'Yer know Sadie Thompson, don't yer? Well, she had a baby daughter last week.'

Eileen's hazel eyes narrowed into slits. 'I thought her 'usband was away in Germany?'

'Precisely!' Milly nodded knowingly. 'He's been away for eighteen months.'

'D'yer mean . . . oh, my God!' The news brought Eileen upright. 'She's one I never expected to hear that about!'

'Well, it's true!' Milly leaned closer. 'There'll be ructions when her husband gets home.'

'Ructions! He'll bloody kill 'er!' A smile tugged the corners of Eileen's mouth. 'I know I shouldn't be laughin', but I can't 'elp it! All these married women have been swanning around with the bloody United Nations, 'aving a ball while their fellers have been away fightin'! Well now the time's come to pay for their bit of fun, an' I 'ope they think it's been worth it. They deserve everythin' they get, an' I've no sympathy for them.' Her smile disappeared. 'I feel bloody sorry for their 'usbands though! Fancy comin' back to that!'

Eileen waddled down the street, her thoughts with the husband of Sadie Thompson. Poor bugger, he deserved better than that. It wouldn't be any consolation to him, but there were hundreds of men coming home to find their wives had cheated on them.

'Come on, our kid!' Rene and Mary were standing outside Eileen's house. 'You can't half talk!'

'Hark at her!' Eileen made to brush past them but Mary barred her way.

'You've to stay in the hall until we call you in.' Mary pushed Eileen up against the hall wall. 'We want to go in first so we can see your face when you see what we've done.'

Left alone, Eileen chunnered to herself. 'I feel like a bloody kid playin' hide an' seek!' But her inside was turning over with excitement. She couldn't wait to see what her room looked like. The minutes passed and she became impatient. 'What the 'ell are yez doin' in there! It is my 'ouse yer know!'

'You can come in now.' It was Rene's voice bidding her enter.

'About bloody time!' Eileen pushed the living room door open and the first thing she noticed was the group standing inside the kitchen door. Her mother was flanked by Rene and Mary, and behind them towered Harry and Alan. 'Yez are like a gang of kids!' Eileen told them before her eyes swept the room. 'Oh, my God! Am I in the right house?' Her hand on the door knob, she took in the new curtains, the lovely shining table with a vase of flowers standing proudly in the centre and a chair on each of the four sides. And the matching sideboard also boasted a vase of flowers with ornaments either side that Eileen had never seen before. Lost for words, she could only shake her head.

'Come in and shut the door, love,' Maggie said softly. 'You'll be able to see the room properly then.'

Eileen shut the door and leaned against it, and as she did, she caught her breath. Along the back wall, where the old couch used to stand, was a new couch, in coffee-coloured cut moquette. Eileen screwed her eyes up, then opened them again to make sure she hadn't been seeing things. Her legs were threatening to give way under her and she pushed her back hard up against the door. Then the tears started and she covered her face with her hands, her body shaking with sobs.

'Oh, come on, our kid!' Rene and Mary rushed to put their arms around her. 'We thought you'd be pleased!'

'Pleased!' Eileen said through her sobs. 'I'm bloody over the moon! I'm cryin' with happiness, yer silly sods!'

Eileen's tears only lasted until she saw Harry pull a chair out to sit down. 'Not on yer nellie, yer don't!' Eileen threatened. 'Everything's getting covered up till the day my Bill comes 'ome.'

So, old sheets were found to cover the table and couch, and pillowslips for the chairs. 'Now, yez can all park yer back-sides.'

When they were seated, Eileen found out what all the whispering had been about. Rene and Alan, and Mary and Harry, had clubbed together to buy the new couch as a welcome home present for her and Bill, and when Rene was supposed to be at Milly Knight's ringing Alan, she'd actually been making arrangements to have the couch delivered. It was Rene who'd bought the material and made up the new curtains, and Mary who'd bought the vases and ornaments. Maggie, insisting she wanted to do her bit, had supplied the flowers.

All the time they were telling her, Eileen's head was shaking as her eyes went from one eager face to the other. 'I'm not very good at makin' speeches,' she told them, her face flushed with embarrassment. 'I don't know big words like our Rene, who sometimes sounds as though she's swallowed a dictionary.' She ducked a blow aimed at her by her sister. 'All I can say is, I think yer the best mates anyone ever 'ad, an' I love yez all.' She looked into Alan's face. 'Haven't they made a good job of it, Alan? Yer wouldn't think it used to be a pig sty, would yer? I'll probably come 'ome tomorrer an' think I'm in the wrong house!'

'They've done a great job,' Alan agreed. 'I'm only sorry I couldn't do anything to help. But I do have something to give you.'

'Oh, for Christ's sake, don't give me anything else,' Eileen laughed. 'I couldn't take any more!'

'Will you stop taking the Lord's name in vain.' Maggie pursed her lips. 'I know you're excited, but that's no excuse.'

Eileen cast her eyes up to the ceiling. 'I'm sorry, God! I promise I'll turn over a new leaf after today.'

'And I don't think!' Maggie muttered, as Eileen turned to Alan.

'I'm sorry for the interruption, Alan. What was it yer were sayin'?'

'That I have something for you.' Alan brushed a non-existent speck from his coat trying to appear nonchalant.

'Bill's on a ship on his way home.'

'Yer what!' The table moved as Eileen jumped to her feet. 'Are yer 'aving me on?'

'At this very minute, Bill is on a ship sailing towards England,' Alan told her. 'He should be on English soil in a few days.'

Harry was the first to notice the colour drain from Eileen's face, and he reached her just in time to save her from dropping to the floor in a dead faint.

Chapter Six

'Mam, are you sure this dress looks all right?' Eileen pulled the skirt of her navy and white spotted dress down over her tummy, but the second her hands let go, the dress wrinkled up again. 'It makes me look like a bloody big whale!'

Maggie clicked her tongue impatiently. 'For the umpteenth time, the dress looks fine!' Secretly Maggie wondered how anyone with a figure the size of her daughter could have bought a spotted dress. But to say that now would only make Eileen more agitated than she was already. 'For heavens sake, lass, will you sit down and try to relax! You've got my nerves on edge, and the poor kids are frightened to breathe!'

The three children were sat on the couch, hands clasped in their laps. Dressed in their new clothes, they'd been warned that a clip over the ear hole was what they could expect if they got themselves dirty before their dad arrived.

Joan and Edna were feeling badly done to and very fed-up. The excitement they'd felt when they knew their dad was coming home had changed to apprehension. They'd been very young when he went away and their memory of him was hazy. But they'd imagined his homecoming would be a happy and joyous occasion. Now they were not so sure. If today was a sign of things to come, life was going to be very miserable

51

from now on. They weren't allowed to play out, and when they'd asked if they could have a game of Ludo, their mother had nearly bitten their heads off. Not a thing was to be out of place when their dad walked through the door.

Billy was lost in his own thoughts, which were far removed from those of his sisters. He remembered everything about his dad, and he couldn't wait to have him home again. They'd be going to see Liverpool play on a Saturday afternoon like they used to, and when their team was playing an away game, they'd go fishing.

A smile crossed Billy's face as he ran his fingers down the crease in his new long trousers, remembering how his dad used to lift him up at the match so he could see over the heads of the men in front. His dad would have a job to lift him now, because Billy reckoned he'd probably be as tall as his dad now.

Billy's heart was bursting with pride as he pictured his dad's face when he saw him in long trousers. And wait till he knew he had a job to go to when he left school at the summer holidays! The headmaster had let him take a morning off school to go for an interview at the Cable works in Linacre Lane, and he'd got a job as an apprentice mechanic at seventeen shillings and sixpence a week. Oh, he had a lot to tell his dad, did young Billy Gillmoss.

'Edna, stop rubbing yer 'and along the arm of the couch,' Eileen growled. 'Yer'll 'ave it filthy in no time.'

'Huh!' Edna dug her sister in the ribs. 'We can't do nothin'!'

'Why can't we go out and play?' asked a defiant Joan. 'We'll only be in the street, and we'll see our dad comin'.'

'Yez are not goin' out because I say so!' Eileen heard

herself yelling and screwed her eyes up. What was she shouting at the kids for? It wasn't their fault she was so excited she felt sick. 'Look, kids,' Eileen kept her voice calm. 'I know it's hard for yez to understand, but I just want everything to look nice for yer dad. He hasn't seen us for five years, remember, and yez wouldn't like him to come 'ome after all that time to a filthy 'ouse, an' us lookin' like waifs and strays, now would yez?'

'No, Mam,' chorused the two girls. That was the answer their mother wanted, so that was what she got. In truth, they'd rather have been out playing and not worrying about getting dirty.

Eileen paced the floor. 'I still don't understand why I couldn't go to the station to meet Bill. He'll be expectin' me to be there.'

'How many times do you have to be told?' Maggie's patience was wearing thin. 'Alan's picking Bill and another man up in an army Jeep, and civilians aren't allowed to ride in army vehicles!'

'Ssshhh!' Eileen spun round. 'I 'eard a car stop outside.'

'It might not be them.' Maggie stood up and took command. 'You stay here, and, Billy, you go and see.'

Eileen couldn't have gone anyway. Her legs were threatening to buckle under her and she had to lean on the table for support. The seconds ticked by, then they heard Billy yelling, 'Me dad's here!'

The two girls flew off the couch, elbowing each other out of the way to be first out of the room, but Eileen was rooted to the spot. Her mouth opened and closed but no words would come. Maggie took one look at her daughter's face and grabbed her arm. 'For heavens sake, pull yourself together!

Take a few deep breaths . . . that's right.'

When Bill walked through the door, he was alone. Alan, forever thoughtful had invited the children to examine the Jeep, to give man and wife the first few minutes together. And also to give Eileen time to get over the shock she was in for when she saw the man Alan hadn't recognised when he'd stepped from the train at Lime Street station.

Eileen stared, her mouth hanging open. This man wasn't her husband! Her Bill had black hair, a round healthy-looking face, and he was tall and straight. This man was a stranger, with white hair, hollow cheeks, and he was stooped like a man twenty years older than her Bill.

Maggie was the first to recover. Crossing the room she held her arms out. 'Hello, Bill! Welcome home, son.'

Eileen felt she was watching a film, as Maggie put her arms round this stranger's shoulders and kissed him. Then she heard the stranger saying, 'Thanks, Ma, it's good to be home.' When his eyes met Eileen's over Maggie's shoulder, her breath caught in her throat. There was no mistaking Bill's deep brown eyes.

Maggie pulled away. 'You'll be dying for a drink . . . I'll put the kettle on.'

Bill dropped his army bag, his eyes still holding Eileen's. And in those eyes Eileen could see the same haunted look she'd seen in Alan's when he'd come back wounded from the war. What in the name of God had those bastards done to make her Bill look as he did?

Eileen's head was filled with mixed emotions . . . disbelief, horror, pity and anger. Bill's appearance had really knocked the stuffing out of her. But she sensed him watching her reaction closely, and knew it was vital she didn't let her feeling show. This was her husband and she loved him with all her heart. Mustering a strength she didn't know she possessed, Eileen willed herself forward, her arms outstretched. 'Don't I even get a kiss, after waitin' five years, or are they on ration, too?'

Bill kicked his army bag out of the way and walked into her arms. He lay his head on her shoulder and tears rained down his face. And while Eileen held him, the anger in her grew. He was like a skeleton! All she could feel was skin and bones, hidden from sight in the ill-fitting navy blue suit. My God, if she could get hold of the people responsible for doing this to her Bill, she'd strangle them with her bare hands.

The clattering of cups in the kitchen brought Eileen back to life. 'I love you, Bill Gillmoss, and I'm bloody glad to 'ave yer home again,' she whispered softly in his ear. 'Now give us a kiss before the kids come in.' Ashamed of his emotional display, Bill couldn't meet Eileen's eyes as he planted a feather like kiss on her mouth. 'I'm sorry, chick! I couldn't help meself.'

At the sound of the old pet name, Eileen's anger resurfaced, but this time it was overshadowed by the power of her love for Bill, and a strong determination. Whatever damage those bastards had done, she'd spend the rest of her life repairing it. Surrounded by love and understanding, he'd soon get better. And she'd feed him up to get some flesh back on those bones, even if she had to scrounge food coupons to do it.

Outside in the street, the driver of the Jeep kept the girls amused while Alan took Billy to one side. The look of bewilderment on the boy's face frightened him and there were things he thought Billy should know before he faced his dad again. 'Billy, I think you're grown up enough now to be told what your dad's gone through. I'm not going to tell your mother, and I don't want you to, either. If your dad wants her to know, he'll tell her in his own good time. So anything I say now, is man to man, d'you understand?'

Billy was staring down at his shoes, his heart broken. He looked up briefly and nodded. 'Okay, Uncle Alan.'

'This prisoner of war camp your dad was in was one of the worst in Germany. The guards were hard and cruel, and they treated the prisoners like animals. They only had to look sideways to be punished, and they barely had enough food to keep them alive. A lot of the prisoners, those not as strong as your dad, didn't survive. It wasn't only the hardship and the lack of food they had to put up with, but they were robbed of their dignity and their pride.'

Billy was now watching and listening closely, and Alan chose his next words carefully. 'Your dad has been to hell and back, and is going to need all the help he can get. And with you being the only other man in the house, he's going to need your understanding. Forget that he doesn't look like the man who went away five years ago, just remember that your dad is a hero.'

Billy lowered his face quickly. Boys of fourteen don't cry, he told himself. Only cissies cry. Gulping back the tears, he said, 'I'll look after him, Uncle Alan, I promise! And me mam and me nan . . . they'll take care of him, too!'

'I knew I could rely on you.' Alan patted the boy's shoulder. 'And if your dad sometimes gets bad tempered, you will remember what I've told you, won't you?' When Billy nodded, Alan said, 'You're a good lad, Billy.'

* * *

Rene came later that day with Victoria, and the family sat around talking, telling Bill all the things that had happened in civilian life during the war years. The blitz, shortage of food and clothes, and the blackout. But the conversation was laboured as Bill merely nodded or shook his head. He said nothing about his imprisonment, and as though by mutual consent, the others didn't ask. He seemed ill at ease and nervous. Every sound outside made him jump and look towards the door. And watching him, Eileen's heart bled. What a fool she'd been to expect him to come home looking and acting the same as he had when he went away. And what a good job she'd taken Alan's advice and not arranged a coming home party. She had intended to have all the neighbours in for a knees up, but now she knew how stupid she'd been to have even thought of it.

Joan and Edna were all mixed up. For years their mam had talked about their dad, how he'd done this and that and what he'd said. And yet, here he was, and he hadn't even said a word to them. Never asked how they were getting on at school or anything. In fact it could have been a complete stranger sitting in the chair with nothing to say for himself. They couldn't have put into words what they expected of their dad, but it certainly wasn't this serious man who didn't even have a smile for them.

Billy sat on one of the dining room chairs, listening to the conversation and watching his dad closely. Not a word had been said about how tall he'd grown, how he suited his long trousers, or how lucky he'd been to have found a job. But he didn't mind. His Uncle Alan's words kept running through his brain and he viewed the man sitting quietly on the couch, not as a stranger, like his sisters did, but as a hero.

* * *

It was nine o'clock when Rene said it was time to take a sleepy Victoria home. And while Alan helped the child on with her coat, Eileen nodded to the girls. 'Time you two were in bed, too!'

'Ah, ay, Mam! We don't 'ave to go to school temorrer!' Joan saw her dad's head turn sharply, and decided that today wasn't the best time to argue. 'Okay! Come on, our Edna.'

Edna gave Eileen her goodnight kiss, then as she waited for Joan to perform the nightly ritual, she stuck her thumb in her mouth and sucked furiously. 'Goodnight, Mam.'

'Goodnight and God bless, sunshine.' Eileen saw the indecision on the faces of her two daughters and acted quickly. 'Kiss your dad goodnight.'

Edna pushed Joan forward. 'You first.'

Joan hesitated, then slowly walked towards her dad. 'Goodnight, Dad.'

Her kiss was fleeting, her exit through the door even more so. And fast on her heels went Edna. They could be heard running up the stairs, and Eileen managed the first smile of the evening. 'They probably think you're the flippin' milkman!'

Everyone had gone to bed and Eileen and Bill were alone at last. Eileen didn't know how she felt. For five years she'd waited for this night, and now it had come she felt shy and unsure. Everything was so different from what she'd planned. In her dreams she'd imagined Bill coming home looking exactly the same as the last time she'd seen him, and the house would be filled with laughter and love. Then came the thought that five years was a long time, and Bill could probably see a change in her!

'I suppose yer've noticed I've put weight on?' she ventured. 'In this bloody dress you couldn't help but notice.' Oh, God, I've done it again, she groaned inwardly. Me mam warned me about swearing.

'I think we've both changed,' Bill said softly. 'Me, far more than you.'

'Oh, yer've got a bit thinner, that's all!' Eileen waited to see if Bill was going to tell her anything about the last five years, but he stayed silent. 'A couple of pans of me mam's scouse, an' yer'll soon put the weight back on.'

Bill closed his eyes. It would take more than a pan of scouse to erase the scenes of pain, suffering and humiliation he'd had to witness. He shook his head to chase away the memories. Even if he tried to tell Eileen, she wouldn't understand. You had to go through it yourself to know what it was like.

Eileen watched his pencil-thin fingers twisting a button on the navy striped jacket. 'Where did yer get the suit from?'

'The Army.' A grimace passed over Bill's face. 'Every soldier is issued with one when they get demobbed.'

'Oh, it's one of those demob suits they're all talkin' about!' Eileen kept her tone light. 'I don't think it's your colour, love! Yer suit grey better.'

Bill fingered the coarse, cheap material. 'Not much to show for five years of a man's life, is it?'

'D'yer want to talk about it?' Eileen leaned closer. 'It might make yer feel better.'

'I doubt that very much,' Bill said. 'Perhaps I'll tell you about it some day, but not now . . . not yet.'

'Then shall we hit the hay? Yer must be tired out.'

'You go first, and I'll follow when I've had a ciggie.'

'Uh, uh!' Eileen said emphatically. 'Not on yer nellie! I've 'ad five bloody years of goin' up those stairs on me own, but not any more! When I go up, you go up! Yer can 'ave yer ciggie in bed.'

Eileen watched the smoke from Bill's cigarette spiral up to the ceiling, her mind filled with conflicting emotions. She'd waited so long for this night, and her body was tingling with a desire born of need. But Bill didn't seem to understand. Instead of being wrapped in each other's arms, Bill was sitting with his back to her, smoking! She felt like grabbing the cigarette from him and stubbing it out. But a warning bell sounded in her mind, telling her to let Bill move at his own pace. They had to get used to each other once again, just like a newly married couple.

At last she felt the bed move, as Bill leaned down to put the ash tray on the floor. Then he slid between the sheet and lay beside her. Seconds ticked into minutes, but still he made no move. Then Eileen could stand it no more. She pulled him towards her and held him tight. 'I'm over the moon to have yer back in me bed, love! Tell me it's the same for you.'

'I'm sorry, chick!' Bill kissed her briefly on the lips, freed himself from her arms and turned on his side. 'Goodnight.'

Eileen felt as though she'd received a body blow that had knocked the wind out of her. Her first impulse was to reach out to him, but once again the warning bell sounded, and instead she whispered, 'Goodnight, Bill.'

But for Eileen it was far from a good night. She tossed and turned, her mind in a turmoil. What had she done to deserve that rejection? Didn't he love her any more? All night the questions came, but not one answer.

The answers were all in the mind of the man lying next to her, pretending to be asleep. Bill could feel her torment but couldn't bring himself to face her and tell her the truth. The day would come when he'd have to, but he was too weak in mind and spirit to tell her now.

Chapter Seven

The next morning Eileen waved the children off to school, then five minutes later her mother hurried out to be first in the queue at the fish shop in County Road. It had been hard trying to behave normally when her mind was so troubled, and it was with a sigh of relief that Eileen closed the front door. 'I'll 'ave five minutes to meself while the coast is clear.'

Eileen often held conversations with herself, and as she pulled a chair out to sit down, she continued. 'It's like bloody bedlam in here when the kids are in! It's a wonder they didn't wake Bill up!'

Bill! The cause of her splitting headache and upset tummy. She couldn't get last night out of her mind . . . and the picture of Bill turning his back on her. If he'd made an excuse, that he was too tired or something, she'd have understood. But with that one gesture, all the dreams she'd had over the years of the joy she'd feel on having him back again had disappeared like a puff of smoke.

Eileen cupped her hands and rested her chin on them. Her Bill wouldn't have behaved like that unless there was something drastically wrong. But what?

The silence and peace in the house wrapped itself around

Eileen's body, calming and clearing her mind. He's my husband and I love him dearly. Whatever it is that's troubling him, we'll work it out together. Perhaps it's just the strangeness of being home, and in a few days, when he's had a chance to get used to us again, he'll be all right and everything will be back to normal. Until then I'll just have to grin and bear it. Be the same old easy going, laughing Eileen everyone thinks I am, and pretend that everything in the garden's rosy!

The sound of next door's grate being raked out reminded Eileen there was a tub full of dirty clothes waiting to be washed and she scraped her chair back. 'I'd better get this fire lit for some hot water, then I'll take Bill a cup of tea up. He might be feeling better after a good night's sleep.'

Eileen opened the bedroom door softly, and her nose wrinkled as the smell of moth balls invaded her nostrils. We'll never get rid of the smell of the blasted things now, she thought, his things have been wrapped in the smelly balls for too long. I'll have to get his suit out on the line for a few days in the fresh air before he'll be able to wear it.

Eileen approached the bed and looked down on the sleeping form. God, he was thin! There wasn't a pick on him! His face was haggard and the white hair made him look like an old man. And all this because of some power hungry maniac called Hitler! May he rot in hell, the bastard!

'Wake up, sleepy head!'

Bill shot up in bed, his hands waving so violently the cup was almost knocked out of Eileen's hands. Like a man demented with fear, Bill's eyes darted round the room, finally coming to rest on Eileen's startled face. There was no sound in the room except the ticking of the alarm clock and Eileen's pounding heart. Although it was only seconds, it seemed like an eternity before the fear left Bill's face and his eyes showed recognition. He lowered his head as though ashamed. 'I'm sorry, chick! I couldn't make out where I was for a minute.'

Eileen almost blurted out that he'd frightened the life out of her, but that inner voice told her to be careful. 'I've brought yer a cup of tea, but don't expect to get waited on every day, Bill Gillmoss! This isn't an 'otel, you know!' Eileen's shaking hand held out the tea. 'I don't know 'ow yer slept through the racket the kids made! They made enough noise to waken the dead!'

'I'm not quite dead.' Bill took the cup thinking of the hundreds of times he'd wished he could die. 'Thanks, chick! I'll get up when I've drunk the tea and had a ciggie.'

Eileen speared a piece of bread with a fork and leaned forward to hold it in front of the fire. 'It's no use askin' what yer want for yer brekkie, 'cos we've got nothin'! So it's Hobson's choice, I'm afraid.'

Bill watched as she turned the piece of bread to toast the other side. 'I'm not very hungry.'

'Hungry or not, yer've got to eat something.' Eileen waited till the bread was nicely browned, then swivelled round. 'Come an' sit at the table, where I can see yer.' She scraped some margarine thinly on the toast before placing it in front of Bill with an unlabelled jam jar. 'Cissie Maddox made the jam with apples, an' she sent it up for yer.' The floorboards creaked as Eileen's massive body shook with laughter. 'Yer must be well in, there! Cissie's usually that mean she wouldn't give yer last night's *Echo*!' Eileen waited expectantly for a smile to appear on Bill's face, but he concentrated on his toast and made no comment. Oh, God, Eileen groaned inwardly, it's going to be hard going. But she had to keep trying to get some response from him. 'Who was the other feller Alan picked up at the station?'

'A bloke called Arthur Kennedy.'

Eileen persisted. 'Did Alan take 'im 'ome first? Where does 'e live?'

'Somewhere down the Dingle, off Mill Street.' Bill chewed half-heartedly on the toast, offering no further information.

'Was 'e in the prisoner of war camp with yer?'

Bill shook his head. 'I met him in the repatriation camp.'

It's like getting blood out of a stone, Eileen thought. But I've got to keep talking otherwise we'll never get anywhere. 'Had 'e been a prisoner of war?'

'I don't know!'

Eileen winced at the tone of Bill's voice. He may as well have told her to shut up, 'cos that's what he meant! And what was the good of trying to talk to him when she had to drag every word out of him? Keeping her sigh silent, Eileen stood up. 'The water should be 'ot by now, so I'll start the washing before me mam gets back. She may as well 'ave a bit of a rest while I'm off . . . God knows she deserves one.'

Eileen watched the water fill up the old tin tub through the hose attached to the tap, her mind deep in thought. They'd been separated for nearly six years, and you'd think they'd have lots to talk about. But Bill didn't seem to want to talk about his life during those years, nor was he showing any interest in hers or the kids. It just wasn't natural! You couldn't pretend those years had never been, or that there hadn't been a war!

Eileen turned the tap off, unscrewed the hose, then sprinkled

Persil powder in the tub and swished it around. Her movements automatic, she picked up the posser and began to press up and down on the clothes. There's nowt I can do about it, she told herself. Only hope that each day will bring him out a bit more. Perhaps she was expecting too much too soon.

Eileen rubbed the handle of the posser briskly between her two palms, swishing the clothes around in the tub. She should leave them to steep for half an hour, but she couldn't bring herself to go back in the living room and face Bill's indifference. Perhaps when her mam came back it might be better. He always got on with her mam, and he might be a bit more talkative when she was there.

Eileen added softly, please God!

'What are you doing out here?' Maggie asked sharply. 'Fancy leaving Bill on his own!'

'What does it look like, Mam?' Eileen's voice was equally sharp. 'I'm certainly not bakin' a cake!'

'There's no need to be so sarcastic!' Maggie's face was flushed. 'I'm not in the mood for your sense of humour.' She waved a paper bag under Eileen's nose. 'I've stood for two hours in a flipping queue to get this! A piece of cod that will barely feed two, never mind six of us! We'll need a magnifying glass to see it!'

Eileen draped some of the wet clothes over her arm and picked up a handful of pegs. 'I bet it's at times like this yer wished yer used swear words, like I do.' A grin lit up her face. 'Tell yer what, Mam, I'll do it for yer an' it'll get it off yer chest.' Eileen brought her brows down in a frown and wiped the smile from her face. 'Two bloody hours in a bloody queue for a bloody tiddler that probably gave itself up! Now, does that make yer feel better?'

'No, it doesn't!' Maggie said. 'And you can just leave that washing and go in to Bill. I'll hang the clothes out.'

'This is the last lot, so I may as well finish it off.' Eileen waddled towards the door. 'If yer want somethin' to do, stick the kettle on for a cuppa.' She was in the yard when she remembered and hurried back. 'We 'aven't got much tea, so take it easy. Just one teaspoonful will 'ave to do, or we won't last till our next ration. It'll look like maiden's water, but that can't be 'elped.'

Satisfied with her mother's startled expression, Eileen went back to hang the clothes out. With a peg between her teeth, she muttered, 'If I lose me sense of humour, I may as well die off!'

Maggie glanced at Eileen, who shrugged her shoulders to the question in her mother's eyes. Even Maggie's gentle efforts to get Bill talking had met with the same response as Eileen's. He answered questions as briefly as he could without being rude, but contributed nothing off his own bat to the conversation. It crossed Eileen's mind that he was like a lodger who they were meeting for the first time. Maggie talked about the weather, the neighbours and the shortage of food in the shops. But not once did she mention the war . . . guessing that the subject was taboo with Bill.

Eileen heard her mother try to interest Bill in the new furniture and muttered silently, 'God loves a trier!', then her eyes went to the mirror over the mantlepiece where the old photograph of Bill was stuck in the wooden frame. It had been taken when he'd first come home on leave in his army uniform, and he had his head back, laughing. It was hard to believe that the man in the photograph, tall and straight, with black hair and white teeth bared in a smile, was the white-haired man sitting hunched up on the couch. Tears threatened as Eileen tore her eyes from the photograph. How long, dear Lord, will it be before we get Bill back to health, and will we ever see that smile again? And how long before I feel his arms around me, holding me tight like he used to?

Maggie shook Eileen's knee. 'I can hear the kids.'

Shrieks of laughter preceeded the entrance of the two girls, fighting to be first in the room. 'Mam,' Edna's face wore a proud smile. 'Teacher said I was very good today, an' she let me give the pens out.'

Eileen noticed the frown on Bill's face. 'Hold yer 'orses! Don't yez even say "hello"?'

The smiles faded as two pairs of hazel eyes turned to Bill. 'Hello, Dad!'

Bill ignored their greeting. 'Do you have to make so much noise when you come in?'

The girls looked so dejected, Eileen sprang to their defence. 'Oh, come on, love! They're only kids!'

'They're old enough to know how to behave themselves.' Bill's eyes, sunk back into his head, glared. 'If you treat them like babies, then that's how they'll act.'

Stung by the injustice, a hot retort sprung to Eileen's lips, but she managed to bite it back. What the hell did he think she'd been doing for the last five years . . . sitting on her backside?

'Can we go out to play, Mam?' The joy of being prefect for the day had gone for Edna. She was expecting to be praised, but instead had been told off! It wasn't fair! Her mam would have told her how pleased she was if it hadn't been for . . . him! Edna glared defiantly at her father. It was his fault, he'd spoiled it all!

Joan, two years older, had the sense to know when to be quiet. If she left it to Edna, they'd end up getting sent to bed. 'Can we go out, Mam?'

Eileen nodded. 'Don't go out of the street, though, 'cos I'm goin' to start on the tea.'

'D'yer know where me top and whip are?' Edna asked.

Bill turned his body. 'Don't you know how to say "please"?'

Eileen screwed her eyes up so she couldn't see the hurt on the faces of her two daughters. All these years she'd told them how marvellous their dad was, and now this! She heard a tiny voice saying, 'Please, Mam,' and felt like holding the two thin bodies close, and murmuring words of comfort. But taking sides now would set a pattern for the future, and she couldn't do that to Bill.

'Your top and whip's in yer bedroom, on the bottom of the wardrobe.' Eileen forced a smile. 'Don't forget, stay in the street or I'll smack yer backsides.'

It was with a heavy heart Eileen prepared the tea. If this was a sign of things to come, she dreaded what the future held for herself and the kids. Okay, so she'd ruined the kids by giving them all their own way, but she wasn't a bloody miracle woman! She couldn't be out at work every day, and see what the kids were up to at the same time!

When the fish came to the boil, Eileen lowered the gas under the pan and walked back into the living room just as Billy came in from school. He looked so proud and handsome in his new long trousers, and so like the Bill in the faded photograph, Eileen's heart turned over. If Bill starts on him, I will have something to say, she vowed silently. I'm not going to let him upset the whole household. So she waited, ready, if necessary, to spring to the defence of her son.

'Hi, Mam! Hi, Nan!' Billy grinned at them before turning to his father. 'Hi, Dad!'

Bill looked up. 'Hello, son!'

Eileen heaved a sigh of relief. Thank God for that!

Billy turned one of the wooden dining chairs to face the couch. 'How've you been today, Dad?'

A ghost of a smile flickered across the gaunt face. 'Not so bad, son! And you?'

Eileen's relief was tinged with jealousy. She was his wife, why couldn't he look her straight in the eye, like he was with Billy? Then Eileen scolded herself. What difference did it make who got through to him, as long as somebody did! It was a step towards . . . what was the word Alan used, rehabilitation, that was it!

Billy, oblivious to the tension in the room, sat forward, his elbows resting on his knees. 'Has me mam told yer I leave school in two weeks, Dad, an' I've got a job to go to?'

A flicker of interest showed in the tired eyes. 'I think your mam thought you'd rather tell me yourself.'

That was what Billy had been hoping for. His account of the interview he'd had for the job was given in great detail, his words accompanied by gestures with his hands. He'd been polite, he told his dad, like his teacher had told him, and hadn't forgotten to address the man who interviewed him as 'Sir'. Flushed with pride, he explained what the work entailed and what his weekly wage would be. Then sitting back with a smug smile on his face, he said, 'There's only two of us in

71

our class got jobs so far, so I'm very lucky.'

'You've done well, son,' Bill said softly. 'I'm proud of you.'

Well, I'll be blowed! Eileen drained the water off the fish and turned the light out under the potatoes. It looks as though our Billy's done the trick!

She looked at the piece of fish she had to share between the six of them and shook her head. She'd do without, and give Bill her share. He needed it more than she did.

Spooning the potatoes on to the plates, Eileen's thoughts were on Bill. Now young Billy had got him talking, perhaps he'd come out of his shell and talk to her. If he didn't, then there was something definitely wrong. She put the empty pan in the sink and ran the water on it. All I can do is wait and hope.

Eileen picked up two plates in each hand. They say patience is a virtue, well I'm going to be very virtuous from now on.

Chapter Eight

Her wide hips swaying, Eileen walked through the door of the shell inspection department. The familiar smells and noise of the shop floor brought a smile to her face. 'Hasn't changed much, 'as it?'

'Blimey! What did you expect?' Jean Simpson asked. 'You've only been away a week!'

'Seems like a million years!' Eileen mumbled under her breath, linking her arm through Jean's. 'When's the big day, then, kid?'

'Don't ask me!' Jean pulled a face. 'If it was up to me and Ivan, we'd get married by special licence at Brougham Terrace. But the two families are at loggerheads over whether the wedding should be here or in the States! Ivan's family wrote to say they'd like us to be married over there, but yer should have heard me mam when Ivan told her! "Over my dead body," she said. "It's only right and proper that a girl should be married from her own home with her own dad to give her away."'

'I'm on yer mam's side, kid!' Eileen removed her arm as they neared their machine. 'An' fair's fair, yer know! Your family won't see much of yer when yer go to live in America, so the least yer can do is give them the pleasure of seein' yer get married.'

Sally Molloy was hopping impatiently from one foot to the other, willing Eileen forward. 'Come on, slow coach! We have a home to go to, you know!'

'Blimey! Anyone would think Clark Gable was in yer bed, waitin' to ravage yer!'

'An' who says he isn't?' Sally laughed, glad the long night shift was over. 'Who needs Clark Gable anyway? My feller's as good as him, any day!'

With a cheery wave, Sally made a dash for the door, leaving Eileen with the moving conveyor belt and her thoughts.

The last week had been a nightmare, and no mistake. She didn't know how she'd got through it! Bill looked so ill, his face so full of despair, every time Eileen looked at him she wanted to take him in her arms and hold him tight. But he was so withdrawn, he gave her no opportunity to show how much she cared. Most of the time he just stared at the grate, even when there was no fire lit. The only time he showed any real emotion was when there was a knock on the door, and then his eyes would fill with a look of fear that frightened Eileen. Some of the neighbours had called to see how he was, and although it went against Eileen's hospitable nature, she'd kept them standing on the step while she explained that Bill wasn't feeling too well.

Eileen took a suspect shell from the conveyor and placed it on the trolley standing at the side of the machine. If only Bill would tell her what was worrying him, share his fears with her, she would know what to do! As it was, she felt so helpless. That he had suffered was written all over him, but she was at a loss to know what to do. Thinking he might be in pain, she had suggested asking the doctor to call, but Bill had given her such an emphatic 'No', Eileen was afraid she'd do more harm than good if she went against his wishes.

An anger started to build up in Eileen. The Army had no right to send men to war, then forget about them! Surely they couldn't just dump a sick man at home when they'd finished with him, without making a check that he was all right.

A lump formed in Eileen's throat and she swallowed hard. Crying was one luxury she couldn't afford, and it wouldn't help, anyway! What she had to do was find someone who could help Bill, and quick! Otherwise he was just going to fade away before her eyes, and the whole family would disintegrate. The two girls were frightened of him and spent as much time playing in the street as they could. And at bedtime they were up those stairs without a murmur, glad to be in the safety of their own bedroom.

Eileen had followed them up one night, and had sat on the side of the bed explaining that the war had made their dad the way he was. But he was going to get better, she told them, and when he did they'd find out he was the best dad in the whole world. Two pairs of wide hazel eyes, set in two solemn faces, had nodded agreement when Eileen asked if they'd help her to get their dad better again. But as she descended the stairs, her heart heavy, Eileen had told herself she couldn't really expect them to understand. After all, they were only kids, and you can't put an old head on young shoulders.

Eileen caught a movement out of the corner of her eye and turned to see the labourer, Willy Turnbull, pulling the full trolley away from the machine so he could replace it with an empty one. 'Hello there, Willy! Had any clicks while I've been away?'

Willy's smirk showed yellowing teeth. 'Ah, that would be telling!'

'Of course it would be telling, yer silly sod! That's why I'm askin' yer!'

Willy Turnbull must be the only man who's sorry the war's over, Eileen thought. Small, thin, sickly-looking, he had a yellow complexion that matched his teeth, and a bald head that he tried to hide by growing the little he had on the sides long enough to comb over the top. He carried a comb in the top pocket of his overalls, and every hour he would disappear into the toilets to make sure the thickly plastered on Brilliantine was holding his hair in place against all the laws of gravity, and to snatch a few puffs on a Woodbine.

Before the war started Willy hadn't had any luck with girls, but with all the young men being called up, he'd managed to catch a few the Yanks had turned their noses up at. Now he considered himself a real ladies' man. 'Got a date tonight, 'ave yer, Willy?' Eileen persisted. 'Is she blonde or brunette?'

'Blonde, if yer must know.'

Eileen watched him struggle with the heavy trolley and was suddenly sorry for him. He couldn't help the way he was, and when she remembered how she'd skitted him over the years she was filled with remorse. 'You enjoy yerself tonight, Willy, d'yer hear? An' I want to know all about it in the mornin'.'

Harry appeared by Eileen's side. 'Do my ears deceive me, or have I just heard you being nice to Willy Turnbull?'

'Well, God love 'im, the poor bugger doesn't get much out of life! An' he'll get even less now with all the men comin' 'ome.'

'Me and Mary were going to call on you, then we thought you might want to have Bill to yourself for a while.'

Eileen concentrated on the passing shells. What was she to do now? Should she tell Harry the truth, or pretend everything was fine? In the end she decided to compromise. 'I'm glad yez didn't come, 'cos Bill's not strong enough yet for visitors. But in a couple of weeks he should be feelin' better, an' then we'll 'ave a knees up, eh? It'll be jars out then all right!'

'Give him time, Eileen! It couldn't have been a picnic being a prisoner of war, and you shouldn't try to rush him.'

'Oh, I'm not goin' to rush 'im! I don't care how long it takes, as long as he gets better!' Eileen's thoughts didn't match her words. It did matter to her how long it took! It was agony to lie awake every night after Bill had turned his back on her. Feeling his body next to hers, so near and yet so far away.

Harry was eyeing her thoughtfully. He'd worked with Eileen for over five years, and he'd never seen her without a smile on her face and a joke on her lips. But there was no joke on her lips today, and her smile was hollow. 'You let us know when Bill's ready for visitors, and me and Mary will be up like a shot. We can't wait to meet this husband we've heard so much about.'

'Will do, Harry!' Still Eileen didn't meet his eyes.

'And if we can help in any way, you know you only have to ask.' Harry saw one of the other machine operators beckon, and he waved to say he was on his way over. 'I'll see you later.'

Eileen watched him walk away. He was her friend, and right now she needed a friend to confide in. 'Harry!'

But when Harry turned, Eileen was filled with doubt. Bill would go mad if he knew she was talking behind his back. So she grinned, and called over the noise of the machine. 'You're still me best mate, Harry!'

Eileen rubbed the back of her hand over her forehead, then shouted across the conveyor to Jean. 'Can yer manage on yer own for five minutes, I'm dyin' to go to the lavvy?'

Without waiting for an answer, Eileen walked away. She needed some time alone to think. The toilets were empty, for which Eileen was grateful. She was in no mood to answer questions, exchange gossip, or crack jokes. In fact, the way she felt now, she'd never crack another joke in her life!

The tiles on the toilet walls were nice and cool, and as Eileen rested her head against them, she tried to marshall her thoughts into some sort of order. Bill needed help, there was no doubt about that. And as his wife, it was up to her to make sure he got that help, not anyone else.

Eileen stood up and pulled hard on the lavatory chain. 'I've got to stop feelin' sorry for meself,' she muttered, 'an' think of something! Come hell or high water, an' if I kill meself into the bargain, I'm goin' to find a way to make my Bill better.'

Eileen's determination lasted until she got home and saw the forlorn figure of her husband. Fighting talk was all right until you were faced with the reality of the situation.

Bill was sick, mentally and physically. She could feed him up as much as she liked, and in time he would probably put some flesh back on that skeletal frame, but she couldn't rid his mind of the fears she knew were tormenting him. What he needed was professional help, but if he refused, what could she do?

If Doctor Greenfield was back home she could go and have a word with him on the quiet, 'cos he was a man you could let your hair down with. But the doctor who had taken over when Doctor Greenfield joined the army was a stranger to Eileen. She'd only met him once, when young Edna had the measles, and she hadn't been very impressed with him.

'Have yer had something to eat, love?' Eileen slipped her coat off and folded it over her arm. Since the advent of the new furniture, the kids weren't allowed to throw their clothes over the backs of chairs, and while Edna often cursed having to take her coat upstairs, she knew if she went back to her old habits the kids would follow suit and the place would soon look like a pig sty again.

'Your mam made me some porridge.' That it was an effort to even talk could be seen on Bill's face. 'And before you ask, yes, I did eat it.'

'Good for you! Where is me mam, by the way?'

'Nipped to the shops for a packet of ciggies for me.'

'I'll 'ave to settle up with Milly Knight, when I get the chance.' Eileen didn't tell Bill that most of the cigarettes he smoked came from under the counter. She'd given Milly all her sweet coupons, 'cos on your ration book you could either have sweets or cigarettes, but they didn't cover the number of packets Bill smoked.

Eileen was in the bedroom putting her coat in the wardrobe when she heard her mother's key turn in the lock. Then their Rene's voice drifted up the stairs. Eileen hadn't seen her sister or Alan since the day Bill came home, and until now she was glad they'd kept away.

Eileen bent down to pick up the folded wad of paper that was used to jam the wardrobe door shut. The key had been lost years ago, and without the paper to keep it closed the door would swing open on its hinges. She couldn't hear a sound from downstairs, and Eileen's heart began to sink. She'd been hoping for the sound of Alan's voice, thinking it might do Bill good to have a man to talk to.

Eileen moved to the landing and leaned over the banister, her head cocked, listening. Yes, there it was! That low, well-modulated voice that had always inspired confidence in her. Please God, let it have some effect on Bill! At that moment a seed was sown in Eileen's mind, and as she stepped down the first stair, she squared her shoulders, determined not to let the seed wither and die.

Chapter Nine

Eileen untied the belt of her overall with one hand, while holding her outdoor coat ready in the other. Her intention was to slip into her coat before any of the women noticed she was wearing her best dress, but she hadn't reckoned on the sharp eyes of Maisie Phillips.

'Well! The state of you an' the price of fish!' Maisie pulled Eileen's arm aside to reveal the spotted dress which stood out in stark contrast to the drab walls of the cloakroom. 'Where d'yer think you're off to, me lady, all dressed up to the nines?'

'Jealousy will get yer nowhere, Maisie Phillips.' Eileen pulled her arm free and quickly slipped into her coat. 'You're a nosey bugger, but if yer must know, I'm goin' to visit a friend.'

'Sounds like dirty work at the cross roads.' Ethel Hignet's teeth clicked back into place as she added her twopenny worth. 'Does yer 'usband know about this?'

Eileen snorted. 'Yer've worked with Maisie that long, Ethel, she's got yer as bloody nosey as she is! It's a friend of Bill's I'm goin' to see, if yer that interested! An' as it's in your neck of the woods, yer can tell me 'ow to get there.'

'If yer want to get to the Dingle from here, yer best bet is

to go down to the Pier Head, and get another bus from there.'
Ethel tried to get more information by offering to travel with
Eileen, but the big woman wasn't having any. What they
didn't know wouldn't hurt them, and they'd have nothing to
gossip about. 'No, ta, Ethel! I'm in a hurry.'

'Northumberland Street!' The conductor tapped Eileen's
shoulder. 'This is your stop, love.'

Eileen stepped off the bus in Mill Street and immediately
on her left saw the street sign she was looking for. Her
mission was to find Arthur Kennedy, and although she'd
been able to get the name of the street off Alan by casually
asking about the bloke he'd picked up at the station, she
didn't have the nerve to ask the number of the house for fear
of rousing his curiosity. It had seemed a good idea at the time
to find out whether Arthur was suffering the same as Bill, and
if he was, how his family were coping, but now she was filled
with misgivings.

The journey down on the two buses hadn't helped her
nerves, either! It was the first time she'd seen how much
damage had been inflicted on the city and it added to her
misery. She knew that most of Liverpool had been affected
by the German bombing, especially down here near the docks,
but the scale of the damage took her breath away. Everywhere
you looked there were bombed-out houses and shops.

Eileen waddled up Northumberland Street looking at the
names on the signs at the corner of the small side streets with
their rows of two-up two-down terrace houses. She could feel
the sweat running down her neck, caused by exertion and
apprehension, and asked herself what she had let herself in
for. Then the image of Bill came into her mind, and with it a
determination to finish what she'd started.

At last she came to the corner of the street she was looking for. All she had to do now was find out which house the Kennedys lived in. She hesitated, wondering whether to knock on the first door and hope for the best, or ask at the corner shop. Then a young boy came along rolling a hoop, and she stepped in front of him. 'D'yer live in this street, son?'

The boy brought the hoop to a stop, his eyes curious. 'Yeah!'

'Can yer tell me what number the Kennedys live in?'

'I don't know the number, Missus, but I can show yer the 'ouse!'

Eileen took a penny from her purse. 'Here yer are, son, buy yerself something.'

The boy's face lit up. 'Ooh, ta, Missus!'

Eileen noticed the neat windows of the houses they passed, and the well-scrubbed steps. She smiled as she remembered how her mother was always reminding her that no matter how poor you were there was no excuse for being dirty, 'cos water costs nothing.

'This is the 'ouse, Missus!' The boy pointed, then fled in the direction of the corner shop to buy the catapult he'd had his eye on for weeks. Eileen's eyes took in the shabby appearance of the house. Unlike its neighbours, the windows were dirty, the step filthy, and through the open front door Eileen could see a dark hall with peeling wallpaper and a threadbare carpet. God, I used to think my house was bad, Eileen thought, but it had nothing on this!

It took a lot of willpower to knock on the door, but Eileen urged herself on. She'd come this far, she couldn't back out now.

It was so gloomy in the hall, Eileen didn't see the woman

until a voice came through the darkness. 'Yeah? What d'yer want?'

'Are you Mrs Kennedy?'

'Who wants to know?' The woman came nearer and Eileen's heart sank. Bleached hair framed a face that would have been pretty but for the heavy, cheap make-up, and the purple dress she wore was far too short and tight. A cigarette dangled from the side of her mouth as she stood with her hands on her hips, eyeing Eileen up and down. 'Well?'

'I came to see if yer can help . . .'

Eileen's words were cut off by a cynical laugh. 'Listen to me, whoever yer are! If it's help yer after, yer've come to the wrong 'ouse! I can't help me bleedin' self, never mind you!'

'Are you Mrs Kennedy?' Eileen's dander was up, but she tried to keep her temper in check as she waited for the woman's nod. 'It's really your 'usband I came to see. I think he was in the Army with my 'usband, and I wanted to have a word with 'im.'

'Why didn't yer 'usband come 'imself?' The woman's eyes were half closed against the smoke wafting up from the cigarette still dangling between her thin lips. 'Can't he do his own messages?'

'My husband's ill.' Eileen counted slowly up to three. She didn't want to lose her temper, but if this woman didn't stop looking her up and down as though she was a piece of dirt, she'd clock her one! 'And besides, he doesn't know I'm 'ere. He'd kill me if he did!'

'I don't know what it is yer after, but whatever it is yer'll be lucky to get it from my feller! If I can't get anythin' out of him, I'm bleedin' sure you won't!'

They were sizing each other up like opponents in a boxing

ring. Eileen felt at a disadvantage because standing on the step, the woman was able to look down on her. But Eileen wasn't going to be intimidated. Thinks she's tough, does she? Well she's met her match! And I feel sorry for her husband if this is what he had to come home to. 'Well, are yer goin' to let me talk to 'im?'

The woman threw her cigarette into the street, missing Eileen's face by inches. 'Please yerself! But yer'll get nothin' out of 'im!'

As Eileen followed Mrs Kennedy down the hall the smell hit her with full force. It was a combination of dirt and bugs, and Eileen could feel herself retching. She pressed hard on her tummy and tried not to breathe in, but the smell was so overpowering she could feel herself going weak at the knees. 'There he is.' Mrs Kennedy nodded to the man sitting in a chair, staring into space. 'Sits there all bleedin' day and never opens 'is mouth.' A look Eileen could only describe as hatred, flitted across the woman's face. 'He may as well 'ave stopped where he was, for all the good 'e is.'

Swallowing her distaste, Eileen stood in front of the man who seemed not to hear his wife's voice. 'Hello, Mr Kennedy! My name's Eileen Gillmoss, an' my 'usband came up from the army camp with yer.'

Tired eyes, filled with hopelessness and despair, met hers. And Eileen felt she could have been looking into Bill's eyes, except that this man's were blue. He wasn't as thin as Bill, and he still had his mousey-coloured hair, apart from a few odd streaks of white. But the sadness written on his face told Eileen that here was someone suffering as Bill was. 'I 'ope yer didn't mind me comin',' Eileen knew she'd wait till Doomsday before Mrs Kennedy invited her to sit down, so she pulled up a chair and placed it next to Arthur's, 'only Bill was wonderin' how yer were gettin' on.'

'Yer wasting yer time!' Mrs Kennedy picked up a packet of cigarettes from a sideboard that was thick with dust and finger marks. As she lit up, Eileen noticed they were the same American Camel cigarettes that Ivan smoked. 'He sits there all day like one of Lewis's! Neither use nor ornament!'

Eileen flashed her an angry look before turning back to Arthur. 'I guess yer like my Bill! He doesn't feel too good, either!'

'If he feels like me, then he knows what hell is like!' The strength of tone surprised Eileen, and from the sharp intake of breath behind her, it had also surprised his wife.

'Well, my God, it can talk!' Sarcasm dripped from Mrs Kennedy's lips, and Eileen could have willingly strangled her. Fancy a sick man having to put up with a wife like her!

'How would you know?' Arthur stared hard at his wife. 'You're never in the house!'

Eileen's eyes rolled from one to the other. Her brain was working overtime, putting together the American cigarettes and Arthur's statement. It sounded as though his wife was a fly turn! She certainly looked like one, with her made-up face, and tarty clothes. She was probably one of the many women who hung around the American camps waiting to be picked up.

You could almost touch the tension in the room, and Eileen felt partly responsible for upsetting a man who obviously needed help as much as her Bill. 'Have yer seen a doctor since yer came 'ome, Arthur?'

He shook his head. 'When we were in the rehabilitation camp, they told us it would take a long time to adjust.' He flung his arm out to encompass the room, and there was such bitterness in his voice, Eileen's heart went out to him. 'How do you adjust to this? And how do you adjust to your wife going out every night all tarted up?'

'There's nothin' to keep me in, is there?' Mrs Kennedy stood with her hands on her hips, a sneer on her hard face. 'Yer can't even . . .'

'Shut up, Sylvia!' The words were like a shot out of a gun. 'Why don't you go where you go every night, and leave me in peace?'

Oh, Lord, what have I done? Eileen screwed her eyes up. I came here for help and end up causing a row! Then she thought, no, I haven't done any harm! I've probably given him the chance to let off steam, and that can only do him good!

Sylvia Kennedy tapped Eileen on the shoulder. 'I suppose yer expect a cup of tea?'

Thinking of the dirty state the kitchen would be in, Eileen shook her head. Besides, she wanted nothing from this woman. Fancy being a prisoner for years and coming home to this! At least Bill had her and the kids, and a clean home! 'No, ta!'

Eileen's eyes showed her dislike, and Mrs Kennedy's lips curled. 'Please yerself!'

If I could please myself, Eileen thought, I'd have you hung, drawn and quartered! She sniffed her disapproval and turned back to Arthur. 'Have yez got any family?'

'Two boys,' he told her, 'they should be home from school soon.'

Eileen looked at the clock. Her kids would be home soon, and she'd told Bill she was only calling to Mary's for half an hour and would be home in time for their tea. So Eileen decided to stop pussyfooting around and get on with it. Otherwise her visit was going to be a wasted one.

'Would yer leave us alone for a few minutes?' Eileen's face told Sylvia she would be ill advised to refuse.

'I was goin' to the shops, anyway! Yer can 'ave all the time in the world!'

'I'm sorry about that,' Eileen said when they were alone. 'But I'm so worried about me 'usband, I don't know where to turn! I thought you might be able to 'elp, seein' as yer went through what he did. He won't tell me anything . . . never talks about what 'appened when he was a prisoner, and he's so quiet and withdrawn. I'm at me wits end, wonderin' what to do to help 'im.'

'He's a lucky man, having someone who cares about him! My wife, as you have seen, couldn't care less!'

'Can you talk about what yer went through, or is it too painful?'

'Oh, I can talk about it all right, but no one wants to know! It's over now, so forget it! That's what they say! What they don't understand is that you can't just forget!' Arthur's voice was filled with passion as his story poured out. Every now and again he would stop, close his eyes and struggle to compose himself. Eileen could see and hear his distress as he recounted tale after tale of torture and degradation.

Eileen sat silent, hardly breathing. Never in her wildest dreams had she imagined prisoners of war being treated in the way Arthur was describing. It wasn't human!

'But who cares?' Arthur asked, his voice filled with bitterness. 'You're home now, so forget about it, they say! But how the hell can you forget things like that?'

Arthur dropped his head for a few seconds, and when he

raised it his eyes met Eileen's. 'I'm sorry about that! I've been wanting to get it off me chest, but I shouldn't have put you through it. It's just that you're the only one who's shown any interest!'

'I'm glad yer've told me, and I thank yer, because it will 'elp me understand what Bill's gone through.'

'It's me who should be thanking you!' Arthur told her. 'I really needed to talk it all out of me system. Perhaps I'll be able to sleep tonight, now.' Then Arthur remembered why Eileen had come. And a picture flashed through his mind of the man who'd sat next to him in the Jeep for the short journey from the station. The man had never opened his mouth, but he didn't have to. That he'd suffered more than most was written all over him. Arthur looked into Eileen's eyes and saw the kindness there that was missing from his own wife's. 'I don't know what your husband went through, because we weren't in the same prisoner of war camp. But after we were liberated and came back to England, we heard that some camps were a lot worse than the one I was in.'

Eileen met his gaze. 'You've helped me more than yer know, Arthur! And when yer feel up to it, come and see me an' Bill! Yer'd be more than welcome.'

After giving the address, Eileen held her hand out and impulsively kissed Arthur on the cheek. Then she made her departure.

Chapter Ten

Eileen held on to the door frame while she stepped sideways into the street. With her bust being the size it was, she couldn't always see where her feet were landing. 'If there was any justice in this world, Arthur, I'd be as thin as a rake!'

Arthur had followed Eileen down the hall, and he understood when she gulped in the fresh sea air wafted in from the Mersey. After the sickly stench of the house, the air smelled like Evening in Paris perfume to Eileen. 'She wasn't always like this, you know!' A wistful expression crossed his face as he remembered the young girl he'd married. 'She was nice looking, took pride in her appearance, kept the house clean and was a good mother to the boys. Then the war came, and I've been away for so long she probably got lonely. Unfortunately she got in with the wrong company, and you can see for yourself how she's ended up.'

Eileen's feelings were a mixture of sadness and anger. She'd got on like a house on fire with Arthur, and she'd learned a lot from him. He'd needed someone to talk to, and Eileen felt a burning anger against the wife who couldn't be bothered to listen. But she hadn't come to cause trouble between man and wife, so she kept her own counsel. 'The air's lovely and fresh down 'ere! Good as a dose of medicine!'

'We're right on the sea, that's why! You can't see it from here, but if you look straight ahead when you turn the corner, you'll see the ships in the Mersey.'

Eileen lifted her hand in farewell. 'Ta-ra, Arthur! Don't forget what I said about comin' to see us! Yer'd be very welcome, and it'd do Bill good to 'ave a man to talk to.'

'We'll see!' Arthur returned Eileen's wave. 'Give him my regards.' He watched her retreating back for a while, then sighed as his mind returned to his own worries. He didn't know what was going to happen with him and Sylvia. She'd changed that much he didn't know her any more. He'd tried reasoning with her, but she wouldn't listen, and she adamantly refused to give up her friends. Sometimes he thought she was sorry he'd come home.

Head down, Eileen started to walk quickly. The kids would be home from school and there was nothing in for the dinner. It'd have to be something from the chippie, like it or lump it! The kids would be happy, they liked nothing better than proper chips, wrapped in newspaper.

Eileen was so deep in thought when she turned the corner she didn't see anyone before her until they collided. 'Ooops! I'm sorry, I . . .' The automatic apology died on Eileen's lips when recognition dawned. 'Oh, it's you!'

Mrs Kennedy, her actions slow and deliberate, drew heavily on the cigarette she was smoking, then blew the smoke directly into Eileen's face. 'Yer know what they mean now on the posters that ask "is your journey really necessary", 'cos I bet your journey's been a complete waste of time. I said yer'd get nowt out of my feller! He's had it! He's not even any good in bed!'

The cocky expression fled, leaving a look of alarm on her face when Eileen moved in on her, pressing her back against the wall. 'What the 'ell d'yer think yer doin', fatty?'

'What I'd like to do is put me fist right in yer gob!' Eileen hissed. 'But instead, I'll give yer a piece of me mind! I wouldn't normally waste me breath on a tart like you, but I will for Arthur's sake! Yer've got a good man there, far too good for the likes of you! All he needs is someone to talk to, someone to understand, and he'd be as right as rain in no time. So I suggest yer take my advice an' get 'ome an' clean the place up for a start, 'cos it stinks! Then sit down and get to know yer husband again.' Eileen's hand was on the wall behind Mrs Kennedy, keeping her prisoner. Their faces were almost touching. 'That's if he'll let yer, of course! Not many men would fancy a tart for a wife! If it was my 'usband, yer'd be out on yer ear!'

Eileen's hand dropped and Arthur's wife quickly stepped away. 'You don't frighten me, fatty! Why don't yer toddle off 'ome and mind yer own business?'

'Oh, I'm goin', don't worry! In fact I can't get away from yer quick enough! The gas works smells better than you do!' Eileen said. 'But when Arthur walks out on yer, don't say yer weren't warned!'

Eileen stepped off the bus at the Pier Head just as one of the ferries landed, and she was caught up in the rush of people making for the buses which would take them home after a day's work. She groaned when she saw the queue and knew she wouldn't be getting on the first bus. It was half past five now, and it would be at least another three quarters of an hour before she got home. There'd be blue murder when her mother got hold of her, for leaving Bill for so long.

The first bus filled up and pulled away, leaving Eileen sixth in the line for the next one. Her eyes were on the people in front of her, but she didn't see them. Her mind was in a whirl, thinking of what Arthur had told her, the little set to she'd had with his wife, and what excuse she was going to make when she got home. That was the worst of telling lies, you always had to tell more to get away with the first one!

But it had been worth it, Eileen told herself. Talking to Arthur had been a great help, and she'd had her eyes opened. She understood a bit more about how Bill felt, and what he'd gone through, and how patient she was going to have to be. And she swore she'd have the patience of a saint, 'cos she loved her Bill very much.

Eileen's thoughts turned to Arthur and his wife. Fancy going away to fight for your country and coming home to that! How in the name of God was he going to get better living in filth, with a wife who was little better than a prostitute?

Eileen shivered. It was well known that the girls who hung around the docks ended up with VD. And then they passed it on to other people. Wouldn't it be terrible if that happened to Arthur?

A frown crossed Eileen's face when she recalled his wife's words. 'He's not even any good in bed!' And into Eileen's mind came the picture of Bill turning his back on her. It had to be a coincidence! She wasn't a tart like Mrs Kennedy! She could understand Arthur not wanting to touch his wife, knowing she was messing about with other men! But it was different with her and Bill! She'd never let another man touch her, and Bill knew that! And since he'd been home she'd showed in every way that she loved and cared for him.

The bus screeched to a halt and the line moved forward. Eileen pulled herself on board with the thought that she was letting her imagination run away with her. I'm being daft, she told herself, taking a seat by the window and leaving a quarter vacant for a man who equalled her in size. She didn't even notice when he tried in vain to push her up, so he could at least get part of his backside on the seat. As it was, the poor man spent the entire journey sitting on air with a prayer on his lips.

Maggie was standing in the street with the girls when Eileen turned the corner, and they made a dash for her. 'Where the hell have you been?' Maggie demanded. 'There was nothing in for the tea, so we've had nothing to eat!'

'Don't get off yer bike, Mam, I'll pick yer dummy up!' Eileen managed a smile. 'The world won't come to an end because yez got yer tea late!'

'But you've left Bill all this time! I'm really surprised at you, our Eileen! Where've you been till now?'

'Mam, will yer keep yer 'air on, for heaven's sake! Anyone would think another war had started!' Eileen opened her scruffy purse. 'Here's five bob, Joan, run to the chippie and get five lots of chips, four fishcakes and one fish.'

'Ooh, great!' Joan grabbed the two half-crowns and legged it down the street fast, with Edna close on her heels. That's two satisfied customers, anyway, Eileen smiled to herself. Now to smooth things over with Bill and me mam.

'Come on, Mam, let's set the table.'

Maggie grabbed her arm. 'Hang on a minute, I've got something to tell you. Father Younger called before, but I told him Bill wasn't too well, and I didn't let him in. I felt terrible keeping him on the step, but I didn't know what to do!'

'Well, yer weren't tellin' lies, so what yer worryin' about? An' he knows Bill was a prisoner of war for five years, so he should understand!'

'He said he'd come back at seven o'clock, when you were in.' Maggie spoke quietly, but when she saw the look of dismay on Eileen's face, her voice rose. 'What the heck was I supposed to say? That he wasn't wanted?'

'Shit!' Eileen screwed her eyes up and stamped her foot. 'Bill's not in the mood for visitors, Mam! Couldn't yer 'ave just told Father Younger that? He wouldn't have minded!'

'I did try, love, but he wouldn't have it! Said it was his duty to see Bill! And you know what Father Younger's like! I'd rather face a raging tiger than him! Would you have had the nerve to turn him away?'

'No, Mam, I'd 'ave been a coward, just like you!' Eileen took her mother's arm and led her to the front door. 'We'd better get our skates on and see to the tea before he comes.'

Maggie could feel her daughter's body start to shake and she looked at her with surprise. 'Don't tell me you can see anything remotely funny in this? Your sense of humour is beyond me, sometimes!'

'I was just thinkin', I should 'ave asked our Joan to get an extra fish for our visitor.'

Chapter Eleven

It was half past seven and there was still no sign of Father Younger. The tea had been hurriedly eaten, with Maggie standing by ready to snatch each plate as the last mouthful was eaten, to wash and put away out of sight. That the priest would never see the kitchen didn't deter Maggie. He was a very important person in her eyes and it was out of respect for his station in life that everything in the house had to be just so. No newspapers could be left to litter the floor, Bill's ash tray was washed every time he finished a cigarette, and if she straightened the runner on the sideboard once, she straightened it a dozen times. Billy had been allowed to go out when his mates had called for him, but much to the disgust of his sisters, they were made to stay in and told to behave themselves, or else! So far they'd sat quietly together on the couch, but as the minutes ticked by, they were starting to get restless. 'It's not fair!' Joan whispered to Edna. 'Why could our Billy be let out, but not us?'

Bill had watched all the hustle and bustle silently. He'd made no comment when told the priest was coming, which gave Eileen hope that the visit would go smoothly. But now Bill looked towards his daughters, having heard their complaint. 'You seem to forget that Billy is older than you.

He leaves school next week, and starts work. So don't set him up as an example of what you two can do or not do.'

Eileen was fed up sitting with her arms folded, waiting. After rushing round like a blue-arsed fly, here they were sitting like lemons! 'I'm goin' to put the kettle on! I swallowed me tea that fast before, it didn't touch me throat.'

'I'll give you a hand.' Maggie followed her daughter into the kitchen. Keeping her voice low, she said, 'Now you can just explain where you've been today! Bill might have believed you were at Mary's, but I don't! I'm not as green as I'm cabbage looking, and I've known you far too long to be taken in by a lie.'

Eileen was saved from answering by a loud rat-tat at the front door. 'I'll go!' She had a smile on her face when she opened the door, but it didn't reach her heart. Father Younger was one of the old-fashioned priests who preached fire and brimstone, and all his parishioners were afraid of him. And if the kids didn't want to go to Church on a Sunday all you had to do was remind them that Father Younger would be at the school tomorrow asking those who hadn't been to Mass to put their hands up. That never failed to do the trick.

'Come in, Father!' Eileen pressed herself back against the wall to allow the priest to squeeze past. 'Sorry I wasn't in when yer came before.'

'I believe you were up at the Sedgemoor's?' Father Younger twirled his old-fashioned, round-crowned hat, in his fingers. 'I hope they are keeping well?'

'They're fine, Father!' That's not a lie, anyway, Eileen thought. And if it is, it's only a little white one.

The priest greeted Maggie and the girls with a nod of his head before standing in front of Bill. 'It's good to see you again, Mr Gillmoss.' Bill shook the hand that was held out to him, but stayed silent.

'Here yer are, Father.' Eileen touched the back of a dining chair. 'Sit down and take the weight off yer feet.'

The two girls watched the proceedings, wide-eyed. They were in awe of the tall, gangling priest, who never seemed to smile. Many's the time they'd felt his wrath when they didn't know the answer to a question he'd asked them from the Catechism. He was very handy with the cane, too! When you got six of the best off Father Younger, your hand would still be stinging hours later. In fact, many of the kids would rather tell a lie than get the cane off the heavy-handed priest. They reckoned, and prayed, that Our Lord would be more lenient with them than Father Younger!

'I haven't seen you at Church since you came home, Mr Gillmoss!' The piercing eyes turned from Bill to Eileen. 'Nor you, Mrs Gillmoss!'

'No, Father, I've been . . .'

Bill's voice, stronger than she'd ever heard, cut off her words. 'For your information, I have no intention of ever, ever, setting foot in a church again!'

Eileen and her mother stared at each other in astonishment, their eyes asking what had come over Bill? He'd always been a softly spoken, mild-tempered man, not given to outbursts of anger such as they'd just heard. 'I can't believe you mean what you say, Mr Gillmoss,' the priest leaned nearer, 'and I'll ask God to forgive you for saying it.'

'God!' Bill spat the word out. 'What God? If there was a God, why would he allow wars to happen? Why would he allow men to kill and torture each other? Why . . .'

Eileen stood up abruptly, knocking the chair to the floor.

'I think it's time for the girls to go to bed! Come on, you two, up those stairs!'

'Ooh, ay, Mam.' Joan's face, like her sister's, was as white as a sheet.

'Why did me dad say that?'

Eileen rubbed her forehead and sank on to the bed. 'I don't know, love!'

'We won't half get it in the mornin'!' Edna nodded knowingly. 'He'll 'ave us out in front of the class an' tell everyone what me dad said!'

'No, he won't, sweetheart!' Eileen gathered them both close. 'Father Younger knows yer dad's not well, an' he won't take it out on you two, 'cos I won't let 'im!'

'You won't be there!' Edna reminded her. 'He will take it out on us, Mam! Me dad 'ad no right to say what 'e did!' She rested her head on Eileen's shoulder and whispered, 'There is a God, isn't there, Mam?'

'Of course there is, sweetheart!' Eileen's head was swimming. She had no idea Bill felt so bitter against the Church. Why didn't he say something before Father Younger arrived and she could have stopped the priest from coming in? Then again, there was a lot she didn't know about Bill these days.

'You two get undressed while I 'ave a listen.' Eileen opened the door a crack and listened. She could hear voices raised in anger, but couldn't make out the words. Then she remembered her mother was down there, in the thick of it. She should go down herself, but she couldn't. How could she take sides, when one was her husband, the other a priest? No, better not get involved! She wasn't going to argue with her

Bill, and her upbringing wouldn't let her speak out against everything she'd been taught to believe in.

'Get yerselves into bed, and don't worry!' Eileen pulled the eiderdown over them and tucked them in. 'If Father Younger says anything to yez tomorrer, tell 'im I said to see me! Okay?' Eileen looked back from the door to see two pairs of wide eyes staring at her from behind the bedclothes which were pulled up to their chins. Poor things, they looked terrified! 'Tell yez what, how about me tellin' yer a story till yez go to sleep?'

Eileen was half way through 'The Boy On A Dolphin' when she heard the slam of the front door. The girls' eyes were drooping, so she let her voice drone on for a few more minutes until she was sure they were fast asleep. Then, with butterflies in her tummy, she made her way down the stairs.

When Eileen entered the room, Maggie stood up. She looked at Eileen, shrugged her shoulders and sighed. 'I'm going round to Vera Jackson's for half an hour. I met her at the shops this morning and she asked me to call round sometime for a chat.' Vera Jackson had been one of Mary's neighbours before she married Harry and moved to Orrell Park. It was through Mary that Eileen had met Vera and they'd become good friends. Vera's husband, Danny, was in the army, and when she was feeling lonely, she would often call round to Eileen's with her seven-year-old mongol daughter, Carol, who was adored and spoiled rotten by Eileen and her mother. Maggie reached the door and turned. 'I'll take the key in case you two want to go to bed before I get back.'

Eileen waited for the sound of the door closing before turning to face Bill. 'Well, what was that all about?'

'What was what all about?'

'Oh, come off it, Bill! All this shoutin' at Father Younger about there bein' no God, and you not goin' to church any more!'

'I told him the truth! It's the way I feel, and there's no use pretending otherwise!'

'But why?'

'If you'd seen what I have, you wouldn't have to ask!' Bill tore a strip from the *Echo* and leaned forward to light it from the fire. He puffed on his cigarette till it was lit, then threw the paper in the grate. 'I'm not asking you or Ma, or the children, to stop going to church, if that's what you want, but don't expect me to go.'

It's taken an argument over God to get him talking to me, was Eileen's thought. But now we are talking, and he's got some of his feelings off his chest, it's about time I aired mine.

'I told you a lie today.' Eileen folded her arms and pinched nervously at the fat on her dimpled elbows. 'I didn't go to Mary Sedgemoor's.'

'Where did you go then? And why did you have to lie?'

'Because if I'd told yer, yer wouldn't 'ave let me go.' Eileen rested her elbows on her knees, her face level with Bill's. 'I went to see Arthur Kennedy.'

'Arthur Kennedy?' Bill looked puzzled for a second, then he remembered the man Alan had introduced him to when they'd got off the train at Lime Street station. 'What did you go to see him for?'

'I thought he might tell me somethin' that would explain why you're behavin' the way yer are.'

'But I don't even know the man!' Bill threw his cigarette into the grate. 'And what d'you mean, the way I'm behaving?'

The chair creaked as Eileen shifted her weight. 'Bill, the man who left here to go in to the army was my husband! The man who came back is a stranger!' Tears started to form, but Eileen was past caring. She was fighting for everything she valued most in the world.

'Not once, since yer came back, 'ave yer cuddled or kissed me, or told me yer love me! An' for five years I've been tellin' the kids about how marvellous their dad is, and they were so excited when they knew yer were comin' 'ome! But the only time yer speak to them is when yer tellin' them off!' Eileen sniffed loudly, the tears now streaming down her face. 'The kids are all mixed up, like me! We don't know what we've done wrong!'

Bill dropped his head. 'It's not you, chick! You've done nothing wrong, neither have the kids! And I do love you, all of you! But I can't help the way I am! It's like living through a nightmare, every day and all day! I can't get out of my head some of the atrocities I've seen, and the way some of me mates died!' Bill raised his face and Eileen could see his suffering. 'I know I shouldn't take it out on you or the kids, but I can't stop meself!'

'Then let me help you! Don't keep me on the outside, Bill, let me in, where I want to be! Tell me what the prisoner of war camp was like, and keep telling me, over an' over again, till yer've got it out of yer system!'

'You have no idea what it was like, chick, or you wouldn't be asking! They talk about man's inhumanity to man, but I never believed there could be such barbaric, evil people in the world.'

Eileen used the hem of her dress to dry her tears. 'I'm glad I went to see Arthur Kennedy, 'cos it's brought us closer together! He told me some of the things he 'ad to endure, but 'e did say that the camp 'e was in was a lot better than others he'd heard of.' Eileen almost blurted out what Arthur had come home to, but decided against it. Perhaps some other time! Right now Bill's problems were more important. 'Come on, sweetheart! Marriage is all about sharing . . . the good things and the bad. Share yours with me.'

It was half past eleven when Maggie quietly closed the door behind her. She expected Eileen and Bill to be in bed, but she saw a shaft of light coming from under the living room door, and as she reached the bottom stair she heard Bill's voice. It wasn't raised in anger as it was when she heard it last, but low and even.

Maggie gripped the banister and pulled herself over the second stair which was given to creaking. It was about time her daughter and Bill sat and talked to each other, and Maggie didn't want to interrupt. Although Eileen had never complained, Maggie knew how unhappy and worried she'd been since Bill came home. Please God that was all behind them now.

Eileen heard her mother come in, but her eyes never wavered from Bill's face. In the last two hours she'd heard such tales of cruelty that her blood ran cold. She couldn't take it all in . . . men kept in cages like animals, others beaten senseless . . . it was a wonder Bill didn't go out of his mind! And she could tell by the way he kept stopping, that he was holding a lot back for fear of upsetting her.

'D'you remember me telling you about the man I'd made friends with on the day I joined the army?'

'Yer mean Mick Sullivan? Of course I remember 'im! Yer always mentioned 'im in yer letters?' Eileen saw a cloud pass over Bill's eyes. 'Why?' Bill could no longer contain his emotions. He dropped his head in his hands and his body shook with violent sobs. Frightened, Eileen ran to kneel in front of him. Stroking his hair, she begged, 'What is it, darlin'?'

Gulping for air, Bill shook his head. 'Leave me for a minute.'

As she waited, Eileen took in the thin fingers and the sharp shoulder blades sticking out beneath his jacket. She wanted to break down, to scream out that no man should have to go through what Bill was going through. He hadn't done anything to deserve this! But Eileen knew she had to be strong for both of them. So gently stroking his hair, she waited. Bill breathed in deeply, and when he spoke his voice was so low Eileen barely heard what he was saying. 'The last time I saw Mick, he was being dragged away by two guards after they'd beat him nearly senseless. I never saw him again after that, and neither did anyone else. He was one of the many who disappeared mysteriously, without any explanation.' Bill shivered as though someone had walked across his grave. 'But Mick's screams as they were dragging him away have been ringing in my head ever since that day. And I think they'll be with me until the day I die.' His eyes pleaded with Eileen for understanding. 'That's why I can't stand it when the girls laugh and scream.'

Eileen held him in her arms. 'Oh, Bill, I'd do anythin' to take all this hurt away from yer, yer know that don't yer?' She rocked him like a baby. 'But I promise yer, sunshine, that together, we'll come through this.' When Bill's sobbing eased, Eileen struggled to her feet. 'Come on, let's go to bed. Tomorrow's another day, and I know every day's goin' to get a bit better from now on.'

Chapter Twelve

'There's no weekend overtime, Eileen!' Harry watched the smile fade from the chubby face. 'They're slowing production right down!'

'Blimey, Harry, just when I need the money more than ever! I knew it was bound to 'appen sooner or later, but I was 'oping the work would last until Bill was fit enough to find a job.' Eileen pushed the turban back out of her eyes. 'It's my money we rely on! Bill got a few bob when 'e was discharged, but that won't last very long, and all he'll get now is peanuts! And when our Billy starts work, his money won't go very far. By the time I give 'im his pocket money, pay 'is bus fares an' carry out, there'll be nowt left!'

'You should be all right for another six months' work here,' Harry said to reassure her. 'Even though they're running production down, it'll be a while before they shut down completely. And a lot of women are asking for their cards already, so I can't see them having to sack anyone till the factory closes altogether.'

'Oh, that's a blessing!' Eileen mopped her brow. 'For a while there I thought we were goin' to end up on the parish!'

'Oh, by the way,' Harry watched her face closely. When he'd told Mary yesterday that Eileen wasn't her usual chirpy self, Mary had insisted on going to see her today. Harry wasn't too sure that was wise, and he waited now for Eileen's reaction. 'Mary said she might pop up and see you this afternoon.'

'Great!' Eileen beamed. 'Tell 'er I'll 'ave the kettle on!'

'Yer've 'eard me mention Mary Sedgemoor, 'aven't yer?' Eileen asked as she bustled round tidying up. 'Well, she's comin' this afternoon, so yer better behave yerself.' She bent to wag a finger under Bill's nose. 'She's a crackin' lookin' girl, so keep yer eyes in yer 'ead, an' yer 'ands in yer pockets! Okay?'

'Yes, boss!' Bill still didn't feel up to meeting strangers, but he didn't have the heart to disappoint Eileen. She was doing her best, God knows, but he needed more time. More time to forget, more time to gain back a feeling of self-respect, and more time to gain some confidence.

Eileen leaned on the brush handle. 'An' 'er 'usband's bigger than you!'

Maggie popped her head round the kitchen door. 'You could always stand in front of Bill! If Harry hit you, he'd bounce off!'

'Ho, ho! Very funny, Mother dear!' Like her mother, Eileen felt as though a weight had been lifted from her shoulders. The gloomy atmosphere that had pervaded the house over the last weeks had been partially lifted. There was still a long way to go, but the start had been made. Even the secret that Bill had shared with her last night couldn't dim her happiness. It was just another hurdle they'd cross together.

'Bill, my sweet one,' Eileen's posh accent came into play, 'would you mind very much moving your feet, so hi can brush hunder them? Thank you hever so much!'

'Cooeee!'

'Here's me mate now, so get ready for an eyeful!' Eileen whispered, before calling, 'Come in, Mary!' She rushed to the kitchen to put the brush away and when she came back the first thing that hit her was the look of bewilderment and shock on Mary's face as she stood uncertainly by the door looking at Bill.

'This is the feller yer've been fed up 'earing about for the last five years! He's lost a bit of weight since 'e went away, but he's still as 'andsome as ever!' Eileen kept on talking to cover up the tension as she introduced her best mate to Bill.

Eileen wasn't joking, was Bill's first thought, Mary certainly is a lovely girl. And when she turned her shy smile on him, he knew instinctively that she was as gentle and modest as her smile. She and Eileen were as different as chalk and cheese in every respect, but it was obvious they were very fond of each other.

'Where's my two god-children?' Eileen asked.

'I've left them with Harry.' Mary turned to Bill and pulled a face. 'They're just at the age when they're in to everything and won't sit still for five minutes.'

'Yer didn't know I was a god-mother, did yer?' Eileen pulled her tongue out at Bill. 'Twice over!'

Maggie's head reappeared. 'Hello, Mary, love! Will you tell your friend to give her mouth a rest, and come and see to this tea? There's no bottom left in the kettle.'

'Ay, missus! Who was yer servant before I came along?' Eileen grinned mischievously. 'Thinks she's Lady Muck, my mother, yer know! She needs takin' down a peg or two.'

'It'll take a better man than you, Gunga Din!' Maggie called out. 'I might be small, but you know what they say . . . there's "good stuff in little parcels".'

'Aye, and poison!' Eileen winked broadly before swaying her way to the kitchen. 'Either yer gettin' too big for yer boots, missus, or yer've been at the Stout again!'

Rummaging in the kitchen cupboard to find a saucer to match the only china cup she could find that didn't have a crack in it, Eileen muttered, 'Just wait till I come up on the pools! I'll be down to T.Js like a streak of lightnin' to buy meself a lovely tea set with flowers on it. And we'll 'ave to learn to stick our little fingers out when we're drinkin', just like the posh people do! I won't call the King me Aunt, then!'

Maggie tapped her shoulder. 'Bill seems to be getting on all right with Mary, they're talking away to each other.'

'She's just right for Bill, Mam! Nice and quiet.' Eileen stood up holding a saucer aloft triumphantly. 'I knew we 'ad one somewhere!'

When Eileen carried the tray through, Mary was telling Bill about how her mother had coped since she'd had the stroke during an air raid. 'She's been marvellous, hasn't she, Eileen? You should see how she gets around the house on her crutches!'

'When yer feelin' better, Bill, we'll go up an' see Mrs B! An' yer can see the posh 'ouse me friend lives in!'

Mary blushed. 'Take no notice of her, Bill! It's not posh at all!'

'Then I'll swap yer for this one!' Eileen grinned. 'We could do with a bigger 'ouse with our gang!'

'I've told Bill I'll call in with the children one afternoon,' Mary said. 'Is that all right?'

Eileen didn't need to say thank you, it was written in her eyes. This was just what Bill needed, another step in the long journey back to normality. 'It'll 'ave to be in the next day or two, 'cos I'm on afternoon shift next week. Unless, of course, yer want to come when yer've got Bill on 'is own!'

'Honestly, your wife is past the post, Bill!' Mary turned her shy smile on him. 'She never takes anything seriously.'

Bill met Eileen's eyes, both thinking of the secret they shared. 'Oh, she can be serious when she likes!' He brought his gaze back to Mary. 'Not very often, I admit, but she does have her moments!'

'Bring the kids tomorrow,' Eileen said suddenly. 'I 'aven't seen them meself for ages.'

'Are you sure?'

'Course I'm sure! Yer'd like that, wouldn't yer, Bill?'

Bill nodded, surprised to find that he wasn't just agreeing to please Eileen. Then he realised why. For the last hour his head had been free of the memories that had been haunting him day and night. For while Mary had been telling him about her children, he'd found himself going back in time to when his own children had been little. This house used to ring with the sound of laughter then, and he'd been part of it.

'Yes, I would like that,' Bill smiled. 'Come tomorrow, Mary!'

'Honestly, I couldn't believe it!' The children were in bed when Mary got home, and now she was sitting telling Harry and her mother about her visit to Eileen's. 'He looks terrible! You could take him for Eileen's father, he looks so old!'

'Poor Eileen, she must be worried to death.' Martha rocked

back and forth in her chair. 'And there's nothing we can do to help!'

'Yes there is, Mrs B!' Harry said. 'We can be there if she needs us, and give her all the backing we can.'

'She's asked me to take the children up tomorrow.' Mary played with a stray curl that had fallen on her cheek. 'Apart from Rene and Alan, they've had no visitors because Bill said he didn't want anyone in the house.'

'I'll come with you.' Harry stretched his long legs out. 'You'll need help getting on and off the buses with the children.'

'No, Harry!' Mary shook her head. 'When Eileen came to the door with me, she said she thought it best to take things one step at a time with Bill. She's frightened if she tries to rush him, it will do more harm than good.' Harry went to object, but Mary put her foot down. 'Harry, if you saw him you'd understand! He went through hell in the prisoner of war camp, and believe me, you can see it written all over him! So, I'll go on me own tomorrow with the kids, and just stay half-an-hour in case it's too much for him.'

'Mary's right, son!' Martha shook her head sadly. 'I remember men coming back from the first world war like that. It took years for some of them to get over it, and they were the lucky ones. There were thousands who never recovered.'

'It's a good job Eileen's strong,' Mary voiced her thoughts, 'and got a good sense of humour! She was laughing and joking this afternoon, but how she managed it I'll never know, because her heart must break every time she looks at Bill.'

'Eileen has a natural sense of humour, but there are times

she uses it as a shield to hide her worries.' Harry felt angry because he didn't have it in his power to help the one person who always found time to listen to people's troubles and hold out a helping hand. 'I just wish there was something we could do.'

'There may be, Harry! Perhaps when Bill picks up a bit, and feels like going out, you can take him for a pint.' Mary knew how Harry felt about Eileen because she felt that way herself. But, as Eileen had said, one step at a time.

Joan and Edna ran up the street laughing and pushing each other boisterously. But when they reached their front door their laughter died down. They'd been warned by their mother to behave themselves, no shouting and screaming 'cos it gave their dad a headache. So it was two very subdued girls who entered the house, with the unspoken agreement to change out of their gymslips as quick as they could and escape back into the street to play.

'Hello, Dad!' They could hear their mother talking to their nan in the kitchen, so they turned to go upstairs. But the sound of their dad's voice stopped them in their tracks.

'How did school go today, girls?'

They spun round, surprise written on their faces. 'It was all right, Dad!' Joan was the first to recover, then Edna ventured. 'I came fourth in arithmetic, Dad!'

'That's good! Keep that up, and you'll get yourself a good job when you leave school.'

Not to be outdone by her sister, Joan told him, 'I'm next to top in our class.' She was thoughtful for a second, then decided that she was stretching the truth a little too far. 'I'm not very good at history or geography, though!'

'English and arithmetic are the subjects to concentrate on. They're the ones you'll need to be good at to get a decent job.'

'Yes, Dad!' Edna kicked Joan's shin, and the action wasn't lost on Bill. They wanted to go out and play, to get out of the house, and it saddened him that he was to blame. He was their father, but he'd made himself a stranger to them. If he wasn't careful, he'd alienate them forever.

'You can play out till the tea's ready, if you like.'

'Ooh, thanks, Dad.'

The noise they made scrambling up the stairs brought Eileen hurrying from the kitchen. 'What are those two monkeys up to?'

'It's all right! I told them they could go out to play.'

'I didn't 'ear them come in!' Eileen's eyes narrowed. 'Have they been givin' yer cheek?'

'No!' Bill shifted sideways to get to the packet of cigarettes in his trouser pocket. 'As a matter of fact, I've just learned that both my daughters are doing quite well at school!'

'If yer believe that, yer'll believe anythin'!' When she saw Bill's eyebrows shoot up, Eileen's cheeks moved upwards in a smile. 'I'm only jokin', Bill! They can be little bug . . .' Eileen hesitated, seeking another word that would describe her daughters and not bring a frown to Bill's face, 'little horrors, when they like, but they're all there! Our Joan takes her school work very serious, but she's not as quick as Edna. That one will leave us all standin'. She can add up a grocery bill while I'm still on the first item, an' she's only ten.'

Eileen picked a stray hair off her dress. 'I'd better get goin' on the tea. Our Billy will be 'ome soon, an' he wants to go to the first house at the Astoria to see William Powell and

114

Myrna Loy. His mate's mother is going to take them in.'

'He starts work next Monday, doesn't he?'

'Yep! He's got to work a week in 'and, but I can't wait to see 'is face when 'e brings 'is first wage packet home! There'll be no stopping 'im then! He'll be struttin' round like King Tut, an' the 'ouse won't be big enough to 'old 'im!'

Eileen disappeared into the kitchen only to reappear with her face stretched in a cheeky grin. 'I was goin' to say the girls were little buggers, but I thought you wouldn't appreciate a woman of my standin' usin' swear words.'

Eileen wheeled around before Bill could answer, but had she stayed she would have seen a gleam of humour in his eyes.

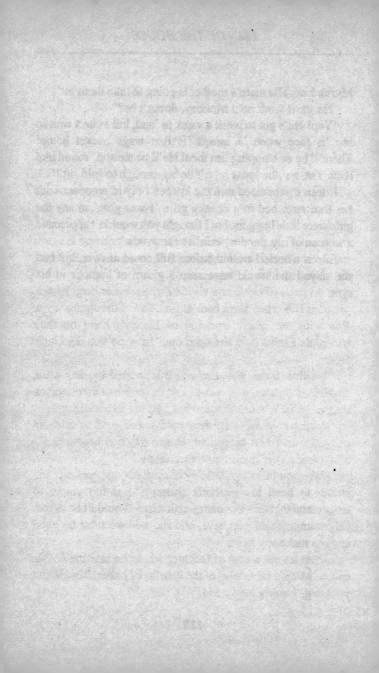

Chapter Thirteen

'Say "hello" to yer Uncle Bill!' There was pride on Eileen's face as she urged her two godchildren forward. 'Shake 'ands, an' show 'im how clever yez are!'

Two pairs of eyes, one vivid blue, the other deep brown, gazed at Bill. They hung back at first, shy of the strange man. But with the gentle pressure of Eileen's hand on their shoulders Emma held her hand out. 'How do you do, Uncle Bill?'

'I'm fine, thank you, Emma!' Bill clasped the tiny hand, smiling at the grown-up words and the serious expression on the pretty face. 'Auntie Eileen has told me all about you.'

Bearing in mind what their mother had told them about being on their best behaviour, Emma touched her brother's arm. 'And this is my little brother, Tony.'

'Have you been sick?' Tony blurted out, his curiosity too strong to heed his mother's warning, and too young to understand that this was one question that shouldn't be asked. 'My mummy said you have, and she said we must be good and not make any noise.'

Eileen let out a peal of laughter when she saw the colour rise on Mary's face. 'Out of the mouths of babes! They'd get yer hung, wouldn't they, kid?'

'I have been sick,' Bill kept his face straight, 'but I'm getting better now.'

'We could kiss you better, couldn't we, Mummy?' Tony's eager face looked at Mary. 'Like you do when we're sick!'

Mary nodded. 'That's a good idea, sweetheart!'

Immediately two pairs of arms went round Bill's neck and he was smothered in kisses. 'There now,' Emma pursed her rosebud mouth and nodded knowingly as she did when playing a game of pretend with one of her dolls, 'you'll soon be better.'

Bill's eyes were moist. 'You know, I feel better already!'

Eileen lifted the children, one in each arm, and swung them round. 'A pair of crackers, yez are!' She lowered them on to the couch and began to tickle their tummies. Soon the house was ringing with shrieks of childish laughter and all Mary's good intentions flew out of the window.

It was Mary who noticed Bill become quieter, his face more drawn. They'd been there an hour, and he'd kept up with the talk and the laughter. But now he looked tired. 'Come on, it's time to go.' Mary lifted her hand to stop the children's protests. 'We've got to get home and make the tea for Daddy and Grandma.'

'Can we come tomorrow?' Emma pleaded.

'Not tomorrow, but we'll come again soon,' Mary promised, with a smile at Bill, 'that's if you can put up with us?'

'I'll look forward to it.' Bill had enjoyed their company, but for the last ten minutes it had been an effort and he was feeling drained. He watched Eileen follow Mary and the children out of the room before closing his eyes and letting his head fall back against the chair.

* * *

'I think we've tired Bill out.' Mary looked at Eileen who was standing on the step. 'I hope we haven't overdone it.'

'He'll be all right, kid! He does get tired quickly, but believe me he's a lot better than 'e was! I'm feedin' 'im up as much as I can, but it's hopeless with the rationing!' Eileen's eyes rolled. 'Half a pound of shin beef to make a pan of scouse for six of us! Now I ask yer, kid, what good is that? Talk about blind scouse isn't in it!'

Mary was facing down the street and was the first to see Joan and Edna running towards them. 'Here's your family!'

'Oh, God!' Eileen groaned. 'Yer don't want to adopt two girls, do yer, kid? Yer can 'ave 'em cheap! They're young an' healthy, can go yer messages for yer . . . an' they're bloody cheeky into the bargain!'

'Go way with you,' Mary smiled. 'You love the bones of them!'

'Oh, I love the bones of them, all right,' Eileen's cheeky grin appeared, 'it's the rest of them I can't stand!'

'Aah, yer not goin', are yez?' Joan was breathless. 'Stay for a bit longer, Auntie Mary!'

'Yeah, go on!' Edna added her weight. 'We can play with Emma and Tony!'

'Never mind playin'!' Eileen waved her arm up the street. 'Yez can just run up to Mrs Knight's for us, and get a large tin loaf.'

'Ah, ay, Mam!' There was a petulant droop to Edna's mouth, 'we've only just got 'ome!'

'An' if yez don't do as yer told, yez'll just be goin' up to bed!' Eileen pointed a finger. 'Now go!'

As she watched the four twig-like legs running up the

street, Eileen grinned. 'Poor buggers! Fancy bein' lumbered with a mother like me!' Too late she remembered Emma and Tony. 'Here y'are, Emma, give Auntie Eileen a smack for bein' naughty and usin' bad words.' She held out her hand. 'Go on, smack me! You too, Tony!'

The two laughing children took it in turns to punish their Auntie, then Mary firmly took their hands and turned them towards home.

Eileen was in the kitchen when Edna ran in, plonked the tin loaf on the drainer and ran out again. Shaking her head and thinking it was no wonder the girls were so thin when they did everything on the run, Eileen dried her hands before picking up the loaf. It was then she noticed the large chunk missing from the end. 'The little flamer's 'ad a bit out of it!' Loaf in hand, Eileen marched through the living room, down the hall, and into the street. 'Hey!' Holding the loaf aloft, Eileen called to Edna who was playing skipping rope with one of Cissie Maddox's girls. 'Come 'ere!'

Her head bowed, Edna came forward slowly. 'D'yer want me, Mam?'

Eileen thrust the loaf under her nose. 'What's the meaning of this?'

'I didn't do that, Mam!'

'Oh, a piece of bread just dropped off, did it?' Eileen thundered. 'How many times do I 'ave to tell yer about takin' bites out of the bread?'

'I didn't do it, Mam! Honest I didn't!' Edna made a cross on her chest. 'Cross my heart an' hope to die!'

Eileen had to bite the inside of her mouth to keep back a smile. This one put Bette Davis in the shade for acting. 'If you didn't do it, then who did, eh?'

Her lips trembling, Edna was torn. If she snitched on Joan she'd get a smack, but if she didn't she'd get a bigger one from her mother. In the end she decided this was no time for bravery. 'It was our Joan, Mam! I told 'er yer'd shout!'

'Where is she?'

'In the entry, Mam! She's playin' with Mary Cooper.'

'Tell 'er I want 'er . . . now!'

Eileen leaned back against the wall, the loaf hidden behind her back. It was no good going back in the house and upsetting Bill. She'd sort it out here, and there'd be no need for him to know. As she waited, Eileen remembered the number of times she'd had a hiding off her mam for doing exactly what she was going to tell her kids off for! Still, she couldn't let them get away with it! If she did, they'd eat half the blinking loaf next time!

'Clat tale tit!' Joan was shaking her sister by the arm when they emerged from the entry. 'Yer little sneak!'

'Eh! Cut that out!'

When Joan heard her mother's voice she dropped Edna's arm as if it was a red hot poker. 'She's tellin' lies, Mam! I didn't bite the loaf, a piece came off in me 'and!'

'Oh?' Eileen raised her brows. 'An' what happened to the piece, might I ask?'

Taken back by the unexpected question, Joan stuttered, 'It . . . it . . . fell on the ground.'

'Joan,' Eileen grimaced. 'Even next door's cat could 'ave come up with a better excuse than that! Anyroad, yez can both go up to yer bedroom an' stay there till the tea's ready.'

'Ah, ay, Mam!' Edna protested, 'that's not fair! I 'aven't done nothin'!'

'Yes, yer 'ave, our Edna!' Joan wasn't going to suffer

alone. 'She got the cane in school today, Mam, for bein' naughty!'

'Oh, no, not again! What did yer do this time, yer little madam?'

Eyes down, foot kicking at a raised flagstone, Edna whispered, 'I only did it as a dare, Mam! I didn't mean for Miss Wright to sit on it!'

'Sit on what?'

There was silence for a moment, then a squeaky voice said, 'A drawing pin.'

Eileen was flabbergasted. 'Yer mean yer put a drawing pin on Miss Wright's chair?'

Tears were running down Edna's face. It was bad enough that the whole class had clatted on her, but for her own sister to give her away was the last straw.

Eileen looked up at the sky. 'What, dear Lord, have I ever done to deserve these two little faggots?' Then, with a menacing look on her face, she roared, 'Up the stairs with both of yez, and not a sound or I'll tell yer dad what yer've been up to, an' then yer'll know what for!'

Eileen didn't have to say it twice. She followed them down the hall and watched them pushing each other to be first up the stairs. Bony elbows were dug into ribs, and arms were pinched as they whispered accusations of 'sneak' and 'clat tale tit'. Eileen waited for the closing of their bedroom door before moving. They were probably battering each other up there, but by tea time they'd be as thick as thieves again.

Eileen held the loaf at her side, out of sight of Bill, as she walked through the living room. Her mother was in the kitchen rinsing a few clothes through in the sink.

Maggie eyed the loaf. 'Been up to the shops, have you?'

Eileen shook her head. 'No, but I'll 'ave to slip up later to settle up with Milly. I 'aven't paid her for a week, so I must owe 'er a fortune!'

Eileen weighed her mother up. Should she tell her, or not? Yeah, why not! They could do with a laugh!

'Mam,' Eileen pointed to where the cob was missing from the loaf, 'would you say they were teeth marks?'

Maggie squinted. 'Look like it to me . . . why?'

Eileen quickly gave an account of the last ten minutes. And by the time she had finished, her huge tummy, her enormous bust, and her layers of chins were wobbling up and down as her body rocked with laughter. Sucking in air, she croaked, 'What makes it so funny, is that Miss Wright's got a bigger backside than me! An' I'm bloody sure that if I sat on a drawing pin, I wouldn't feel a thing!'

Maggie tried to keep her face straight, but couldn't. It was such a long time since she'd seen her daughter laughing so heartily, she wasn't going to spoil it by reminding her that although what Edna had done might seem funny, it really was very naughty. She waited till Eileen's bout of laughing eased before asking, 'I wonder who they take after?'

Eileen's eyes were lost in the folds of flesh. 'Oh, I know, Mam! I was ten times worse than them when I was their age! But the funny thing is, I can't remember you seein' the funny side, like I do!'

'Funny! Did you say funny?' Maggie smoothed her pinny before putting her hands on her hips and glaring at Eileen. 'I suppose you think I should have laughed when Mrs Porter found you bathing their cat in their kitchen sink . . . nearly drowning the poor thing? And when you pushed Alice Jones in the lake at Walton Park and left her to walk home, all on her own, dripping wet, I suppose I should have been splitting me sides laughing!'

'Gerroff yer high horse, Mam, I was only jokin'!' Eileen breathed in deeply and held her tummy to stem the laughter, but to no avail. Bending double, she gasped. 'Yer've left the best one out! Have yer forgotten the time I put some of yer Andrews Liver Salts in our Rene's tea, 'cos she snitched on me?'

Maggie gave up. Memories flooded back, and her laughter was louder than Eileen's. 'I'd forgotten about that!'

'I'm glad our Rene 'as, or she wouldn't be speakin' to me yet!' Eileen held on to the sink, gasping for breath. 'She was sittin' on the lavvy for a whole week!'

'So would you, after two teaspoonsful of Andrews!' Maggie wiped her eyes with the corner of her pinny. 'You're only supposed to take enough to cover a sixpence!'

They both jumped when Bill appeared in the doorway. 'What's going on?'

'Bill, your wife has definitely got a screw loose!' Maggie fought hard against the rising tide of laughter. 'She needs certifying!'

'What's she been saying now?' Bill wanted to know.

Eileen could hear the wireless in the background. It was Henry Hall's band playing their signature tune, *Here's To The Next Time*, and this brought forth a fresh burst of giggles. 'Can yer hear what they're playin', Mam? Appropriate, eh?'

'Oh, take her in, Bill, for heaven's sake! I'll never get me washing done at this rate!' Maggie dipped her hands in the soapy water. 'She's worse than the flippin' kids!'

'I came out to say there's a knock at the door.' Bill looked at Eileen. 'Will you answer it, chick?'

'Okay, love!' Eileen gave her mother a dig as she passed. 'It might be Miss Wright, bringin' the drawin' pin back!'

Eileen's smile disappeared when she opened the door and saw the man standing on the step. He was wearing a navy pin-stripe suit, and the brim of his trilby hat was pulled low over his eyes. 'Arthur!'

Arthur Kennedy saw Eileen's red-rimmed eyes and blotchy face, and stepped back. 'Have I come at an inconvenient time?'

Eileen looked puzzled. 'No! Why?'

'You look as though you've been crying!'

'Nah! I always cry when I laugh!' Eileen held the door. 'Don't be standin' on the step, come on in!'

As she walked back down the hall, Eileen was praying. Please God, let Bill be all right with him!

'Look what the wind's blown in!' Eileen entered the room first. 'It's Arthur Kennedy come to see yer!'

Arthur stood awkwardly in front of Bill. 'I thought I'd call and see how you're getting on, Mr Gillmoss! How are you?'

Bill took the outstretched hand. 'So-so, you know! And what about you?'

Eileen turned a chair from the table. 'Sit down, Arthur! And never mind the mister business . . . his name's Bill!'

Eileen hovered as Arthur placed his trilby on the table before sitting down. If she stayed around, Bill would never open up. It would be better if she made herself scarce and left the two men together for a while. 'I'm just slipping up to the corner shop, so I'll leave you two to have a chin-wag. I'll get me purse, then leave yez in peace.'

Maggie had peeped through a crack in the door to see who their visitor was, now she looked at Eileen with curiosity written all over her face. 'Who's that?'

'I'll tell yer all about it later!' Eileen took her purse from the cabinet drawer. 'I'm goin' up to Milly's to pay me bill, but I'll be back to make them a cup of tea. In the meantime, don't go in the livin' room, Mam, please! Let the men be on their own for a while.'

Leaving her mother more curious than ever, Eileen slipped into the yard, then made her way up the entry to the corner shop.

Chapter Fourteen

'Hiya, Milly!' Eileen rested her elbows on the shop counter. 'How goes it, me old cock sparrer?'

'Well, you're a stranger!' Milly was serving at the far end of the counter and she signalled to Eileen to hang on while she showed her customer that the fragile gas mantle in the little box was intact. If she didn't, and they broke it on the way home, they'd be back saying it was broken when she'd sold it to them! She'd been done too many times to fall for that one! She took the twopence, rang it in the till, then waved goodbye to the customer.

'I didn't think any of the 'ouses round 'ere still had gas light,' Eileen said. 'I thought they were all leccy!'

'No, there's still a few only got gas.' Milly Knight didn't seem to have aged a day since the war started. She was a big woman, almost as big as Eileen, but her figure was well corseted and always looked trim. There was no sign of grey in her neatly waved, dark hair, and not a line on the round, happy face. And yet she worked harder than anyone! The shop opened at six in the morning and didn't close until ten at night. And that went on for seven days a week. There were some nights when Milly crawled into bed around midnight thinking she just couldn't carry on another day, but at six

127

o'clock the next morning Milly would be behind the counter again, and still with a smile on her face for the early customers who called in on their way to work for a morning paper or a packet of cigarettes. She tried to give each customer a bit extra on their ration book, but it wasn't always possible to please everyone and it grieved Milly to have to refuse.

It hadn't been so bad when she and her husband worked it together, but when he was called up Milly only had a couple of part timers to help.

It was a busy little shop, too, and kept her on the go all the time. Mind you, she stocked everything under the sun. Firewood, paraffin, hair nets, milk, potatoes, bread, babies' dummies . . . you name it, and Milly Knight sold it. It was a homely, happy shop, and Eileen felt like one of the Bisto kids every time she went in . . . sniffing in all the different smells.

'It's ages since I've seen you,' Milly said, 'I was beginning to think you'd fallen out with me!'

'The last few weeks 'aven't been the best in me life, Milly!' It was funny, but Eileen could talk to Milly where she couldn't talk to others. 'My Bill came 'ome in a terrible state! I've been nearly out of me mind worryin' about 'im!'

Milly didn't say that Maggie had already told her all about Bill. One thing about Milly Knight, she never repeated anything anyone told her in confidence. 'How is he now?'

Eileen crossed her two fingers. 'I'm keepin' these crossed an' hopin' for the best! That's all I can do!' Eileen considered for a while, then decided she had to talk to someone. So the whole lot poured out, even the visit to Arthur Kennedy's, and as it did, Milly prayed no customers would walk in. She knew how important it was for Eileen to get it all off her chest. What she didn't know was that Eileen was keeping one secret back. A secret only to be shared with her husband.

Eileen ended by telling Milly that right now, Arthur Kennedy was sitting in their living room. 'I only 'ope he can get through to Bill! Bein' man to man, it might be just what Bill needs.'

'It'll take time, Eileen. You can't expect him to go through what he did and come home and forget all about it.'

'I know.' Eileen screwed her face up. 'An' I know I'm lucky compared to some poor buggers, who'll never see their 'usbands again. But it doesn't stop me from worryin'.'

'Hasn't he improved at all since he came home?'

'I think he's put a bit of weight on, an' he is talkin' a bit more, but things are not movin' fast enough for me.'

'Everything comes to him who waits, Eileen,' Milly quoted. 'You're too impatient.'

'I'm bloody selfish, too!' Eileen smiled. 'I'm lumberin' you with all my troubles, an' haven't even asked how your feller is!'

'He's coming home on leave next week!' Milly clapped her hands in joy. 'After four long years, he's coming home!'

Eileen straightened up, her face alight. 'Well, that's the best news I've 'eard for a long time!' Then she cocked her head to one side. 'Did yer say he was comin' 'ome on leave, or for good!'

'Only on two weeks' leave. He's got to go back to Greece, but it won't be for long. He's hoping to be home for good in about two months.'

'Oh, I'm glad fer yer, Milly, I really am! Yer'll be able to 'ave a lie in now an' again . . . no more gettin' up at five every mornin'. Yer won't know yer born!'

'You're telling me! I won't know what's hit me!'

'Eh, I better be gettin' back!' Eileen brought her purse out. 'I'll settle up with yer for the things I've 'ad on the slate.'

'You can leave it if you're skint,' Milly said kindly. 'Next week will do.'

'No, I'll settle up now. If my Bill knew he'd been smokin' ciggies I'd got on tick, he'd 'ave choked on them.' Eileen grinned. 'My feller doesn't believe in gettin' things on the never-never, but what the eye don't see, the heart don't grieve.'

'Would he object to you getting half a pound of Spam from under the counter?' Milly asked mischieviously.

'Milly, for half-a-pound of Spam, I wouldn't care whether 'e objected or not! Are yer sure yer can spare it, 'cos I've got no coupons left?'

'I can spare it.' Milly moved down the counter to the cutting board. 'And I can spare half of bacon for his breakfast, too!'

'Milly Knight, yer an angel!' Eileen's cheeks moved, a sure sign a laugh was on its way. 'Pity yer not a chicken instead of an angel, then I could 'ave 'ad some eggs to go with the bacon!'

Milly laid down the knife, her shoulders shaking. 'Your face would get you the parish, you know that, Eileen Gillmoss! Okay, you twisted me arm! I'll slip in a couple of eggs for your cheek!'

'D'yer know what I feel like now, Milly? D'yer remember when we were kids, an' our mams used to say, "close yer eyes and open yer mouth, an' see what God'll send yer"? Well with all the goodies yer givin' me, I feel like a kid again! Yer might not look like God, Milly, but yer'll do for me, kiddo!'

* * *

Eileen practically skipped down the road. The precious Spam and bacon were together in a brown paper bag, but because bags were scarce, she carried the two eggs loose in her hand.

She hummed softly to herself. Bill could have bacon and egg for his breakfast for the next two days, with a couple of rounds of fried bread. And if Jean Simpson's American boyfriend sent in a piece of meat like he'd been doing for the last few months, she'd be quids in! She'd be able to feed Bill up, and she'd soon have him strong again.

Eileen's high spirits lasted till she reached her front door. Then her tummy filled with butterflies, wondering what she was going to find inside. When she was halfway down the hall, she could hear the sound of men's voices.

They were too low to distinguish, but they filled her with hope. She pushed the door open with her hip in time to see Arthur and Bill leaning towards each other, deep in conversation. They broke apart when she entered, like two children found doing something they shouldn't, and Eileen wished she'd stayed out a bit longer.

'I'll make yez a cup of tea now, fellers!'

'We've had one, chick,' Bill told her. 'I asked Ma to make us one.'

Arthur noticed the eggs in Eileen's hand and grinned. 'With Bill calling you chick, I'm wondering if you laid them yourself!'

Eileen chuckled. Thank God he had a sense of humour! 'There's many a time I've laid an egg, Arthur, but not a real one!' She put her ill-gotten gains on the table, then asked, 'How 'ave you two been gettin' on?'

Bill left it to Arthur to answer. 'We've had a real good

chin wag, swapping experiences and ideas.'

'Are you all right, Bill?' Eileen asked. 'Yer very quiet!'

'I'm fine, chick! Me and Arthur get along just fine!' And Bill really meant it. It had been good to unburden himself to someone who knew and understood what it was like to be a prisoner of war. And who, like himself, felt less of a man than he had before he was captured.

'Then yer'll 'ave to come again, Arthur! Come one day next week an' 'ave some dinner with us.' Eileen shrugged expressively. 'Yer'll 'ave to take pot luck, with things as they are, but yer won't mind, will yer?'

'Eileen, bread and jam are a luxury to me! So don't worry or put yourself out on my account!'

'Eh, you, bread and jam are a luxury to us, an' all! We 'aven't been livin' the life of Riley, yer know!' Eileen leaned on the table, causing it to slide backwards in protest. 'We don't 'ave any puddin's, so yer know in advance! For afters we usually 'ave a few jokes, so yer'd better learn a few before yer come.'

Arthur rose and reached for his hat. 'I'll have to ask my sons! I'm afraid it's a long time since I heard a good joke!'

After goodbyes were said, Eileen followed Arthur to the front door. 'What d'yer think of 'im, Arthur?'

'What I went through pales into insignificance when you hear what Bill suffered! I thought we were badly treated, but I know now that in our camp we were some of the lucky ones.'

'I'm so glad yer came, Arthur! I'm sure it's done Bill good to 'ave yer to talk to, an' I do thank yer!' Eileen folded her elbows and leaned against the door. She couldn't let him go without asking how he was faring, but she worried that he might think she was just being nosey. 'I've thought about yer quite a lot, and wondered 'ow yer were gettin' on. How are things with you? Are you feelin' any better?'

A shadow crossed Arthur's face. 'You saw how it was, Eileen, and it hasn't changed. Sylvia barely speaks to me, and the house is still the pig sty you saw.' Arthur put his trilby on and pulled the brim down, the action reminding Eileen of Humphrey Bogart. 'She still goes out every night and nothing I say will make her change. In fact, I can't see any future for us. If it weren't for the boys, I'd pack me bag and walk out, and that's what she's hoping for. With me out of the way she could please herself, with no one to ask questions or criticise.'

With Eileen shaking her head and tutting, Arthur went on, 'I often wonder what happened to the boys when I wasn't at home to mind them while she goes out every night. I haven't asked them, because I don't think it's fair to question them about their mother, or ask them to take sides. But it makes me wonder if she even cares about them.'

Arthur turned his head to gaze up and down the street, and when he spoke there was sadness in his voice. 'I haven't been quite truthful with you, Eileen. The reason I haven't questioned the boys is because I'm afraid of the answers. I don't think I'd be far wrong if I said Sylvia is used to bringing her boyfriends home with her, and I'm just a bloody nuisance because my being there has put a stop to it.'

Eileen gasped. 'She wouldn't do that!'

'Eileen, if you saw the way the neighbours either avoid me, or look at me with pity in their eyes, then you'd know what I'm talking about. They were my friends once, now they can't even look me straight in the eye!'

'What yer gonna do, then?' Eileen asked. 'Yer can't put

up with that for the rest of yer life!'

'If it weren't for the kids, Eileen, I'd have been on my bike the day after I came home. But I can't just walk out on them. They'd have no stability in their lives if I left them with a mother whose only concern in life is to enjoy herself and to hell with everyone else!'

'Oh dear, yer 'ave got problems, 'aven't yer, Arthur? Did yer tell Bill all this?'

Arthur nodded. 'I didn't intend to, but when we got talking it all just came out. And at least he knows now that there are people with bigger problems than his.'

'It's going to be easier sortin' his problems out than it is yours, I can tell yer that for nothin'!' There was determination in Eileen's voice. 'He's got no troubles on the home front like you 'ave.' A loud sigh escaped her lips. 'I wish I could 'elp yer, Arthur, honest, but there's not much anyone can do.'

'Don't worry, you've got enough on your plate.' Arthur managed a smile. 'I'll sort myself out all in good time.'

'Don't forget yer comin' for dinner, will yer? I'll be puttin' an extra spud in the pan for yer!'

'I'll look forward to it, and I won't forget to bring a joke with me, either!'

'Ta-ra, then, Arthur! See yer next week!'

When Arthur was halfway down the street, Eileen bawled after him, 'Yer'd better bring a few jokes, 'cos there's not many I 'aven't heard!'

Chapter Fifteen

Eileen rested her elbows on the table, her hands wrapped around a cup of tea. She'd just finished washing the dinner dishes and when she'd had five minutes' rest she intended tackling the mound of dirty clothes left on the kitchen floor. Her feet were tired and for a fleeting moment she gave way to one of her fantasies. This one consisted of a fairy godmother, complete with a magic wand in her hand, standing in the back kitchen. With one wave of her silver wand the dirty clothes disappeared, and in the blink of an eyelid they turned up, all washed and ironed, in a neat stack on the sideboard.

Eileen grinned into the tea cup. Wishful thinking, my dear, she told herself. Then answered, 'Yeah, but wouldn't it be lovely?'

Her eyes slewed to the couch where Bill sat reading the *Echo*. He'd been home three months now, and what a lot had happened in that three months! The war in Japan was over, and although the celebrations hadn't been as big as the ones for VE day, the people had still taken to the streets to celebrate what the Government had called VJ day.

Nearly all the servicemen were back on civvie street, with only small units left in what were the occupied countries. Factories that had been taken over to produce armaments

135

were now being converted to produce goods for the home market. Rationing was still as tight, but more could be had on the black market if you had the money to pay for it. The spivs were still raking in the money, but they weren't very popular now, especially with the returning servicemen who felt strongly about spivs making money out of the war when they'd been out fighting for their country.

Many of the women Eileen had worked with had left the factory, and half the conveyor belts had been shut down completely. It wasn't the same without all the old crowd, and Eileen didn't half miss them. Maisie, Ethel, Sadie . . . all of them gone! And Jean Simpson had left last month to marry her American, and she'd gone to live in the States.

Eileen sighed inwardly. She'd pack in work tomorrow if she could, but without her money they'd be living from hand to mouth. So it was Hobson's choice! Through lowered lids, Eileen surveyed Bill. He looked a different man to the one who'd walked through the door that day three months ago. He'd put some weight back on, and his face had filled out and lost that sickly yellow look. But although his health had improved, and the nightmares were less frequent, he was still more quiet and withdrawn than the Bill she'd married. It was as if he was frightened of showing any affection, and when she tried to get near him, he didn't respond.

'Any news, love?'

Bill lowered the paper. 'I can't believe it! D'you know that Britain and America are giving money to Germany to help them build up their country again? They want bloody shooting!' Bill swearing was an indication of the anger he felt. 'Why the hell should we help them? They start a war, kill thousands of people, blow this country to pieces, and we want to give them money! They must have lost the run of their senses! Who's going to pay to build this country up again?'

'The world's cock-eyed!' Eileen agreed. 'We're still on rations, but they can find food for our enemies! I can understand them 'elping the likes of Holland and Belgium, 'cos they've 'ad a tough time, but I'm blowed if I can understand why we should 'elp Germany!'

'Because we're stupid, that's why! Anyone would think we started the war!' Bill rustled the paper. 'I'll bet any money that Germany is built back up again before we are. They lost the war, but they'll win the bloody peace, you mark my words!'

'Here's our Billy!' Eileen smiled when her son walked in. 'Well, 'ow did work go, son?'

'We've been busy.' Billy turned to his father. 'How've you been today, Dad?'

'All right, son!' Bill thought young Billy grew taller every day. He was only fourteen but must be nearly six foot tall. And in his dirty, navy blue overalls, he looked older than his years. 'You know, if you grow any taller, you'll not get through the door!'

'I'm taller than most of the men in work,' Billy's chest swelled with pride, 'they call me Lofty!'

'Your dinner's keepin' hot between two plates on a pan,' Eileen told him, 'but get yerself out of those filthy overalls before yer even think of sittin' down.'

When Billy had gone to wash and change, Eileen grinned at Bill. 'Thinks he's the pig's ear, since 'e started work. Gives the girls a dog's life, 'as them runnin' round after 'im as though he was lord and master. But 'e gives them a couple of coppers every week when he gets 'is money, so they don't mind.'

'He's a good lad,' Bill said. 'He never forgets to ask how you feel, or if you want any messages.'

'He's not mean, either. He 'as to pay 'is fares out of the seven and six a week he gets pocket money, so 'e doesn't 'ave that much left! But he still buys you a packet of ciggies, me a bar of chocolate, and gives the girls a couple of coppers.' Eileen chuckled. 'Wait till the girls are workin', an' you an' me can sit back and live the life of Riley!'

'I'll just be glad when you can pack in work.' Seeing his wife going out to work was a source of worry to Bill. He was supposed to be the man of the house, and it should be him going out to fend for his family.

'Oh, I don't mind,' Eileen lied. 'Anyway, it's not hard work . . . it's a doddle, really!'

'Just the same, it's not right. As soon as I feel up to it, I'll get out and find a job, then you can stay home where a wife should be.'

Eileen stared into the now empty tea cup. *Just you get better, Bill, that's all I ask. I'll willingly scrub my fingers to the bone, as long as you get better.*

'Feel like coming for a pint, Bill?' Alan asked. He and Rene called at least once a week, and for the last four weeks he'd managed to persuade Bill to go out for half an hour to the pub round the corner.

Maggie had gone to the first house at the Walton Vale picture house, Billy was out with his friends, and the girls were playing in the street. So when Bill and Alan left, Eileen and Rene had the house to themselves. It was the first time the sisters had been on their own for months, and over a cup of tea, they brought each other up-to-date with local gossip and family news.

Eventually the conversation came round to Bill. 'I must say Bill's looking a lot better,' Rene said. 'Each time I see him he seems to have filled out a bit more.'

'Seein' 'im every day, I don't see the change as much as you do, but, yeah, he 'as put weight on.'

'And is he all right in himself?' Rene asked. 'Are things working out for you?'

Eileen cast her eyes down. No, things weren't working out, but it wasn't something she could talk about. Then an argument raged in Eileen's head. Why couldn't she talk about it? It was nothing to be ashamed of! And, if she couldn't confide in her sister, then who could she confide in?

'There is something, our kid, but I don't know 'ow to tell yer.' Eileen's face was red with embarrassment. 'Bill would do 'is nut if 'e thought I'd told yer, so give me your word of honour it'll go no further . . . not even to Alan!'

'I promise,' Rene said. 'Now spit it out, kid!'

'I don't know 'ow to put it, 'cos it's so personal.' Eileen played with the handle of her cup. Could she do it? Then she thought of all those sleepless nights, and blurted out, 'He can't make love!'

Eileen looked up expecting to see surprise on Rene's face, instead she saw understanding and compassion.

'Oh, our kid!' Rene shook her head. 'Why didn't you mention it before, I could have told you you're not on your own! A lot of soldiers came back from the war impotent. Especially those who were in prisoner of war camps.'

Eileen's mouth gaped. 'Go way!'

'What they went through made them like that. I know because Alan has seen a lot of them, and he told me. They suffered humiliation and degradation, and because they had to put up with it, couldn't fight back, they felt like cowards.' Rene stretched across and touched Eileen's arm. 'Why didn't you tell me before now! I could have told you all this and you would have understood! It'll take time, but eventually Bill will be all right.'

'Yer mean it's not something permanent? That he will get back to bein' normal?'

Rene nodded. 'Of course he will.'

'Oh, God, our kid, yer don't know 'ow worried I've been. I thought 'e didn't love me any more!' Eileen felt a weight had been lifted from her shoulders. 'Now I know, I can put up with anythin'!'

'Seeing as we're baring our souls, I may as well tell you the lot.' Rene gave a half smile. 'I went through the same thing with Alan.'

Eileen gasped. 'Yer never did! I bet yer only sayin' that to make me feel better!'

'Eileen, if I never move from this table again, that's the God's honest truth! When Alan came out of hospital, before he had his artificial arm fitted, he wouldn't let me near him. He was so ashamed, he wouldn't even get undressed in front of me. And I felt the same as you . . . I thought he didn't love me any more!'

When Eileen didn't speak, Rene went on. 'I was out of my mind too! I didn't know where to turn. It went on for two months . . . two months of hell! Then Alan must have seen what it was doing to me, and he sat me down and explained that he loved me very much, but he wasn't capable of making love. And once I understood, it made so much difference! Sex isn't the be-all and end-all, and I didn't mind as long as he loved me. Then, when he had his artificial arm fitted, I wouldn't let him go to the bathroom to get undressed. I made him show me how he put the arm on, and I talked openly about it. And I must have done the right thing, because after a while he wasn't embarrassed any more. Then, slowly, he regained his confidence, and nature took its course.'

'Our Rene, yer don't know what this means to me!' Eileen was near to tears. 'I must 'ave been bloody stupid not to have thought things out for meself! It's taken me kid sister to make me see sense!'

'It's hard to see sense when your husband turns his back on you in bed, isn't it, Eileen?' When Rene saw Eileen's eyebrows shoot up, she grinned. 'Oh, yes, I went through that too. And so have thousands of other wives. But it will all come right in the end, if you go about it in the right way. Don't try to rush things . . . just be kind and considerate, and, above all, patient!'

Rene wet her finger, ran it across her arched eyebrows. 'If it helps, you can tell Bill what I've told you.'

'Ooh, I couldn't do that! Bill would 'ave kittens if 'e thought we'd been talkin' about 'im!'

'Please yourself, Eileen, but you might be doing Bill a big favour by telling him. He may be worrying, thinking there's something wrong with him. If he knows there's many more like him, and if you can talk about it openly, then he'll know it's not such a big thing. But it's your life, so you must do as you think fit.'

'I don't think I could, kid! I 'aven't got your way with words,' Eileen pressed a finger in the fat of one of her hands, and watched as the dent filled out again. Almost without thinking, she found herself telling Rene about Arthur Kennedy and his wife. 'It was when yer said to be kind, considerate and patient, that I thought of Arthur. His wife's as hard as nails. Not much chance of her being kind or patient. I felt sorry for him before, but now I feel ten times more sorry.'

'Eileen, you always try to take the world's troubles on your shoulders. Think of yourself for a change, will you? Get yourself sorted out, then worry about the Arthurs of this world!'

Eileen straightened up and gave a mock salute. 'Aye, aye, sir!'

It was then they heard Bill's key in the door, and Eileen put a finger to her lips. 'Ssssh! Not a word, our kid, please?'

Chapter Sixteen

There was a droop to Eileen's shoulders as she watched the conveyor roll by. She couldn't remember ever being so fed-up and downhearted in all her life. In fact she'd been happier when the war was on! For although she'd had the worry of Bill being a prisoner of war, at least she'd had her dreams and hopes to keep her going.

Eileen could feel her turban slipping over her ear, and she pushed it back impatiently. Since she'd had the perm her hair was a mass of frizz and she couldn't keep the scarf straight even with six hair clips trying to anchor it down. She turned her head sideways and her eyes lit on the woman standing the other side of the conveyor. As though things weren't bad enough without having to look at that misery guts five days a week. Apart from having a face like the back of a bus, Florrie Maskell had this terrible habit of re-arranging her false teeth every few seconds. And Eileen had to put up with her at break time, too, which was enough to give anyone the willies! If Florrie didn't have a pain in some part of her body, then one of her family or neighbours did. She seemed to thrive on doom and gloom, and where Eileen used to look forward to break-time, now she dreaded it. She had enough problems of her own without listening to Florrie's moans and groans.

Florrie sensed Eileen's scrutiny and waved, bringing a flush of shame to Eileen's cheeks. She really shouldn't be calling Florrie for everything because it wasn't her fault Eileen felt so depressed. It was like kicking the cat when you had no one else to take your temper out on.

While she scratched at an itch in the region between her tummy and bust, Eileen decided she couldn't remember a time when she felt less like smiling. And she was sure she'd never had a temper like she had now, which flared at the least thing. She was moody, unhappy and depressed, and wondered how long she could carry on with things the way they were before she exploded.

After her talk with Rene, Eileen had been full of hope. Her sister said it was nearly three months before Alan had been able to make love to her, and with this in mind, Eileen did everything Rene said she should. She'd been kind, compassionate and patient. But how much longer she could keep it up she didn't know. She wanted her husband back. Wanted to feel his arms around her in bed, wanted to hear him tell her he loved her. She needed it to keep her sanity.

A sigh escaped Eileen's lips. She felt like walking away from the conveyor putting her coat on and saying to hell with it. She'd done more than her share and she'd had enough. She was mentally and physically drained.

Eileen sniffed. There was a lump forming in her throat and tears were stinging the backs of her eyes. If she wasn't careful she'd break down and make a fool of herself. 'Snap out of it,' she muttered under her breath, 'and stop feeling sorry for yourself.'

But she found it harder to talk herself out of it today because there was an extra reason for her sadness. Harry

Sedgemoor had gone for an interview for another job, and if he got it she'd be losing the only pal she had left in the factory.

Eileen could understand Harry wanting to find other employment before the factory closed down, but she wouldn't half miss him. He'd been part of her life for the last six years and the shop floor wouldn't be the same without him.

Harry came to a halt a little way from the machine and stood for a while watching Eileen. She looked so down in the dumps it took some of the shine off his good spirits. Although she'd never said anything, Harry had known her too long not to notice the deterioration in Eileen. Her round fat face had lost its glow, she seemed to be losing weight, and her smile wasn't so ready. She put on a very good act, but Harry wasn't taken in by it. And because they were friends as well as work mates, he was worried about her.

Harry coughed to announce his approach. 'I hope you haven't been skiving while I've been away?'

Her smile forced, Eileen tried hard to put some enthusiasm into her voice. 'Yer a cheeky bugger, Harry Sedgemoor! Who's been keepin' this place goin' for the last six years? It certainly wasn't you!'

'Well, aren't you going to ask me how I got on?'

Eileen eyed the dimple in Harry's chin, and although her heart ached, she managed a smile. 'Yer got the job, didn't yer?'

'I sure did! I start two weeks on Monday, as a supervisor.'

Eileen felt like lashing out at the moving shells, knocking them to the ground in one fell swoop. Instead she grunted, 'If yer put yer 'and down a lavatory, yer'd come up with a gold watch, you would! An' where is this job, might I ask?'

'Napiers, on the East Lancs Road. They made aero engines during the war, but now they're turning part of the factory over to making electrical goods for the home market and abroad.' Harry's excitement came over in his voice. 'I passed the interview with flying colours, and the man even said that when the factory is organised properly, they'll be looking for men with my experience for managers.'

'Stop braggin', Harry. Don't forget I knew yer when yer 'ad nowt!' The smile slipped from Eileen's face. 'I won't half miss yer, Harry. Who can I 'ave a laugh with now, or tell me jokes to?'

'You've still got Willy Turnbull,' Harry laughed.

'Sod off, will yer, Harry! Willy Turnbull wouldn't know a joke if 'e fell over one!'

'When I've settled in me new job, perhaps I can speak for you,' Harry said. 'That's if you intend going to work again when this place closes.'

Interest flared in Eileen's eyes. 'By that time, Bill might be ready for work. Would yer put in a good word for 'im?'

Harry gave a low bow. 'For you, Madam, I'd do anything.' He placed his two hands on Eileen's shoulders and turned her to face him. His face creased in a grin, he started to croon, '"I would take the stars out of the blue, for you . . . for you."'

Eileen struggled free, but there was laughter in her eyes. 'Yer silly bugger, yer'll 'ave the shells all over the floor!'

When Harry walked away, Eileen's eyes followed him, her mind ticking over. And while her thoughts might never bear fruit, they had at least lifted her spirits.

Maggie was waiting by the front door when Eileen walked up the street.

'Father Murphy's been to see Bill.'

Eileen put a hand to her forehead. 'Oh, no, Mam, not another row?'

'No, him and Bill got on fine!' Maggie told her. 'I made them a cup of tea, then went up to Milly's to get out of the way. Father Murphy was just leaving when I got back, and him and Bill were on the best of terms.'

'Thank God for that! I've neither the inclination or the energy for another argument.'

Maggie followed as Eileen ambled down the hall, and there was sadness on her face as she took in the weary droop to her daughter's shoulders and the legs swollen from standing too long. 'You sit down, love, and I'll make you a nice cup of tea.'

'Ta, Mam! Yer'll never see what I buy yer for Christmas!' Eileen put her bag on the sideboard then faced Bill. 'I believe yer've 'ad a visitor?'

Bill nodded, 'Yes, Father Murphy called. He's a different kettle of fish to Father Younger, isn't he?'

Eileen sat down and winced as she pulled one of her shoes off. 'Ooh, that's better. Me feet are practically talkin' to me.'

Bill stared at the red marks made by the too tight shoes. 'You could do with buying yourself a pair of comfortable shoes. Those are far too tight for you.'

'I could do with a lot of things, Bill, but we can't afford them.' Eileen had never moaned in front of Bill before, but today she just couldn't summon the energy to put on a cheerful face. 'When I was a kid and I asked me mam for anythin' she couldn't afford, she always used to say I'd get it when "Donnelly docks". I could never make out who this

"Donnelly" was, and why I 'ad to wait for 'is ship to dock.' Rubbing her swollen foot, Eileen went on, 'I must 'ave been fourteen before me mam told me that Donnelly would never dock because 'e didn't 'ave a bloody ship!'

Maggie came through with a steaming cup of tea. 'That's not quite how I said it, now is it?'

'No, Mother dear, yer don't swear, do yer?' Eileen turned her attention to her other foot. 'How yer managed to bring our Rene and me up without swearin', I'll never know.'

'You don't need to swear to get your point across, chick,' Bill said quietly. 'And there's nothing worse than to hear a woman using bad language.'

'Oh, for Christ's sake, Bill, put a sock in it!'

While Bill was stunned into silence, Maggie lowered her head. She'd been wondering when Eileen would finally erupt. Though her daughter had tried to keep up the pretence that everything was normal, Maggie knew that deep down, her daughter was confused and unhappy. She knew why, too! But she'd die rather than tell Eileen.

When Maggie came to live with Eileen and Bill, she'd been given the bedroom next to them. And she couldn't help but hear the sounds that came through the dividing wall, the sounds of a happily married couple enjoying their love for each other. But since Bill came home, four months ago, the only sound coming from their room once their bedroom door closed, was the sound of silence.

Maggie was worried sick about her daughter's health. Eileen had always had a good appetite, eating anything and everything. But lately Maggie had noticed her picking at her food, as though she had no appetite for it. There had been the excuse at first that Bill needed the food more than she did, and Maggie accepted that. But not any more. If Eileen wasn't careful she'd make herself ill.

Maggie lifted her head. 'There's someone at the door.'

'You go, Mam, will yer? I'm not puttin' these shoes on again.'

Her head cocked, Eileen listened. 'Oh, it's Vera Jackson! Yer 'aven't met 'er yet, Bill, but yer'll like 'er.'

Maggie came in first, hand in hand with Carol, Vera's six-year-old mongol daughter. Vera followed, her face, as ever, anxious in case they were intruding. 'You're not having your tea or anything, are you?'

'It wouldn't matter if we were!' Eileen pushed herself from the chair and padded in her bare feet to pick Carol up. 'This is Vera, Bill.' She waited till the introductions were over then placed Carol in front of Bill. 'This is Carol, Uncle Bill. She's one of me favourites, aren't yer sunshine?'

The flat, moonlike face, beamed. 'Yeth, Auntie Eyeen.'

'Well, you clever kid!' Eileen smiled at Vera who was hovering near her daughter. 'She's speakin' better, isn't she? Be tellin' me to shut up, soon.' Carol's arms went round Eileen's legs, clinging on tight. She was afraid of men, and her big round eyes viewed Bill with suspicion.

Eileen ruffled the blond hair. 'She'll come round in a minute if we don't make a fuss of 'er.'

Vera was still moving from one foot to the other. She was an attractive woman with a neat slim figure, hazel eyes and an abundance of rich auburn hair. But she didn't have a lot of confidence and was ill at ease with strangers. She hadn't always been like that, Mary had once told Eileen. It was only after Carol was born, and she'd had to suffer the curious stares of ignorant people, that Vera had become withdrawn.

Her husband hadn't helped either. Ashamed of having sired a daughter who, as he put it, wasn't right in the head, Danny Jackson lay the blame at Vera's door and treated her like a punch bag. But when he'd been called up for the army a miraculous change had come over him, and to outsiders he was the perfect father to Carol and her two older brothers, and a caring husband to Vera. But to Eileen he was a bad taste in the mouth.

'Vera, will yer sit down?' Eileen gave her a gentle push. 'Yer makin' me nervous standin' there like the nit nurse.'

Bill was winking at Carol, trying to persuade her to come from behind Eileen's skirt. She kept turning her head away, then peeping back. In a few minutes she was smiling back at him, and a few minutes later was sitting on his knee.

Maggie went to put the kettle on and find a biscuit for Carol, while Eileen flopped back on the chair. 'How's Danny? He'll soon be 'ome, won't he?'

'He's in Holland, but I had a letter yesterday saying he should be home on leave soon. He reckons he'll have to go back again for a short while though, till things are straightened out.'

'Yeh, that's what Milly Knight's 'usband 'ad to do,' Eileen said. 'He was 'ome for two weeks, then went back last week. He's 'oping to be 'ome for good in a month or so.' Eileen's eyes narrowed. She wouldn't trust Danny Jackson as far as she could throw him. She'd seen Vera's bruised face after he'd given her a beating, and Eileen had no time for men who hit women. In fact, whenever her mind went back over the war years, one incident always stood out. That was when Harry Sedgemoor had given Danny Jackson a good hiding for ill treating Vera. Harry had zoomed up in Eileen's estimation after that. If anyone had deserved a hiding, it was Vera's husband, and if Harry hadn't sorted him out, Eileen would have done it herself.

In those days, Eileen only knew the Jacksons as neighbours of Mary's, but since that time Vera had become a very dear friend. So some good had come out of Danny's wickedness.

'Yer'll be glad to 'ave 'im home, won't yer?'

'It'll be strange, 'cos I haven't seen him for two years,' Vera said, 'but I suppose we'll get used to it.' Her eyes strayed to Carol, sitting happily on Bill's knee. 'Carol won't remember him.'

'He won't know her, either! She's come on like a 'ouse on fire in the last year. And wait till he sees your Colin, all grown up and workin'.' Two things crossed Eileen's mind as she spoke. Was it because Danny was away that Carol was coming on in leaps and bounds? And if Danny does revert to his old ways when he's back in civvie street, will he be as quick to knock Vera around now that Carol's big enough to stand up to him?

Eileen's train of thought was interrupted by a knock on the front door. 'We're gettin' very popular, aren't we, Bill?' When Eileen saw Bill run his finger gently down the silky skin on Carol's cheek, her love for him surged. He was so kind and gentle, and she loved him dearly. If only he would show her the same affection her cup of happiness would be filled to the brim. She sighed as she pushed herself off the chair. 'I suppose I'd better answer the door, me Mam seems to 'ave gone missing.'

Vera looked down at Eileen's bare feet. 'Shall I go?'

'If yer don't mind, Vera! But whoever it is, don't let them in.'

Chapter Seventeen

A flustered Vera hurried back down the hall. 'It's a man at the door, he says he's a friend of yours. His name's Arthur.'

'Oh, lord, throw me shoes over will yer, Vera?' Struggling and groaning, Eileen winced as she pushed a swollen foot into one of the shoes. 'Yer 'aven't left Arthur on the doorstep, like one of Lewis's, have yer?'

'You told me not to let anyone in!'

'I didn't know it was goin' to be Arthur! I thought it would be one of the neighbours on the cadge.' The other shoe was proving more difficult and huffing and puffing, her face screwed up in pain, Eileen said, 'Tell 'im to come in, Vera.'

When Arthur entered the room, Eileen had her two legs stuck out, one foot shoeless. 'Yer'll 'ave to excuse me, Arthur, but I'm 'avin an argument with one of me shoes . . . it refuses to do as it's told.'

Arthur grinned. 'It's got guts, arguing with you . . . I wouldn't!'

'Well, that's nice, isn't it? Anyone would think I was a big bully!' Eileen waved a hand. 'This is me mate, Vera, and this little angel is her daughter, Carol.'

Vera returned Arthur's nod before stepping towards Carol, who was completely relaxed on Bill's knee. 'I'd better be going and leave you with your visitor.'

'Don't be so daft! Arthur's not a visitor, he's a friend, aren't yer, Arthur?'

'I'd like to think so.' Arthur smiled at Vera. 'Don't go on my account, please!'

Vera was wringing her hands nervously. 'You'll have things to talk about, and you wouldn't get much talking done with Carol taking up Bill's attention.'

'Nonsense!' Bill held the little girl close. 'She's as good as gold, aren't you, sweetheart?'

When Vera saw the pleasure on her daughter's face, her heartbeat doubled. It didn't take much to make Carol happy . . . just a little love and kindness. And she hadn't had much of that in her short life. None of the children in their street ever knocked to see if she could play out, and the only people who showed her any affection, or treated her like a human being, apart from herself and the two boys, were the Sedgemoors and the Gillmoss family. Without them to visit, Carol would never see anyone and Vera's life wouldn't be worth living.

'Arthur, you sit next to Bill on the couch, so yez can 'ave a natter, while me and Vera sit at the table an' pull everyone to pieces.' Eileen raised her brows, 'I'm sure yer wouldn't be interested in Mrs Smith 'avin' it off with the milkman, would yer?'

'No, but I might be interested in where Mrs Smith lives! She sounds very interesting!' Arthur put his trilby on the back of the couch and sat down, watched with suspicion by a wide-eyed Carol. She'd been enjoying herself, and now this man had come along and spoilt it. She withdrew further into the safety of Bill's arms.

But it was as if Arthur knew that he needed to take things

quietly and slowly, so as not to frighten the child. So he ignored her and focused his attention on Bill. 'Have you had the wireless on, Bill? Churchill's calling an election in a couple of weeks.'

'Aye, and I'll be first there to put me cross on to get this lot out,' Bill answered. 'Not that they stand a snowball's chance in hell of getting in.'

Eileen was halfway through telling Vera about Harry's new job when she heard what Bill said. 'What d'yer mean, they won't get in? It was through Churchill we won the war!'

'Oh, was it?' Bill's voice rose, making Carol look up at him with apprehension. 'I thought it was the men out there fighting that won the war?' Bill heard Carol whimper, and lowered his voice as he cradled her. 'Don't be frightened, sweetheart, Uncle Bill's only playing.'

But the look of anger on Bill's face belied his words. When he spoke, his voice was low but filled with bitterness. 'The ones dodging the bullets and bombs, and watching their mates being blown to pieces, they won the war.'

'Hitler, started the war, Bill, not Churchill!' Eileen twisted round in her chair. 'Would you 'ave sat back and let 'im walk through all the countries in Europe, an' not do anythin' about it? The man was a raving lunatic who wanted to rule the whole world! If we hadn't stopped 'im, he'd 'ave been over 'ere, an' where would we 'ave been then?'

Vera's eyes were moving from one to the other, as though watching a game of tennis. She gave a nervous smile when she caught Arthur watching her, and he winked as though to say, don't worry, they won't come to blows.

'I know we had to stop Hitler, and I'm not suggesting we should have sat back and done nothing,' Bill said. 'But there's a world of difference between sitting round a table in an underground bunker giving orders, and being the ones to carry those orders out! A lot of young men were killed fighting for freedom, and those that have been lucky enough to come back won't forget it. They'll want a better life for themselves and their families.'

'Bill's right, Eileen,' Arthur was nodding agreement. 'The men that have come back will expect more than they had when they went away. That means a fair living wage and better working conditions.'

'You've hit the nail on the head, Arthur,' Bill said. 'Otherwise, what's it all been for?'

The subject was dropped when the two girls came in from school, and the tension eased with Eileen's loud gasp at the sight of Edna as she stood inside the door with one leg of her navy blue knickers hanging loose around her knee. 'Oh, my God, will yez look at the state of 'er! Talk about gettin' yer knickers in a twist isn't in it!'

With all eyes on her, Edna became indignant. 'It's not my fault the elastic broke, is it?'

'No, sweetheart, it isn't,' Eileen sighed, 'but I don't suppose yer thought of borrowing a safety pin, did yer?'

Her thin nostrils flared, Edna flounced out. 'I'm goin' to change them.'

'Yer'd 'ave a job! Yer Nan's washed all yer knickers, an' they're not dried yet.' But Eileen was talking to fresh air. Edna was already up the stairs. 'Go up and get her knickers,' Eileen jerked her head at Joan, who hadn't so far opened her mouth. 'I'll put a knot in the elastic an' they'll do 'er to play out.'

Eileen tutted at Vera, 'Kids . . . who'd 'ave 'em?' She

turned her gaze to Carol, who had now decided that Arthur was no threat and was playing with the buttons on his demob suit. 'Got yerself a click, there, Arthur!'

'Looks like it, doesn't it?' Arthur lifted a tiny hand and pressed it to his lips. 'She's a little love.'

Eileen stood on the step and watched Vera and Arthur walk down the street, each of them holding one of Carol's hands. Every so often they would swing her off the ground, and Eileen found herself smiling at the child's infectious laughter.

Long after they had disappeared round the corner, Eileen's thoughts were still on them. Two nice people who'd married the wrong partners.

With Vera being there, Eileen hadn't had a chance to ask Arthur how things were on the home front. But in her own mind she couldn't see much chance of their marriage surviving. Even if by some miracle Sylvia changed, Arthur surely wouldn't want to stay with a wife who'd been with God knows how many men. He might try to make a go of it for the sake of the kids, but what sort of a life was that for him?

Eileen sighed. It was such a pity, 'cos he was a smashing bloke. And now he'd filled out and lost that haunted look, he was a handsome man. He'd recovered quicker than Bill was doing, but then he hadn't been in such a bad state as Bill.

'Are we not having any tea tonight?' Maggie had come up behind Eileen causing her to jump.

'Mam, yer frightened the livin' daylights out of me!' Eileen put a hand over her heart which was thumping like mad. 'An' where the 'ell did yer disappear to?'

'I went out to tidy up the entry and got talking to Cissie

Maddox. Did you know her husband came home yesterday?'

Eileen pushed past her mother. 'The kids told me. I get all the jangle from them. They know more what's going on than I do!' A sly grin was on Eileen's face when she turned her head round. 'I even know that Cissie bought herself new underclothes for the occasion.'

Maggie clicked her tongue. 'Like mother, like daughters!'

'I must be the exception to the rule, then, mustn't I, Mam? Or do I take after you?'

'Not on your life, you don't!' Maggie huffed. 'I'll swear to this day that the hospital mixed the babies up and I got the wrong one!'

'Don't forget to go and vote.' Harry stood by Eileen's machine. Tomorrow was his last day, and as the time drew near he realised how much he was going to miss the place. And in particular he was going to miss this big woman. Without her help he wouldn't be married to Mary, and without her he wouldn't have had so many laughs over the years. 'Did you hear me?'

'I might be daft, Harry, but I'm not bloody well deaf!' Eileen stuck a finger under her turban and scratched her head. 'I don't think I'll bother. I've never voted in me life, so why start now?'

'Everyone should vote! What's the good of having an election if no one can be bothered to go out and put a cross on a piece of paper?'

'I'm all mixed up about who to vote for,' Eileen said. 'I'd vote for Churchill, but Bill's dead against it.'

'Far be it from me to come between man and wife, Eileen, but you should vote for who you want to.' Harry studied the nib of his fountain pen, pushed it into his finger and watched the stain made by the blue ink. 'After all, that's what democracy is all about.'

'Well, I'll think about it.' Eileen noticed Florrie trying to attract Harry's attention. 'Dozy boots wants yer.' As Harry rounded the machine, Eileen called after him, 'Don't forget yer've promised to bring Mary and the kids up on Saturday afternoon!'

'We'll be there!' Harry stuck his thumb up. 'Are you going to bake a cake for the occasion?'

'It's obvious yer've never tasted me bakin',' Eileen's voice boomed over the noise from the machines. 'It's nourishment yer want, sunshine, not punishment!'

Harry was smiling when he reached Florrie's side. God, he was going to miss Eileen!

By Saturday all the results of the election had been counted, and Churchill had been thrashed at the polls. According to the wireless commentators, it was the servicemen who had swung the vote against him. Those still stationed abroad had been given postal votes, and it was they who voted in their droves for a Labour Government.

Bill was delighted. But although she kept her thoughts to herself, Eileen felt sad for Churchill. She could see Bill's argument, but he hadn't been here when Churchill had made those dramatic speeches, urging everyone to be strong and keep going. Listening to him had filled everyone with such pride and patriotism they'd have gone through hell and high water to make sure Hitler was defeated. He was bluffing most of the time, but it was his bluffing that won the war.

When Mary and Harry came in the afternoon, Eileen had

heard enough about the election to last her a lifetime. So, pointing a finger, she warned, 'One word about the election and I'll scream the 'ouse down, so there!'

Emma and Tony were dressed in their Sunday best, and Mary was reluctant to let them play out with Joan and Edna. But seeing the disappointment on their faces, Harry put his foot down. 'There's no children round by us for them to play with, so for heaven's sake let them have a bit of fun while they can.'

Eileen swayed her way to the kitchen, a sly smile on her face. She could be heard giggling and whispering to her mother and Harry raised his brows at Bill. 'What's your wife up to, Bill?'

'Don't ask me, Harry, Eileen's a law unto herself! She's been like a kid with a new toy all day.' Bill was used to the Sedgemoors now and was completely at ease with them. 'You never know with Eileen, what she'll be up to next.' At that moment, Eileen appeared in the kitchen doorway. In her hands she was carrying a cake with a lighted candle on top. But the brightness of the flame from the candle couldn't compare with the glow on Eileen's face. And the twinkle in her eyes told the startled Harry that there was more to come. 'Hurry up, Mam!' Eileen called over her shoulder. Then when her mother was by her side, she started to sing while Maggie waved a white hankie. 'Wish me luck, as you wave me goodbye, Cheerio, as I go on my way'. With her hips swinging to the tune, Eileen belted out the words to Gracie Fields' popular song. What she lacked in melody, she made up for in enthusiasm.

Bill was smiling. 'So that's what you two have been so mysterious about all day, eh?'

Harry's eyes were bright with laughter. 'Eileen, you're incorrigible!'

Eileen looked sideways at her mother. 'Eh, Mam, is that good or bad? What does incorrigible mean?'

'It means you're past help,' Maggie informed her.

'So is this candle.' Eileen looked down at the candle which flickered brightly for a second before going out. 'Anyway, Harry, this is a little leaving present. And don't worry, I didn't bake it . . . me mam did.'

Maggie dug Eileen in the ribs. 'There's someone knocking on the back kitchen window. I wonder who it can be?'

'There's only one way to find out, missus, and that's by opening the flippin' door!'

There was silence until they heard Maggie saying, 'Hello, Vera, come in.'

Carol made a bee-line for Bill, then stopped when she saw her Uncle Harry and Auntie Mary. She couldn't make up her mind who to go to, so she stood in the middle of the room, her eyes moving from one to the other.

'She's spoilt for choice,' Eileen laughed. 'What made yer come round the back, Vera? Was the club man after yer?'

'I knocked on the front door, but we couldn't make you hear above the noise you were making.'

Eileen placed the cake on the table. 'I asked Vera to come round 'cos we never seem to get together these days. And Harry's little leavin' party was as good an excuse as any.'

Carol had finally made up her mind and settled on Harry's knee with one arm round his neck and the other round Mary's. They were making a big fuss of her and her hearty laugh brought a smile to all their faces.

'Give us a hand with the butties, will yer, Vera, while me mam makes the tea?'

'Your mam can sit down, and I'll do the tea.' Mary disengaged herself from Carol's arm. 'I'm not sitting here like a dog's dinner while you do all the work.'

In the kitchen, Eileen looked from Mary to Vera. 'Isn't this nice? All mates together, the way it should be.'

Mary set about cutting the tin loaf, then passed the slices over to Vera to scrape a thin layer of margarine on. Then they were passed to Eileen to be made into sandwiches with the corned beef she'd cadged off Milly Knight.

'Have you heard from Danny lately?' Mary asked.

'He's coming home on Monday, on two weeks' leave.' Vera handed some sliced bread over to Eileen. 'He said in his letter he'd be going back to Holland for another couple of months.'

'Yer'll 'ave to bring 'im round when he's home,' Eileen said. 'I haven't seen 'im for years.'

'I haven't seen him for years meself.' Vera gave a nervous laugh. 'It'll be strange having him home again.'

'Are the boys looking forward to seeing him?' Mary asked.

'It's hard to know with the boys, what they're thinking. They were old enough to remember what he was like, and kids don't forget.'

'I thought he was all right with them now?' Eileen finished the last of the sandwiches. 'He seemed to 'ave changed, last time I saw 'im.'

'We'll just have to wait and see.' Vera didn't want to talk about Danny. The house had been nice and peaceful without him, and if she was to be honest, she'd have to admit she didn't relish the thought of having him home for good. True, he had changed since he joined the army, but Vera didn't trust him to stay that way. If he went back to his old haunts and his old boozing buddies, then like as not he'd go back to his fits of bad temper. Vera sighed inwardly. All they could do was wait and see. But never again would Danny Jackson lay a finger on her or Carol. That was one thing she was sure of.

The three women cleared the table, with Maggie washing the dishes as they were brought out. Then, when everywhere was tidy, and Carol was playing with Edna's game of tiddly winks, Eileen brought a half bottle of whisky and a bottle of port wine out of the sideboard cupboard.

'Well, you are doing it in style, Mrs Gillmoss!' Harry patted his tummy. 'I'm stored. That was a very nice spread, and I thank you.'

'I 'aven't got enough glasses, so me an' you are goin' to 'ave to make do with cups, Bill.' Eileen filled the glasses and cups, then raised her cup to Harry. 'The best of luck in yer new job, Harry.'

'Thanks, Eileen.' Harry took a sip, then raised his glass again. 'Here's to good luck for all of you. To you, Bill, Eileen, Vera, Maggie, and not forgetting my lovely wife, I wish you all the very best of everything. And, above all, may we always be friends.'

'Shut up, before yer 'ave me bawlin' me eyes out.' Eileen took a mouthful of whisky and pulled a face. 'Terrible when yer 'ave to drink this bloody awful stuff to make yerself 'appy.'

Eileen heard the back door open and twisted in her chair to see Joan come in, her hand gripping Emma's, followed by

Edna and Tony. The children's clothes were filthy, but that didn't surprise Eileen. What did surprise her was the tall form of Arthur Kennedy behind the children. 'We brought 'im round the back, Mam, 'cos the front door's closed.' Joan's eyes looked accusingly at the glasses and bottles. 'Yer've been 'aving a party!'

'Mind your manners, young lady,' Bill said sternly. 'And move out of the way and let Mr Kennedy in.'

Arthur looked embarrassed and glared at Joan. 'They didn't tell me you had visitors. I wouldn't have bothered you if I'd known.'

'All the more the merrier, Arthur! You're very welcome,' Eileen said. 'You do the introductions, Bill, while I get another cup.'

'No, I'll not stay. I'll come back another time.'

'Yer'll do as yer told and get yer bottom on that chair.' Eileen pushed Arthur down and flung his trilby on the sideboard. 'An' yer'll get drunk like the rest of us, whether yer like it or not.'

Arthur grinned. 'I told you once, I'm not going to argue with you 'cos I know I'd lose.'

Bill raked over the embers of the coals before putting the fireguard in front of the grate. Hanging over it were two pairs of navy blue knickers airing off for the girls to wear for school the next day. 'I think everybody enjoyed themselves, chick!'

'Yeah, it's nice to 'ave a get together with yer friends.' Eileen was rubbing her tired feet. 'Funny 'ow Arthur's fitted in with us. He comes that regular he's beginnin' to feel like one of the family.'

164

'I think he's a lonely, lost man.' Bill looked down at his clasped hands. 'I feel sorry for him.'

'Well, he's always welcome in this 'ouse.' Eileen yawned. 'I'm glad it's Sunday temorrer an' I can 'ave a lie in.'

'You've made some good friends while I've been away, chick!'

'Yeah, I know! And all because Mary Bradshaw came to work on my machine. I knew Harry of course, 'cos 'e was me boss. But we'd never 'ave become real friends without Mary. And it was through her I met Vera. Small world, isn't it, love?' Eileen stifled another yawn. 'I can't keep me eyes open, I'm off to bed.'

'I'll just finish me ciggie, then follow you up.'

Chapter Eighteen

Bill knelt in front of the newly black-leaded grate willing the rolled-up pieces of burning newspaper to set fire to the sticks of firewood laid criss-cross on top of it. He was waiting for it to take hold before carefully placing the cobs of coal he had laid out on a piece of newspaper on the floor beside him. The trouble was, the firewood was damp and not going to light easily. If only someone would remember to bring the small sticks of wood in the night before, there wouldn't be this trouble.

Bill shook his head, angry with himself. When am I going to stop blaming everybody else in the house when things don't suit me? Seeing as I'm the only one with nothing else to do, surely to God I can at least see to little tasks like this.

Falling back on his heels, Bill shoved the poker between the rails of the grate and gently lifted the slowly burning paper and wood to let the draught get to it. And while he looked into the flickering flames his mind dwelt on his selfishness. It was only this morning, seeing Maggie getting the two girls ready for school, that the truth sank in. He was allowing his mother-in-law, a woman twenty-odd years his senior, to do what he should be doing. He had watched with growing shame as she'd rushed around seeing to the breakfasts, checked the two thin necks to make sure there were no tidemarks, packed their sandwiches and waved them off to school.

The firewood had caught now, and Bill carefully placed the cobs of coal on top. He'd bank it up later with some slack to eke out their meagre coal ration.

'Is me mam in yet?'

Bill turned to see Edna's face poked round the door. 'Your mam won't be home from work for another hour or so.' Then Bill noted the woeful expression on his daughter's face and the signs of recent tears. 'What are you doing home from school so early?'

The question brought forth a wail of distress. 'They sent me 'ome with a note for me mam.'

Bill rose to his feet. 'Come here and tell me all about it.'

Edna came forward slowly, a crumpled letter clutched in her hand. 'Miss said to give this to me mam.'

'Give me the letter and take your coat off.' Bill held the letter in his hand while Edna slipped out of her coat and laid it carefully over the back of a chair. 'Now come and sit next to me and we'll see what the letter has to say.'

'I want me mam!' Edna's cries rose. 'Teacher said to give it to me mam.'

Bill sat on the couch and patted a spot next to him, 'Come and sit here, pet.'

Edna eyed him for a second, then sat down, as far away from her father as the couch would allow. She'd walked home from school slowly, looking in shop windows to pass the time till she thought her mother would be home. Now she was in for it.

Bill moved closer and put an arm round the shaking

shoulders. 'I'm sure there's nothing in this letter that's worth crying over, pet! Let's see if we can sort it out before your mam comes in.'

Eileen eyed the two figures on the couch. At first her heart was lifted to see Bill with his arm around Edna, holding her close. Then suspicion took over. 'What's going on?'

Bill handed the letter over and watched Eileen's eyes run hurriedly over the handwritten note. 'Oh, my God, yer've got nits in yer hair!'

'There's no need to let the whole street know,' Bill said quietly. 'Edna feels bad enough as it is!'

Eileen sank on to a chair. 'Yer can't 'ave nits! None of us 'ave ever 'ad dirty 'eads!'

'The nurse from the clinic said I 'ave.' Edna's tiny voice came from within the depths of Bill's arms. 'Three of us in our class got letters.'

Eileen looked at Bill. 'Where the 'ell would she catch them from?'

'Irene Clarkson sits next to me in class, an' she's got them.' Edna sat forward, the worst was over now. 'Yer can see them in 'er hair.'

'Right!' Eileen jumped up. 'I'll run down to the chemists and get some Sassafras oil and a fine-tooth comb. I'll give yer 'air a good do tonight, then again temorrer night. I'll get rid of the bloody things if it kills me.' Eileen rummaged in her purse to make sure she had enough money, then made for the door. 'I wouldn't get too close to 'er, Bill,' she called over her shoulder, 'otherwise she'll pass them on to yer.'

Eileen spread the newspaper on the table then motioned to

Edna. 'Get yer 'ead down over this.'

The steel fine-tooth comb raked through the thin hair, bringing screams from Edna. 'Ow, our mam, that hurts!'

'I'm sorry, sunshine, but it's the only way to get rid of them,' Eileen said, then she noticed Joan looking on with a smirk on her face. 'You'll be laughin' the other side of yer face in a minute, young lady, 'cos you're next! If our Edna's got nits, then ten to one yer'll 'ave them as well, with sleepin' with 'er.'

Poor Edna's scalp was sore by the time Eileen had finished with the fine-tooth comb, and when the Sassafras oil was rubbed in, her screams were pitiful. And even though the gob stopper that Eileen had had the sense to buy dulled the screams, it didn't stop them.

Maggie looked on with pity on her face. And when Eileen dragged a terrified Joan to the table, she thought it was time to step in. 'Come here, love,' Maggie held her arms out to Edna. 'All kids go through this, you know! I can remember your mam going through the same thing, and screaming her head off just like you.'

Edna was stunned into silence. 'Me ma 'ad nits?'

Maggie nodded, 'So did I at your age! When you've got a classroom full of children, you only need one with nits and before you know it, everyone's got them.' Maggie looked at Bill for support. 'Aren't I right, Bill?'

Bill sniffed in the strong Sassafras oil tang and smiled, 'The smell brings it all back! I can remember as though it was only yesterday, every Friday night my mother used to drag me out to a little lean-to we used to have at the back of the house. And no matter how much I kicked and screamed, she used to douse my hair with that stuff.'

Fine-tooth comb in hand, Eileen turned. 'This 'ouse is too small for any lodgers, so they're gettin' chucked out! These two can stay off school temorrer, and the next day our Edna's takin' a note in with her to tell Miss Wright she's got to be moved away from Irene Clarkson. Let some other sucker 'ave the pleasure of her company.'

Eileen stretched her legs out in front of her and heaved a sigh. 'What a flippin' day! That's the last thing in the world I expected to come 'ome to.'

Bill smiled. 'You should have seen Edna's face . . . she was terrified. I felt heartily sorry for her.'

'It's me mam I feel sorry for, 'avin' to sleep in the same room as them! The stink up there is somethin' shockin'.' Eileen pulled on her bottom lip. 'With all the fuss, I forgot to ask where me mam got to this afternoon.'

'I persuaded her to go to the matinee.' Bill looked sheepish. 'For six months I've sat and watched her doing all the work, and I thought it was about time I did my share.'

Eileen ran a hand through her frizzy hair. 'I'm fed up, Bill! There must be more to life than just bed an' work!' She leaned her elbows on her knees and looked him in the eyes. 'How about comin' into town with me on Saturday? Christmas is not that far off, an' we could look for somethin' for the kids' presents.'

'You know how I hate going into town, chick! You'd be better going on your own, you'd get round quicker.'

'Bill, yer've been 'ome six months, an' the furthest yer've been is the Vale and Walton Road! Apart from doin' you good to get out, don't yer think I'd like to go out with me 'usband now an' again?'

171

Bill cast his eyes down. 'All right, chick, if that's what you want, we'll go to town on Saturday.'

Eileen walked down the street, her arm linked through Bill's, her face creased in a wide smile as she waved and shouted greetings to neighbours who were standing at their front doors. She felt on top of the world. And Bill looked good, too. He was still thinner than he used to be, and of course his white hair made him look older, but to Eileen he looked very handsome in his demob suit. It was like old times waiting at the bus stop, then being helped aboard by her husband. And on the journey into the city she kept the conversation going, pointing out bomb damage and the boarded-up shops. 'But I see all the Mary Ellens are back! Look!' Eileen's head turned each time they passed one of the side streets off County Road and Rice Lane, to where the barrow women stood with their carts full of vegetables. They were part of Liverpool, with their long black skirts and black woollen shawls. And their voices, singing out 'two lemons for a penny', or 'here y'are, love, carrots penny a pound', added a bit of colour to the busy area. When they stepped off the bus in Clayton Square, Bill grabbed hold of Eileen's arm. But she was too busy waiting for a break in the traffic to notice the fear on his face. Pushing her way through the crowds of people, and pulling Bill behind her, Eileen didn't stop until they were outside Reeces. Only then did she notice how pale his face was. 'Are yer all right, love?'

Bill struggled inwardly to get a grip of himself. How did you explain that even after being home for six months, he couldn't forget those five years of being caged in by barbed wire, when the only people you saw were your comrades and the prison guards. He wasn't ready yet to mingle with the hordes of shoppers in the centre of Liverpool, not without the past coming back to haunt him.

Eileen looked concerned. Perhaps she'd done the wrong thing, making Bill come with her. 'I know, let's go in 'ere an' 'ave a cup of tea and a toasted teacake, eh? Yer used to like comin' to Reeces, didn't yer?'

Bill followed Eileen up the steps to Reeces self-service cafeteria. He felt faint and his heart was thumping like mad. But he was determined he wasn't going to let Eileen down. She'd been so looking forward to this, he wasn't going to disappoint her. God knows, she got little enough out of life as it was.

It was crowded in the cafeteria and all the tables were occupied, but Eileen wasn't to be put off. Bill looked as though he needed to sit down, and she stood by the entrance till she saw two people gather their shopping up. 'There's a table, Bill!' Eileen pushed her way forward and beat another couple to the table. She'd have been prepared to fight for it with Bill looking so pale. 'You sit down, love, an' I'll go to the counter.'

The table was near a mirror, and as Eileen slipped her coat off, she caught sight of herself. She closed her eyes to shut out the vision of this huge woman, in a navy and white spotted dress, who looked as big as an elephant. Although she was hot and sweaty, Eileen hastily put the coat back on and made her way to the queue formed at the counter.

All the joy had gone from the day now. It's no wonder Bill doesn't fancy me, Eileen thought as the queue moved forward slowly. No man would fancy someone as big and fat as me.

When her turn came, Eileen ordered a pot of tea and two

toasted teacakes. Her actions automatic, she loaded the plates and cups on to the tray she'd picked up at the end of the counter, and paid her money to the girl at the till. And as she walked back to the table she wished she could shrivel up inside her navy edge to edge coat. It was with difficulty she swallowed the teacake which tasted like straw, and feeling that every eye in the crowded cafe was on her, she couldn't wait to get out of the place.

'Are you all right?' Bill asked. 'You've gone very quiet.'

'I'm fine!' Eileen lied. 'Got to give me mouth a rest sometime, yer know.'

Outside on the pavement, Bill asked, 'Where to now?'

'We'll 'ave a look round the shops, eh? I see most of them 'ave been done up ready for Christmas.'

Eileen walked by Bill's side, making no effort to link arms. Her brain was filled with wild thoughts. He's probably ashamed to be seen out with me! Who'd want a wife built like a battleship?

Bill looked sideways and thrust his arm out, 'Stick your leg in, chick!'

'Yer don't want me 'anging on to yer! I'll wear yer into the ground!'

'Don't be ridiculous! Stick yer leg in in case we get split up in the crowd.' Bill waited for the feel of Eileen's arm and squeezed. 'That's better! I wouldn't be able to find the way home on my own. It's so long since I was down here, and Liverpool's changed that much, I'd get lost.' Bill was puzzled. Eileen had been full of life one minute, then down in the mouth the next. He couldn't make it out. He couldn't understand what had happened to make her change, but change she certainly had. And all in the space of minutes.

They wandered round the shops that had escaped the bombing of the May blitz, but Eileen had lost interest. When Bill pointed out a book that he thought Joan would like in her Christmas stocking, Eileen mumbled that she'd come back another time and get it. 'Me feet are killing me,' she told him. 'Let's make tracks for 'ome.'

'Don't you want to buy something for yourself?' Bill asked. 'Let me treat you to a present?'

Eileen looked away. Money can't buy the only present I'd like right now, she thought. And that's to be nice and slim, so I could wear a glamorous nightie and make yer fancy me. 'Not today, Bill, but ta very much. Yer can buy me something next time we come down, but I'm not in the mood right now.'

They stood at the bus stop, never a word between them. Bill racked his brains for something to say that would bring a smile to his wife's face, but he'd never known her like this and didn't know how to cope. They sat in silence on the journey home, and it was only when they were walking up their street he thought of something that might open her up. 'I thought Vera was going to bring her husband round when he was on leave? His two weeks must be nearly over by now.'

Eileen shrugged. 'He goes back on Monday, so she might bring 'im round temorrer. If she doesn't, I won't lose any sleep! I've never liked Danny an' I never will.'

Chapter Nineteen

'Oh, I forgot to tell you when you got home from town yesterday, our Rene and Alan came with Victoria.' Maggie wasn't going to say she hadn't forgotten at all. It was the sight of Eileen looking so dejected and moody that had put her off. And her daughter wasn't much better today. She was quiet, and she'd hardly touched any of her dinner. She'd expected them to come home talkative and loaded with Christmas shopping, but they came back empty-handed and barely speaking. Eileen's excuse was that she had a headache, and the same excuse took her to bed early leaving Maggie and Bill listening to a play on the wireless. Maggie did think of asking Bill what was wrong, but decided against it. Better to leave man and wife to sort out their own affairs.

'Are they all right?' Eileen settled on the couch, leaving a wide space between her and Bill, while Maggie made for her small arm chair under the window. She smoothed the cloth covering the small table at the side of her, and fingered the embroidery which she'd spent hours working on before her husband died. Never a day passed when she didn't look at the cloth and think of the man she'd adored, who was taken from her in the prime of his life.

'Victoria's got a cold,' Maggie answered, 'but apart from that they're fine.'

'Victoria's always got a cold, but it's their own fault! They're terrified of the wind blowin' on 'er, so consequently she catches cold at the least thing.' Eileen tried to dislodge a piece of meat stuck between her back teeth. 'If they 'ad a couple more kids, they wouldn't 'ave so much time to fuss over Victoria an' she'd come on like a house on fire.'

Bill tutted. 'That's their business, chick, not ours.'

'Oh, God, 'ere we go again! Can't I . . .' Eileen's words were cut off by the rat-tat on the front knocker. 'This will probably be Vera and Danny. Be an angel, Mam, and open the door for us.'

But there was no Danny . . . only Vera and Carol. 'Where's your feller?'

Eileen shuffled forward to the edge of the couch and gathered Carol in her arms. 'I thought he'd be with yer.'

'He got the early train back to camp this morning.' Vera averted her eyes. 'I thought you might be expecting us, that's why I've come to tell you.'

Carol struggled from Eileen's bear-like grip and rushed to Bill, showering his face with kisses. 'Uncle Bill!'

'Yer want to watch this daughter of yours,' Eileen grinned, 'she likes the men too much!'

'She doesn't take after her mother then.' Vera hovered near the door, her anxious eyes on Carol. 'Don't let her make a nuisance of herself, Bill.'

'For cryin' out loud, Vera, will yer relax! Park yer backside down an' make yerself at 'ome.' Eileen noted Vera's jerky movements and the darting eyes. She certainly didn't look like a woman who had had her husband home for two weeks after a two-year separation. Mind you, Eileen pulled a face, I don't suppose I do, either! Oh, well, it's a hard life if you don't weaken! 'We expected yer to call while Danny was 'ome,' Eileen broke the silence. 'What 'appened?'

'Well, you know what it's like! He was out every day visiting his parents and going to see his old mates at the dock. The time just flew over.'

Aye, Eileen thought, that's all me eye and Paddy Martin! I bet he's spent the whole time in the boozer, like he always did. And I'll lay odds that he never took you or Carol over the door. But this was no time for saying what she thought . . . not with Vera looking so miserable and Bill sitting there all ears. 'Were the boys glad to see him?'

'He didn't half get a shock when he saw them.' Vera managed a weak smile. 'They're both taller than him now.'

'An' did Carol remember 'im?'

Vera shook her head. 'He's been away too long.'

'D'you want a cuppa, Vera?' Maggie put her hands on the arms of the chair and pulled herself up. 'I'll make us all one.'

Another rat-tat at the door brought Maggie back from the kitchen. 'Who can that be now?'

'Mam, if I 'ad eyes that could see through brick and wood, I'd be earnin' a fortune on the stage.' Eileen lumbered to her feet. 'Just put another cup of water in the kettle while I go an' see who it is.'

But Maggie stayed put until she heard Eileen greet Arthur Kennedy, then she retreated to the kitchen to add more water to the kettle.

'Hello, Bill, Vera!' Arthur raised his voice. 'Good afternoon, Maggie!' Maggie's head popped round the door. 'I'll swear you can smell a cup of tea a mile away.'

'That's all I come for!' Arthur chuckled. 'You make the best cuppa in Liverpool.'

'Sit down, Arthur.' Bill took Carol on his knee to make room. 'Say hello to my little friend.'

'Hello, sweetheart.' Arthur bent to kiss the upturned, smiling face. 'I wondered if you'd like to come for a pint, Bill?'

'Course 'e would!' Eileen spoke before Bill could answer. 'Yer've got an hour before the pub closes.'

Maggie appeared, hands on her hips. Her face was set in a frown, but there was laughter in her voice. 'If my tea's so good, why go for a pint?'

'Well, I've worked it out so I can have the best of both worlds. I can go for a pint with Bill, then come back for a cup of your delicious brew.'

Carol kicked up a fuss when Bill and Arthur went out, so Eileen called the girls in from the entry where they were having a game of tag. 'Take Carol up to the corner shop for some sweets, then when yez come back yez can go upstairs and play till yer dad gets back.'

When the girls came back their lips were black from the liquorice sticks they'd bought. But for once Eileen didn't complain. She gathered their games together and sent them upstairs to play in their bedroom. It was then Maggie pleaded tiredness and said she'd go and lie down for an hour. It was an excuse to leave the two women alone so they could talk in private. It didn't take a blind man to see they both had things on their minds, and they'd talk more openly without her there.

Maggie, with the wisdom of her years, was right. As soon

as they were alone, Eileen sat at the dining table and pointed to the chair opposite. 'Park where I can see yer, Vera! I've got a kink in me neck an' I'm goin' cross-eyed tryin' to see yer.'

They faced each other across the table, and Eileen grinned. 'Now, let's have it, kid! I gather from yer clock that Danny's leave wasn't all sunshine an' roses.'

Vera closed her eyes, her shoulders sagging. 'He's not changed, Eileen. It was all a show he put on before he went in the army. I thought it was too good to be true, but I went along with it for the sake of the children. Anything for a quiet life, that's me, fool that I am.'

'What happened while 'e was on leave?'

'I didn't see that much of him! He was out every day as soon as the pubs opened and I didn't see him again until nearly midnight!'

'Yer mean he never took yer anywhere?'

'He never took any of us over the door! Not that that worried me, because I didn't want to go out with him. But I was upset and angry that he never bothered with the children.' Vera blinked rapidly. 'I hate him, Eileen! God forgive me, but I hate him. The only time he bothered to even talk to me was when he was cadging money off me to go boozing with his cronies.'

'The bastard!' Eileen clenched her fists. 'Yer mean he never kisses yer, or says nice things to yer?'

'Danny's never said nice things to me, Eileen. He's always been the same. He'd come in from the pub, rotten drunk, wake me up if I was asleep, take what he wanted without a by-your-leave, then turn over and go to sleep. Never one word of love or affection would ever cross his lips. And I used to put up with it because I didn't want the kids upset. I put up with all the beatings as well, because of the kids.' Vera blew out a deep sigh. 'Remember that time Harry caught him giving me a beating, and Harry took him outside and belted him one? Well I swore then that Danny Jackson would never lay a hand on me or the kids again.'

'He's never 'it yer again, 'as he?'

Vera sat still for a while, then, slowly, she undid the buttons of her blouse and whipped away the silky scarf she'd had tied around her neck. She slipped the blouse off her shoulder to reveal red and blue ugly bruises running from her neck to her breasts, and across her shoulders. 'This is a bit of Danny's work!'

'Oh, my God!' Eileen gasped, 'what did 'e do that for?'

'Because I resisted his amorous advances.' Vera buttoned up her blouse and re-tied the scarf. 'He came in rotten drunk every night, stinking of beer and cigarette smoke. I wouldn't let him touch me, just having him next to me made me feel sick. But you don't say "no" to Danny Jackson and get away with it, as you've just seen.'

'I'd bloody kill 'im if I could get me 'ands on 'im!' Eileen pounded the table. 'Why didn't yer come round 'ere, kid? If I'd of known, I'd 'ave gone and sorted 'im out meself, or told Harry. Harry would 'ave given 'im what for, that's for sure!'

'No, I'm not getting my friends involved. Even the kids don't know about this,' Vera pointed to her neck, 'and I'm not going to tell them.'

'But they must 'ave 'eard yer fightin',' Eileen said, 'they only sleep in the next room.'

'I don't think so, 'cos our Colin would have come in if he'd heard. I didn't scream out or anything, I just suffered in silence. And d'you know what, Eileen?' Vera cupped her face in her hands. 'I wasn't even frightened! I was so determined that Danny wasn't going to get what he wanted, he could have killed me before I gave in to him.'

'I wish I'd known, Vera! I'd 'ave been round there like a shot if I'd known what 'e was doin' to yer.'

'I know you would, Eileen. But Danny Jackson is my problem, not yours. I'll deal with him in me own way.'

'What about when 'e gets demobbed? Yer'll 'ave a hell of a life with him, then.'

'If I had the money, I'd move house before he comes home. But without money, where would I go to? I can't get a job because of Carol, and our Colin only brings home peanuts! Even when Peter starts work after he leaves school at Christmas, I couldn't expect two young boys to keep me. I'd be making them grow up before their time, making old men of them. And I'm not going to do that.' A ghost of a smile crossed Vera's face. 'Anyway, Danny might solve the problem for me! He told me a few times that if I wouldn't give him what he wanted he'd find someone who would.'

'He probably meant that as a threat, but if it was me I'd be hopin' it was a promise,' Eileen grunted, her fat face flushed with anger. 'Of all the good men that got killed in the war, Danny Jackson 'ad to come through without a scratch. They say the devil looks after 'is own, an' it's bloody true!'

'He might have come through the war without a scratch, but he hasn't gone back off leave without one,' Vera told her. 'I didn't just lie there letting him do this to me without retaliating, I can tell you! His back is scratched to pieces, and he'll have to come up with some good excuses when his mates see him. He can't say he bumped into a door, like he did when Harry gave him that black eye.'

The hour passed quickly, and it seemed no time before Bill and Arthur were back. This was a signal for Vera to say she'd have to go and get the tea ready. She looked more relaxed, but refused when Eileen asked her to stay for a while. 'Ask the girls to bring Carol down, please.'

'I'm beginning to think I should change me talcum powder,' Arthur smiled at Vera. 'Every time I come in, you say it's time for you to leave.'

'No.' Vera returned his smile. 'I really must get home to see to the tea, and I've got to iron the boys' shirts for tomorrow.'

Carol kicked and screamed but Vera was determined. 'Give everyone a kiss, there's a good girl.'

Eileen walked them to the door. 'I'll slip round one mornin' next week on me way to work, to see 'ow yer are.'

'Thanks for listening, Eileen, you're a pal.'

'It's my turn next week, kiddo! You can sit and listen to my tales of woe.'

Vera's laugh rang out. 'You never look as though you've got any troubles, Mrs Gillmoss.'

'Then I'll make some up!' There was a smile on Eileen's face, but inside she was thinking, if you only knew! But as she closed the door, she admitted to herself that her troubles were nothing compared to Vera's. 'Oh, well,' she said softly, 'no matter 'ow bad things are, yer always find someone worse off than yerself.'

'Carol's a lovely little girl.' Arthur looked up when Eileen walked in. 'And Vera seems a nice, quiet woman.'

'Oh, she's not always quiet.' Eileen sat down heavily. 'But when you think of it, she hasn't got much to shout about, 'as she? Her two boys are lovely and they're very good to her, but she's got her hands full with Carol. An' her husband's no catch, I can tell yer! She deserves better than him.'

'Now, Eileen,' Bill said, 'you should keep your views to yourself.'

'An' Danny Jackson should keep 'is 'ands to 'imself!' Eileen retorted hotly. 'Vera Jackson would be a different woman if it wasn't for 'im! He's a rotter, an' I don't care who hears me sayin' it!'

Bill glared at his wife. 'I don't think we should be discussing Vera's business behind her back.'

'Oh, aye! Is that what yer think, Bill? That I'm just a nosey parker who should mind 'er own business?' Eileen was riled now, and for the moment she forgot Arthur Kennedy was there. 'Answer me somethin', Bill, just out of curiosity. If I told yer that right now Danny Jackson was givin' Vera a bloody good hidin', what would yer do? Would yer sit there an' do nothin', an' tell me to mind me own business? Is that really what yer'd do, Bill?'

'Eileen, this has gone too far! You always were one for exaggerating, but this time you're really surpassing yourself.'

'Oh, I am, am I? Well try this on for size, Bill! Four years ago, Harry Sedgemoor beat the livin' daylights out of Danny Jackson when he found him hittin' Vera. And if Harry hadn't threatened 'im, Danny would have carried on hitting Vera till she was soft in the 'ead.' Eileen was so angry her chest was heaving. Pointing to the door, she said, 'The woman that's just gone out of that door, is black and blue all over 'er body.

185

The scarf round 'er neck is not just an ornament, it's to hide some of the bruises given to 'er by 'er 'usband.'

Bill sat back in the chair, his face drained of colour. 'Oh, no!'

'Oh, bloody yes!' Eileen cried. 'She's been a punch bag for that bastard since the day Carol was born. Danny Jackson couldn't bear the shame of havin' a mongol child so he took it out on Vera.' The tears were released and flowed down Eileen's cheeks. 'The day Harry burst into their house he found Vera hunched over Carol, protecting her from the blows.' Wiping her eyes with the back of her hand, Eileen sniffed. 'D'yer still think I should mind me own business? 'Cos if yer do, Bill, then yer can think again.'

'I had no idea,' Bill said softly, 'I'm sorry, chick.'

'So am I,' Arthur said. 'Sorry because he's not here to tell him what I think of men who hit women.'

'I can't understand the man!' Bill's head was shaking. 'Carol's a lovely little thing, how could anyone not love her?'

'A big-headed bastard, that's who! And just think what it's goin' to be like for Vera when he comes 'ome for good.'

Eileen pushed her chair back when she heard footsteps running down the stairs, and she had her back to the door when Joan burst in. 'Mam, Carol left 'er cardi on the bed.'

'Leave it on the table, sunshine, an' go back an' play for a while.' Eileen waited till the door closed before turning round. 'I'll drop it in their house on me way to work temorrer.'

'Where does Vera live?' Arthur asked. 'If it's on me way to the bus stop, I could pass it in.'

'She only lives a few streets away, but it doesn't matter, Arthur, I can get it to her.'

'It's no trouble to me.' Arthur eased himself off the couch and picked up the small, pink cardigan. 'I'll knock on me way past.'

Chapter Twenty

'Ooh, thank heaven for that!' Eileen staggered up the front step laden down with bags and parcels, 'Me arms are nearly droppin' off!'

Maggie closed the door and followed her daughter down the hall. 'Did you get everything you wanted?'

'I 'ope so. I wouldn't want to go through that again for all the tea in China,' Eileen groaned, holding hands out to show the angry weals on her wrists made by the handles of the shopping bags. She fell exhausted on to the couch and kicked her shoes off. 'It was packed in town, yer could 'ardly move.' Then she noticed Bill standing stiffly on the opposite side of the table. 'What the 'ell are yer standin' like that for, with a grin on yer face like a Cheshire cat?'

Bill stepped aside to reveal the Christmas tree he'd been in the process of decorating. 'We were hoping to have it finished before you came in, so we could surprise you.' He lifted the tree carefully and placed it on the small table in front of the window. 'It'll look nice when we've finished.'

Eileen's eyebrows nearly touched her hair line. 'Where did yer get it?'

'From the greengrocer's.' Bill added a silver ball that Maggie handed to him. 'There wasn't much to choose from, but it'll look nice when we've got all the decorations on.'

'He bought a set of coloured lights, too!' Maggie was looking as pleased as punch. 'Wait till you see it finished.'

'Yer've been busy, Bill!' Eileen closed an eye and cocked her head. 'It sets the room off, makes it look more Christmassy.'

'I'll get on with it while you sort your shopping out,' Bill said. 'I want it finished before tea time.'

Maggie hovered over the parcels, filled with curiosity. 'Let's see what you've bought.'

'You can open them, Mam, I'm whacked.' Eileen pointed to one of the bags. 'But keep yer 'ands off that one, it's private.'

'I feel like a child again,' Maggie said as she brought out boxes of board games, coloured balls, a post office set for Joan and a sweet shop for Edna. There was a shirt and tie for Billy, which brought smiles from Maggie and Bill. 'He'll think he's the whole cheese with these on.'

Another bag contained two dolls, one for Victoria and one for Emma, and a mechanical policeman for young Tony.

'My word you have been busy!' Maggie came to the last bag, and there was puzzlement on her face when she saw the contents. 'Who are these for?'

'The teddy bear's for Carol, an' the fire engine and car are for Arthur's two boys.' Eileen saw her mother's look and said, 'Well I couldn't leave them out, could I? God knows, the poor buggers don't get much out of life.'

'You've spent a few bob, chick.' Bill surveyed the table cluttered with presents. 'Have you won the pools?'

'I'd 'ave a job, seein' as 'ow I don't do them,' Eileen grinned. 'I got me tontine last week, an' I've been in Milly's club all year. Bloody good job, too, or I'd never 'ave been able to buy all that lot.'

'Have you got everything, now?' Bill stepped back to admire his handiwork before adjusting a twisted silver paper dangler. 'I've still got a few pounds if there's anything else you need.'

'No, that's me lot, thank God! Except for the sweets, but I might nip up to Milly's later and get them. I 'ope she's got a few things under the counter for me, otherwise the kids will be disappointed. Then there's the eats, of course, but I should be all right for money. If not I'll come on the cadge.'

Eileen's feet were throbbing, her arms sore, and she felt drained of energy. 'Mam, I 'aven't got the strength to move, will yer see to the tea for us? It's only beans on toast, so it won't take yer long.'

'I'll see to the tea when I've finished this,' Bill said. 'Why don't you put your head down for half an hour and have a rest?'

'William Gillmoss, that's the best idea yer've 'ad all day.' Eileen swerved her bottom round and lifted her legs on to the couch. 'I won't go to sleep, just close me eyes for five minutes.'

'Just come and look at her.' Maggie beckoned to Bill. 'She's out for the count.'

Bill took the pan of beans off the gas and followed Maggie. They stood inside the door and surveyed the sleeping figure. 'I'm worried about her, Bill! She's not the same Eileen at all! Her rosy chubby cheeks aren't rosy or chubby any more, she seems to be losing weight, she's listless all the time, and what she eats wouldn't keep a sparrow alive. Will you try and persuade her to go to the doctor's for a tonic? She needs to do something about herself, or she'll be ill.'

Maggie was voicing what Bill had been thinking for a few weeks. He had an idea what was wrong with his wife, but was afraid to put it into words. 'I'll try, but you know how stubborn she can be.'

'Doctor Greenfield's back in his surgery, and he's a smashing bloke to talk to.' Maggie asked God to forgive her for being underhanded, but this was her daughter's future she was worried about. 'Couldn't you say you wanted to go to the doctor's for a check-up, and ask her to go with you?'

Bill searched Maggie's face for a sign that would tell him that she too knew what was wrong with Eileen, but Maggie's face was one of innocence.

'I'll try and have a word with her tonight,' he promised.

Their whispering must have disturbed Eileen, and she opened her eyes. The first thing she saw were the lights on the small Christmas tree, and a smile lit up her face. Sliding her legs down, she saw Maggie's back disappearing into the kitchen. 'It's all right, Mam, I'm awake! No need to creep around in case yer disturb the sleepin' beauty!'

'I just popped in to see if you were awake,' Maggie said. 'Bill's got the tea ready.'

Eileen rubbed the sleep from her eyes. 'Where's the kids?'

'In Cissie Maddox's back yard. They're playing dressing up.'

'Give them a shout for us, Mam, will yer? I can't wait to see their faces when they get a load of the tree.'

'I've put all the parcels on top of your wardrobe out of the way. I'll help you wrap them up when they're in bed.'

Eileen grinned, 'You're like a big soft kid yerself, aren't yer, Mam?'

'Everyone's a kid at Christmas.' Maggie re-tied the loose bow at the back of her apron. 'Even you, clever clogs!'

The girls were in bed, Billy was out with his mates, Bill was reading the *Echo*, and Eileen and Maggie were busy wrapping presents. 'Are you giving Arthur the presents for his children?' Maggie asked, winding up the bright red fire engine.

'No, I'm going to ask 'im to bring them one day next week when the schools break up. He'll probably come temorrer, so I'll ask 'im then.'

'How old are they, d'you know?'

'I think seven and nine.' Eileen was stroking the blond hair of a small doll wearing a blue dress with white lace round the neck and hem. 'I think their names are Gordon and David, but I'm not sure which one is the elder.'

'He never mentions his wife, does he?'

'I don't think 'e sees much of her! I know 'e makes the children's breakfast, and yer know 'e always leaves in time to be home when school lets out, so I imagine he makes their tea, as well.'

'What a way to live,' Maggie sighed, 'and he's such a nice bloke.'

'Yer want to see 'is wife! She's a real floosie if ever I saw one,' Eileen grunted, and when she heard Bill rustle the paper she winked at her mother. 'Yes, Bill, we're janglin' again! But we wouldn't be women if we didn't pull everyone to pieces. In fact, if we didn't 'ave someone to talk about, we'd never open our flippin' mouths.'

'Are we asking Rene and Alan for Christmas dinner?' Maggie asked. 'I think we should.'

'Yeah, we'll 'ave the family together for Christmas day . . . that's what it's all about, isn't it? Doesn't matter the rest of the year, but come Christmas it's nice to 'ave yer family round yer.' Eileen stretched her leg out and tapped Bill on the shin with her foot. 'How about us 'avin' a party on Boxing day, Bill? It'll be yer first Christmas at 'ome for five years, so wouldn't it be nice to celebrate?'

Bill lowered the paper. 'Who would you ask?'

'I was thinking of Mary and Harry and their kids, and Mrs B. of course. And Vera could bring Carol. Then there's Arthur . . . I'm sure he'd like to come.'

'Eileen, where would you put them all?' Bill's eyes swept the room. 'There isn't room to swing a cat in here.'

'Oh, I wasn't goin' to invite any cats!' Eileen laughed, 'just me mates.'

Bill looked doubtful. 'Well, it's up to you I suppose, but they'd be packed in like sardines.'

Eileen shook her head. 'I worked it all out on the bus comin' 'ome. Our Rene's goin' to Alan's parents on Boxing day, and our Billy won't be 'ere 'cos he's goin' to a party at his mates, so that's three less. And if the kids play upstairs in the bedroom, an' we move me mam's chair so the table can go next to the small table by the window, there'll be plenty of room here for the grown-ups.'

Maggie and Bill exchanged glances. 'She's got it all worked out, Bill.'

'So it seems.' Bill gave a wry smile. 'If you like, Eileen, I could scrape the wallpaper off and that would give you more room.'

'Funny ha-ha!' Eileen pulled tongues at him. 'Anyway, what d'yez think?'

'Do we have any say in the matter?' Bill asked.

'Not really! We've 'ad five lousy Christmases, and I ain't about to 'ave a sixth. If it takes me food ration coupons for the next six months, an' we 'ave to starve, I'm determined that this Christmas is goin' to be a happy one . . . I'll enjoy meself if it kills me.'

Eileen scrambled to her feet. 'I think I'll nip up to Milly's and get me sweet club out. That'll be another thing off me mind. She doesn't close the shop till ten, and it's only 'alf nine.'

There were no customers in the shop and Milly gave Eileen a tired smile. 'Roll on ten o'clock.'

'I thought yer'd be empty. I won't keep yer long, Milly, but I may as well get the sweets in for the kids' stockings.'

'I've put some things away in a box for you . . . hang on a minute, they're in the stock room.'

Leaning on the counter, Eileen watched Milly empty the box. There were liquorice pipes, sweet cigarettes, sugar mice, sherbet dips and chocolate animals with silver hoops for hanging on the tree.

'Milly, yer a pal if ever there was one! I 'aven't seen sugar mice or them chocolate things since the war started. I don't know 'ow to thank yer, not just for these, but for all the times yer've helped us out in the last five years. I don't know 'ow we'd 'ave managed without yer.'

'Now, I'm giving you these on the sly, so not a word to anyone,' Milly warned, 'otherwise there'll be mutiny with me other customers.' She put the goodies back in the box and pushed it towards Eileen. 'Now you can spend your ration coupons on whatever else yer want.'

Eileen eyed the long, shallow tins of toffee in the glass display and licked her lips. 'I'll 'ave some of that, 'cos me mam and Bill like it. A quarter each of banana split, walnut, and treacle. And I'll 'ave whatever is left on me coupons in hundreds and thousands, and dolly mixtures.' Milly took up the toffee hammer and broke up the slab of banana split. It was when she was weighing the broken pieces on the scale, she said, nonchalantly, 'Oh, by the way, Jack's coming home in a couple of days.'

'On leave again?'

'No, for good!' Milly tipped the toffee into a paper bag, flung it on the counter, lifted her arms in the air and shouted, 'Whoopee!' She punched the air with a clenched fist, 'I've been dying to do that all day.'

Eileen looked at the happy, though tired, smiling face. 'I'm very glad for yer, Milly.'

'Just think, Eileen, I'll be able to have a lie in when I feel like it, have time to cook a proper meal and eat it in peace without worrying about that blasted bell ringing, and, best of all, I'll be able to go to the pictures a couple of times a week. Isn't it a lovely thought?'

'Yer deserve it, Milly, honest to God yer do. I don't know 'ow yer've managed all these years on yer own.'

'Well, it'll soon be over, thank heaven. Jack thought he'd be away for another couple of months, but it seems they're demobbing the older men first.' Milly closed her eyes. 'The last five years have seemed like an eternity.'

'Well, yer'll 'ave the rest of yer life to make up for it.' Eileen eyed the round-faced clock on the wall. 'It's ten o'clock, Milly, time for yer to close up. If yer finish me off, I'll leave yer to go to bed and dream sweet dreams.'

Maggie had gone to bed when Eileen got back, and as she emptied the box to show Bill what she'd got, Eileen told him about Milly's husband coming home. 'She's been an absolute angel to me. We'd 'ave been in queer street without 'er.'

'They're a nice couple.' Bill fingered one of the chocolate animals. 'Are you putting these on the tree now? If you do, you'll be lucky if there's any left by Christmas day. You know what the girls are like, they'd have them eaten in no time.'

Eileen was already hanging them on the branches of the tree. 'Oh, no they won't! I'll cut their hands off if they so much as touch them.'

'I've been thinking,' Bill's face was serious, 'I might go along to the doctor's one day this week, for a check-up. It's about time I started thinking about getting a job and I'd like him to give me the all clear.'

Eileen turned. 'D'yer feel up to goin' to work? There's no hurry, yer know. Better wait till yer feel a hundred per cent.'

'I'm as well as I'll ever be,' Bill answered. 'I've got to make the effort some time, I've sat on me backside long enough.'

'Well, it's up to you, Bill. Only you know 'ow yer feel.'

'Would you come to the doctor's with me? I don't know the new doctor that's there now, and I'd feel better if you came along.'

'Yer don't need me to 'old yer 'and, Bill! Doctor Greenfield would wonder what was up if I went with yer.'

'I'd like you to come for some moral support, chick.'

While Eileen transferred a chocolate elephant from one

branch to another, her mind was whirling. It might be a good idea for her to go along and have a word with Doctor Greenfield herself. He was a very easy man to talk to, and being young he would understand her need and her frustration. He might even be able to help. It was worth a try, anyway. Anything was worth it to be put out of her misery. 'Okay, if yer want me to go with yer, I'll go. But can we leave it until we get Christmas over? I'll be workin' till Christmas Eve and I won't 'ave much chance.'

'That's all right with me, as long as you promise, chick.'

'I promise, love.'

Chapter Twenty-One

'Mam! Can we go down now?'

Eileen felt herself being shaken urgently by the shoulder and struggled to sit up. It was pitch dark in the room but in the dim light coming from the next bedroom, she could make out the shapes of her two daughters. 'What time is it?'

Edna whispered, 'We don't know what time it is, but can we go down for our presents now?'

Bill, roused from a deep sleep, glanced sideways at the illuminated face of the alarm clock and groaned, 'It's only half past five!'

'Be good girls,' Eileen pleaded, 'and go back to bed for another hour.'

'Ah, ay, Mam! It's Christmas day!' Edna sat down on the side of the bed. 'You needn't get up, we can go down on our own.'

'Not on yer life, yer won't!' Eileen nudged Bill. 'You stay in bed and I'll go down with them.' She lowered her voice, 'I want to see their faces when they open their presents.'

'No, I'll get up.' Bill swung his legs over the side of the bed. 'You two wait on the landing until me and your mam are ready.'

Hugging her old red woollen dressing gown around her,

Eileen opened the bedroom door to find the two girls, with Billy and Maggie, filling the small space of the landing. 'Oh, my God, they've woken the whole 'ouse!'

'I've been awake for hours,' Maggie told her, dryly. 'I can't wait to see what Father Christmas has brought me.'

'They woke me up, the daft things,' Billy said gruffly, hoping to sound too grown up to be excited about Christmas presents. 'They're like a couple of babies.'

Keeping her face straight, Eileen said, 'You can go back to bed if yer want to.'

'Nah! I'm awake now, so I might as well stay up.'

'Then out of the way an' let me get past.' Eileen looked over their heads to Bill. 'Come on, love, you come with me.'

The laughter and shouting erupted as the children dived for their presents and emptied the stockings hanging either side of the black-leaded fire place. But it was to young Billy, Eileen looked. His face when he saw the grown-up shirt and tie was a study in pride and pleasure. 'D'yer like it, son?'

'Ooh, yeah! They're magic! Ta, Mam an' Dad!' Billy held the dark blue tie against the pale blue of the shirt. 'I'll wear them temorrer night for Jacko's party.'

'If yer don't get a click in them, son, yer'll never get one.' Eileen smiled at him before going to the sideboard and bringing out two parcels wrapped in bright red and green paper. 'Here y'are, Mam, 'ere's your present, and this is for you, Bill.'

'Put it on the chair while I fetch yours.' Bill disappeared into the kitchen to reappear seconds later with two small wrapped parcels. He planted a kiss on Maggie's cheek before handing her one of the parcels, then turned to Eileen. 'Merry Christmas, chick.'

'Open yours first.' Eileen was bubbling with excitement. To see her family so happy was like a tonic to her. Her eyes waited expectantly as Maggie lifted the pale blue jumper from its wrappings. 'D'yer like it, Mam?'

'It's beautiful.' Maggie held it up against herself and preened. 'Don't I look the gear? Thanks, love.'

A bright smile was Eileen's reward for Bill's light fawn pullover. 'Just the job, chick! Keep the old bones nice and warm.' He pointed to the parcel on Eileen's knee. 'Open yours now, chick.'

Eileen tore at the paper to reveal a small jeweller's box. Inside, bedded on a satin covered pad, was an attractive gold plated watch with an expanding strap. It was the most glamorous present Eileen had ever had in her life, and for seconds she was speechless. Then she jumped up and threw her arms round Bill's neck. 'Oh, it's beautiful, Bill! The nicest present I've ever 'ad!'

Bill put his arm round her waist and held her tight. Then a strange feeling came over him. He could feel a stirring in his loins and it frightened him. He moved away from Eileen and forced a smile to his face. 'I'm glad you like it, chick.' He sat down, confused. It was the first time he'd felt any feelings of passion, and he didn't know how to cope. It had been so long, he was beginning to think he'd never again feel desire grow within him, or be able to make love.

Bill smiled at the children but his thoughts were on Eileen. She was a warm, passionate woman who enjoyed the sexual side of married life. Before the war, she'd think nothing of waiting till the children were out playing or in bed, then taking him by the hand and leading him up the stairs to satisfy the need they both had. She was loving and generous, and their marriage was the better for it. And he knew how she must be suffering now. He longed to talk to her about it, but how could he explain something he didn't understand himself? Holding her in his arms just now, he'd felt the old familiar urge to hold her close and prove his love for her. But what if he tried and failed? Another disappointment for Eileen, and for himself humiliation and shame. He couldn't take that chance, a failure would strip him of his manhood completely.

'Here y'are, Bill!' Bill looked up to see Maggie holding out a parcel.

'Happy Christmas, son.'

'Thanks, Ma!' Bill took out the socks and handkerchieves and smiled. 'Just what I wanted.'

'My brooch is lovely.' Maggie fingered the filigree brooch in the shape of a leaf, pinned to her dress. 'Thanks, son.'

'Look what me mam bought me.' Eileen held a link of imitation pearls across her palm. 'I'll be a proper swank with me new watch and pearls. When the neighbours see me all dolled up, they'll think we've come into money.'

It was two o'clock, the turkey was done to a turn, the carrots and turnips mashed ready, and the roast potatoes browning nicely.

'What time did our Rene say they'd be 'ere?' Eileen raised her wrist to look at the time on her new watch. The pearls around her throat showed above the neck of the new dress, and for once her hair was under control, having been rolled in dinkie curlers for a few hours.

'Around two.' Maggie ran her eyes over her daughter. She was getting very worried about her. Eileen used to have a

202

marvellous appetite, but now she just picked at the food on her plate, making stupid excuses like she'd had a sandwich earlier and wasn't hungry. But she couldn't fool Maggie. You only had to look at how much weight she'd lost to know there was something wrong. Not that she couldn't afford to lose some of her fat, but starving herself to do it was asking for trouble.

Maggie sighed. As soon as the holiday was over she'd have a good talk with her daughter. And if that didn't do the trick, whether Eileen liked it or not, she'd tell Bill. She wasn't going to stand by and watch her daughter fade away before her eyes and do nothing about it. But today was a day for rejoicing, so Maggie pushed her worries to the back of her mind for the time being, and smiled. 'You look very smart, love.'

Young Billy agreed. 'Yeah, that dress looks nice on yer, Mam! It doesn't 'alf make yer look thinner.'

Eileen glanced down at the plain, dark blue dress she'd bought. No more spots or stripes for her! 'Thanks, son.'

God love him, he means well, Eileen thought. But even though the label on the back of her dress said it was outsize, instead of the usual *extra* outsize, it wasn't much consolation after practically starving herself to death for the last month or so. How she'd resisted all the temptations she'd never know. Only one crispy roast potato instead of the usual six, one slice of bread with half a dozen chips replaced the doorstep, dockers sandwiches she used to eat, and not one square of her favourite Cadbury's milk chocolate had crossed her lips.

Eileen looked to where Bill was lighting a cigarette. If you only knew what I was going through, Bill Gillmoss, just so you'll fancy me. Please God, don't let me be wasting my time, 'cos I don't know what else to do.

Edna had been standing at the front door waiting for their visitors, now she shouted, 'They're 'ere!'

'My, my, aren't we looking grand!' Rene grinned. 'Christmas presents, are they?'

Eileen nodded. 'Watch from Bill, and pearls from me mam.'

'Did you hear that, Alan?' Rene asked in mock indignation. 'Where's your imagination? All I got was the money to buy meself something.'

'You're so difficult to buy for,' Alan laughed. 'Whenever I buy you anything, you take it back to the shop the next day and exchange it.'

It was a noisy, happy Christmas dinner, with everyone wearing the paper hats found in the Christmas crackers. And when the meal was over and the girls wanted to go to their bedroom, Victoria followed them, clutching her new dolly, already christened Shirley after Shirley Temple.

The grown-ups sat around, their tummies full, to relax and unwind after a hectic day. There were loud protests when Eileen brought a bottle of port out, but not one refused the wine. And Eileen, ignoring the warning glances from her husband, gave Billy his first alcoholic drink. He pulled a face at the first sip of wine, but persevered, telling himself he was grown up now. Then he got to like the taste, and when Eileen went round re-filling the glasses, he held his glass out for more. He felt a nice warm glow run through his body, as he talked and giggled. Then the wine started to take effect and his head became hazy. The room seemed to be spinning around, the light hanging from the ceiling kept changing shape, and the voices in the room sounded as though they were coming through a long tunnel. He remembered nothing after that until he woke in bed with a splitting headache and feeling sick.

'Thanks for everything.' Rene kissed her mother and Eileen. 'I hope young Billy's all right.'

Alan chuckled. 'If he feels anything like I did after my first drink, he won't know what's hit him tomorrow.'

'Well, with a bit of luck, it might put 'im off drinkin' for life.' Eileen patted Victoria's head. 'Yer tired, aren't yer, sweetheart? I think we're all ready for some shut eye.'

'Ta, ra!' Maggie and Eileen stood with their arms around each other waving them off. 'Give our best wishes to Alan's parents.'

As she was shutting the front door, Eileen whispered to her mother, 'I think I'm in for a tellin' off for givin' our Billy that drink.'

'Well he is only fourteen,' Maggie whispered back. 'You should have had more sense.'

'Since when did I ever do anythin' because it was sensible, Mam? He was sittin' there, lookin' all grown up, I couldn't leave 'im out.'

'Oh, well, now you can suffer the consequences.'

But Bill never mentioned it when they went back in, and he hadn't mentioned it by the time Maggie went to bed, worn out with the work and excitement. She looked in on Billy to see if he was all right and found him snoring loudly. Smiling to herself, Maggie crept into the room she shared with the girls. It had been a perfect Christmas Day, the best since before the war. It made all the difference having Bill home again.

Bill brought Eileen a cup of tea up to bed. 'You have a lie in, chick, I'll see to the breakfasts.'

Eileen stretched her arms above her head and yawned. 'Ooh, I could sleep for a week, I'm that tired. It was a long day, yesterday.'

When Eileen lowered her arms the neck of her nightdress opened to reveal the valley between her breasts, and the breath caught in Bill's throat. His head flooded with memories of the times he'd found comfort and joy in the warmth and softness of Eileen's body.

'Here y'are, drink the tea before it gets cold,' Bill said abruptly, then turned to leave the room, away from temptation. Memories were fine, but if you tried to recapture them, and failed, it could cause a lot of misery and pain.

Bill had reached the door when Eileen asked, 'Where are the girls?'

'Playing shop downstairs,' Bill said. 'They've ransacked all the cupboards and drawers looking for buttons to use as money.'

'Ah, happy days! I can remember gettin' a sweet shop for Christmas meself and cadgin' a ha'penny off me mam every day to buy dolly mixtures to fill the bottles up.' Then Eileen's mind clicked. 'Where's our Billy?'

'In bed with a hangover.' Bill twisted the door knob back and forth. 'He was up half a dozen times in the night, running to the lavatory to be sick. Didn't you hear him?'

'Bill, I was out for the count last night. A bomb wouldn't 'ave woke me up.'

'Then make the most of it while you can,' Bill told her. 'I've got the fire going, and I'll see to the breakfast, so you stay where you are for a few hours.'

'Hang on a minute.' Eileen drained the cup and held it out. 'Take this down with yer, love, and I'll do as you say. I don't 'ave to worry about dinner because there was enough left over from yesterday for a fry up.'

Bill took the cup. 'I'll give you a shout at dinner time.' He was at the door again when Eileen spoke, and he turned.

'I forgot to tell yer, I asked Milly Knight and her 'usband to come tonight. Milly said she'd ask Jack, but with 'im only comin' 'ome on Monday, he might not feel like it.'

Bill walked back to the end of the bed. 'Where d'you think you're going to put everybody? That makes nine adults and about seven children.'

'Uh, uh! Mary's got her neighbour, Doris, to mind Emma and Tony. And Vera's two lads won't want to come to a grown-up party. They're old enough to look after themselves, anyway. An' our Billy's goin' out, so there'll only be our two, and Carol. And if it comes to the push,' Eileen snuggled down in the bed, 'we can always sit on each other's knees.'

Bill was shaking his head as he left the room and closed the door behind him.

'Well, this is a surprise!' Eileen looked startled when she saw Arthur with his two sons. She gave a quick glance at the clock that told her it was two o'clock. Arthur was supposed to be coming, on his own, at seven.

Recovering quickly, Eileen grinned at the two wide-eyed boys. 'Now, which one is which?'

Arthur squeezed the shoulder of his taller son. 'This is

David, and this little shrimp is Gordon.'

Eileen kissed the two boys before turning and taking two chocolate figures off the Christmas tree. 'Merry Christmas, boys! Did yez like yer fire engine and police car?'

'Yes, thank you.'

Eileen looked up at Arthur, a question in her eyes. 'I didn't expect to see you this afternoon.'

Arthur nodded in the direction of the kitchen. 'Can I speak to you for a minute?'

Eileen closed the kitchen door. 'What's wrong?'

'Sylvia's going out tonight, so I won't be able to make it. I can't leave the boys on their own.'

'Couldn't she 'ave stayed in for once? God knows, yer entitled to go out once in a while.'

'Eileen, she didn't even stay in last night! Even on Christmas day she wasn't going to miss seeing her so-called friends. Honestly, Eileen, I don't know how I kept me hands off her yesterday. She didn't even want to get up to see the boys open their presents, I had to practically drag her down the stairs.'

Eileen's face was sad. 'What the hell's wrong with the woman? Two lovely children like that, and a good 'usband, the woman either wants 'er bumps feelin', or a bloody good hidin'!'

Arthur let out a deep sigh. 'I thought I'd better come and let you know. I was looking forward to tonight, as well, but it can't be helped.'

'Let's see if we can sort something out.' Eileen had her hand on the knob when she heard Arthur say, softly, 'Don't say anything in front of the boys, Eileen. She is their mother and I don't want to turn them against her.'

Eileen could feel a lump in her throat. Any normal woman would be proud to have a husband like Arthur. 'I won't say anything in front of them, I'm not that daft. But I think your Sylvia must be stark staring mad not to know a good thing when she's got it.'

'It's just one of those things that can't be helped,' Arthur said. 'Don't worry about me.'

'If I want to worry about yer, then I'll worry about yer, so you just shut yer cake 'ole an' let me think.' Eileen folded her arms across her tummy, making a shelf for her bust to rest on. 'Yer could bring the boys with yer, but there's nowhere for them to sleep, an' yer'd never get buses home that late at night . . . not on Boxing Day, anyway.'

Arthur's two sons were in the hallway playing with a game of snakes and ladders, and out of earshot. Bill and Maggie had watched and listened in silence. Now Maggie could see her daughter racking her brains for a solution, and she made an offer. 'If it was okay with Vera, I could go round to her house and mind Carol and Arthur's two boys at the same time. That would give Vera a break, too!'

'No, I wouldn't let you do that,' Arthur said quickly. 'I'm not going to spoil your night.'

'No, Mam,' Eileen added, 'that means yer'd miss the party.'

'I had plenty of parties when I was your age, enough to last me a life time. Even if I stayed, I'd probably go to bed early to get away from the noise. So, if you want to ask Vera, I'll willingly mind the kids.'

Vera came herself in answer to Eileen's handwritten note, sent round with Joan. She said she'd left Carol at home being minded by Colin. Arthur looked embarrassed and tried to intervene a few times while Eileen told the surprised Vera the tale, but Eileen shut him up with a wave of her hand. She didn't go into details about his wife, just briefly mentioned Arthur was having problems finding someone to mind the boys. 'Me mam 'ad a brainwave, Vera, an' we wondered what yer thought of 'er goin' round to your 'ouse. She could mind the boys, and Carol at the same time. That would solve Arthur's problem, an' it would give you a chance to enjoy yerself without 'avin' to worry about Carol all night.'

'Vera, this is not my idea,' Arthur said, looking ill at ease. 'I don't want to cause you, or anybody else, any bother.'

'It's no bother,' Vera said. 'As long as Maggie doesn't mind being landed with a gang of kids.'

'It was me mam's idea, Vera, honest! I didn't twist 'er arm or anythin', did I, Mam?'

Maggie shook her head. 'As a matter of fact, it'll be a rest for me. My party days are over, Vera, I can't stand the loud music or people singing their heads off after a few drinks.'

'Yer a miserable bugger, but yer the best mam in the whole world.' Eileen grabbed her mother by the shoulders and gave her a loud kiss. 'That's settled, then!'

'The boys can sleep at ours, if you like.' Vera smiled at Arthur. 'They'll be a bit crushed, but we'll manage.'

Arthur opened his mouth to protest, but Eileen got in first. 'Yer a pal, kiddo! They can stay 'ere till it's time for me mam to go round. An' we'll see yer about seven, then, Vera?'

When Eileen went to see Vera out, Bill shook his head. 'Have you ever known such an interfering busy body as my wife?' Then a slow smile crossed his face. 'But she gets things done, I'll say that for her.'

Chapter Twenty-Two

'What did you do before the war, Arthur?' Harry was leaning forward, his hands between his knees gripping a pint glass of beer. 'Have you got a trade?'

'Yes, I served me time as an electrician,' Arthur answered. 'I used to work at the British Enka, and I've been thinking about going down and asking for me old job back. But the pay and conditions there were lousy.'

'Napiers is a good place to work. Clean, efficient, and the pay's good.' Harry supped on his beer, then his eyes slid sideways. He knew from what Eileen had said that Arthur's home life wasn't what it should be, and he wanted to help him without sounding as though his offer was brought about by pity. 'You should try and get in there. They're taking on skilled men. I could get you an application form if you like, and put in a good word for you.'

'I'd be grateful,' Arthur said, smiling. 'It's about time I got off me bottom and earned a living.'

'You deserved a rest after what you went through. And I think you, and all the other servicemen, are entitled to a decent job.' Harry put the empty glass down between his feet. 'I'll get you an application form tomorrow and leave it with Eileen. When you've filled it in, I'll take it back and have a word with the personnel officer.'

'Thanks, Harry, I'd appreciate that.' Arthur had a contented look on his face. 'It'll be good to get back to work.'

Bill had been listening intently. Now he asked, 'Are they looking for joiners, by any chance?'

This was what Harry had been hoping to hear, but he didn't let it show in his voice. 'Is that what you are, Bill?'

Bill nodded. 'I served me time with the Corporation.'

'Are you fit enough for work yet?'

'Oh, I'm fit enough, all right! And like Arthur, it's about time I got off me backside, too! The sooner I start work, the sooner Eileen can pack her job in.' Bill leaned forward now and lowered his voice. 'It isn't right for a woman to have to go out to work while her husband sits at home.'

'Then I'll get you a form as well, and drop it off with Arthur's on me way home tomorrow night.' Harry was delighted. In helping Bill, he was helping his mate, Eileen. 'There's a lot of changes going on in Napiers, but it'll be a big concern when they've finished. I've heard it's being taken over by the English Electric Company, but whether that's only a rumour or not, I don't know. All I do know is, I've landed on me feet.'

'Ay, you lot!' Eileen towered over them. 'This is supposed to be a party, an' you, Bill Gillmoss, are supposed to be the host. Get up an' see to the drinks, like a proper gentleman, an' don't be lettin' people see I married beneath meself.'

His tummy doing somersaults, Bill jumped up. 'Okay, chick, I'm on me way.'

He didn't want to put too much store on getting the job, but wouldn't it be fantastic? He might also feel like a man again if he had work to go to every day, it would give him a purpose in life.

Eileen had borrowed a gramophone and some records from Tommy Wilson, a neighbour who lived opposite, and when they'd all had a few drinks and were happy and relaxed, she put a record on. It was a quickstep, and Eileen, determined to push her worries to the back of her mind and have a good time, pulled Bill up from his chair. 'Come on, big boy, let's show 'em how it's done.'

Milly Knight, who had called in 'just for half-an-hour', looked at her husband. 'Are yer dancin'?'

'Are yer askin'?' Jack laughed.

'I'm askin'!'

'Then I'm dancin'!' Jack twirled his wife round the floor. Milly was almost the same size as Eileen, and the two couples filled the dancing space. But Eileen didn't worry about that. 'Get off yer backsides and shake a leg,' she shouted to Harry and Arthur. 'You young ones 'ave got no "go" in yez.'

'We could always dance on the ceiling, I suppose,' Harry pulled a face at her. 'That's the only space there is.'

'Dance in the bloody hall, then!'

'Come on, darling, the hall it is.' Harry took Mary's hand. 'We'll never hear the last of it if we don't.'

Arthur looked across the room to Vera. 'Want to take a chance with me? I'm not very good though, so be warned.'

'That makes two of us.' Vera allowed herself to be led to the hall where Harry and Mary were dancing close together. Vera had her beautiful auburn hair in a sleek pageboy bob, and it swung on her shoulders as she danced. Her face was flushed from the two glasses of sherry, and she laughed as they tried to dance in the narrow space of the hall. She had a loud, clear laugh, and Arthur was put off his steps for a while in astonishment. It was the first time he'd seen Vera in a carefree mood, and he thought what a difference it made to her. She was a very attractive woman.

'Eh, stop canoodlin' out there, you lot!' Eileen bawled. 'I've got me eye on yez.'

It was twelve o'clock when Milly called time. 'I only came for half an hour and forgot to go home. It's been lovely, though, Eileen. We've really enjoyed ourselves, haven't we, Jack? The trouble is, we have to open the shop at six in the morning, so all good things must come to an end.'

'We'll have to be making tracks, as well,' Harry said. 'It's work for me in the morning, too!'

'I've saved one record for the last, so yez can all stay for the last waltz.'

It was a song that was popular before the war, a slow, dreamy song called 'Who's Taking You Home Tonight?' It had been one of Harry's favourites, and he now pulled Mary up and held her close. 'You have to dance cheek to cheek for this one, darling.'

Milly and her husband, separated for so long, melted into each other's arms. 'It's the 'allway for us, sunshine.' Eileen dragged Bill by the hand. 'Just you an' me, babe!'

'Let's pretend.' Arthur held his hand out to Vera. 'All this snogging and us sitting like wallflowers. Come on, let's show them how.'

Vera closed her eyes as she moved to the dreamy, romantic music. It was lovely to be treated like a lady, to be looked at with admiration. It would probably never happen again so she may as well enjoy it while she could. In a few weeks

Danny would be home for good, and she'd become a skivvy again. A woman who walked down the street with her eyes to the ground. A woman with no self respect.

'Thank you, I enjoyed that.' Arthur's voice brought Vera down to earth. She smiled shyly, before moving across to Eileen. 'Will your mam be all right to walk home on her own?'

Arthur was behind her, and he didn't wait for Eileen to reply. 'I can walk you home, then bring Maggie back.'

'You needn't walk me home . . . I'll be all right.' Vera looked flustered. It was very late and there wouldn't be many people about, but what if one of their neighbours did see her taking a strange man in her house? Especially that nosey parker next door but two, Elsie Smith. The local gossip who knew more about people than they knew themselves. And what she didn't know, she made up. A little incident became a drama by the time Elsie Smith had finished adding her tu'penny worth of spiteful fiction. 'Honest, I'll be fine!'

'Don't argue!' Arthur took her elbow. 'I've got to go to yours to bring Maggie back. There's no way I'm going to let her walk home on her own.'

'Me mam's got a key, so we don't need to wait up for 'er.' Eileen had moved the table back into the centre of the room and was now putting the chairs in place. 'It was a good night, though, wasn't it, love?'

'It certainly was . . . in more ways than one.' Bill couldn't keep it to himself any longer. 'Harry's calling tomorrow on his way home from work with two application forms. One for Arthur, and one for me.'

'Application forms?' Eileen put the last chair down. 'What are they for?'

'Jobs!' Bill smiled at the expression on Eileen's face. 'He's going to put a word in for us at Napiers.'

Eileen's hand covered her mouth as she stared at Bill. At first she'd thought he was joking, but now she could see he was serious. 'I don't know what to say! It would be marvellous, but d'yer feel fit enough for work?'

Just the thought of getting a job had given Bill a confidence he hadn't felt for many years. And it showed in the smile he gave Eileen.

'If it comes off, chick, you'll be able to pack in work.'

'Ooh, what a lovely thought!' The corners of Eileen's mouth curved upwards into a beaming smile. She held her arms wide. 'Come 'ere an' give us a kiss, yer great big handsome hunk.'

Bill walked into her arms, but as they wrapped around him and he felt his heart lurch, he stepped back quickly. He saw the hurt in Eileen's eyes and turned his head. If only he could tell her how he felt about his fears, and hopes, but he just couldn't find the right words. Softly, he said, 'If I get the job, things might return to normal.'

Eileen gulped back the tears as she tilted her head. 'I 'ope so, Bill Gillmoss, I really do. 'Cos I love the bones of yer.'

Bill picked up the poker from the companion set and raked it over the coals before placing the fireguard in the hearth. 'If I get through the interview, I've got to go for a medical. So I won't need to go to the doctor's.' He straightened up and faced her. 'But I think you should go, chick. You're not eating like you should, and you look very pale. Why don't you slip along to the surgery tomorrow morning before you go to work?'

The doctor won't be able to cure what ails me, Eileen thought. Only you can do that, Bill Gillmoss. But Eileen kept her thoughts and fears to herself. 'I'm all right,' she said. 'It's just goin' to work that's gettin' me down. I'll be fine when I can pack in an' stay at home, you'll see.'

'It wouldn't take you half an hour to go and have a check-up,' Bill insisted. 'The doctor could give you a tonic.'

'Just leave it for now, Bill, and we'll see how things go.' Eileen turned her back on him and lowered her head. 'Undo the clasp on these pearls for us, then let's hit the hay. I'm almost asleep on me feet.'

When Harry called in at six o'clock the following night on his way home from work, he found Arthur sitting next to Bill, waiting for him. They both looked up, hope in their eyes, and he didn't keep them waiting. He handed them each a form, a wide grin on his face. 'Fill the forms in tonight, and take them with you tomorrow when you go for your interview.'

Two mouths gaped, shocked into silence. Then Bill swallowed hard before croaking, 'We're going for an interview?'

'Yep!' Harry felt sad and happy at the same time. Happy that he was able to help them, but sad because no one seemed to care what happened to men like this who had given so much for their country. 'I had a word with the personnel officer, and as they're looking for skilled men, he's agreed to interview you tomorrow. If you pass, then you've got to go for a medical. But there shouldn't be any problem there, so we'll just keep our fingers crossed.' Harry didn't say he'd had more than a word with the bloke in personnel, who at first had said the applications must go through the normal channels and it was a case of first come first served. Harry had then asked the man if he'd been in the forces, to which the answer was 'no'. Harry said he hadn't, either, but surely some consideration should be given to those who were. He explained that Bill and Arthur had been prisoners of war, and what they'd been through. And by the time he'd finished the man knew he had no argument. So he'd agreed to see both applicants the following day.

Bill and Arthur looked down at the forms, then at each other. Then they started to laugh. 'We've been on pins all day,' Bill told Harry. 'It was worse than waiting for our calling up papers to fall on the mat.'

'Thanks, Harry,' Arthur said. 'I'll never forget you for this.'

'Me neither,' Bill echoed. 'And me neither.'

Harry was looking round and listening. 'Where's Eileen?'

'On afternoon shift.'

'Oh, of course, I forgot.' Harry grinned. 'Let's hope it's not for very much longer, eh?'

Arthur was turning the application form in his hands, and when he spoke, his voice was filled with emotion. 'To think I'd never have known any of you if Eileen hadn't called to our house that day. Now I feel like one of the family, with more good friends than I ever had.'

'My wife did us all a favour that day,' Bill said. 'She likes people, and will go out of her way to help anyone.' He laughed loudly. 'Wait till she hears the news . . . she'll be over the moon.'

'Well, I hope things go all right for you both tomorrow. Keep your chin up and go in fighting. I'll try and get over to the Admin to see how you got on.' Harry looked at his watch.

'I'd better get home or me tea will be burned to a cinder. It's me favourite too, spare ribs and cabbage.'

Harry lifted his hand in farewell, and the thanks of two happy and grateful men followed him down the hall.

'God bless Harry, he's a good mate.' Eileen sat in front of the fire, her legs open to the warmth. It was cold and dark out, and she'd come in shivering. 'I'll say a little prayer for you an' Arthur tonight, love.'

'I've been praying since Harry left,' Bill said with a sheepish smile. 'I know I said I didn't believe in God, but I could be wrong and I'm not taking any chances. I need all the help I can get.'

'Are yer meetin' Arthur down there?'

'No, he's calling for me. We thought we could give each other some Dutch courage.'

Eileen rested her head on her hand. 'I wonder what'll happen if Arthur gets the job? It's to be hoped 'is wife mends 'er ways an' looks after the boys when 'e's not there.'

'It's up to Arthur to sort his own life out, chick, so don't interfere,' Bill warned. 'We've got enough problems of our own.'

Eileen didn't answer. They only had one problem as far as she was concerned, and it was tearing her heart in two.

Eileen couldn't wait till half past ten to find out how Bill had got on, so she told a lie and said she wasn't feeling well and wanted to go home. She'd expected him to be back before she left for work at half one but he hadn't arrived. And her nerves wouldn't let her stand beside the machine without knowing what had happened. So, at four o'clock Eileen was sitting on the bus telling herself it would serve her right if she was punished for telling fibs.

As the bus travelled the familiar route, Eileen wondered how many more times she'd be making this journey. Hopefully, it wouldn't be for much longer. She used to enjoy going to work and having a laugh with the women, but not any more. The factory was like a prison to her now.

The bus neared the Black Bull and as Eileen stood up, she raised her eyes and said a silent prayer. Please God, if you're going to punish me for telling lies, don't do it just yet. Let Bill get the job and I'll make it up to you, I promise.

Eileen hurried up the street, her heart in her mouth. She'd never done as much praying in her life as she had the last eighteen hours. She put the key in the lock and opened the door. She could hear a man's raised voice, then her mother's. She stood for a while in the hall. Did the tone of the man's voice sound disappointed or happy? There was only one way to find out.

The talking stopped when Eileen flung the door open. 'What are you doing home, chick?'

'Because I couldn't bloody well wait to find out 'ow yez got on!' Eileen stood in the middle of the room, her hands on her hips. Her eyes flicked past her mother to rest briefly on Arthur, sitting on a straight back chair by the table, then moved to Bill who was standing in front of the fire. 'Well?'

'We got the jobs!' There was excitement in Bill's voice. 'Both of us!'

'Go way!' Eileen flopped on to a chair. 'Yer not 'avin' me on, are yer, 'cos I'll strangle yer if yer are.'

'I wouldn't joke about a thing like that, chick!'

Arthur couldn't conceal his delight. 'We had the interview, then the medical, then back to the main office to be told we start work next Monday.'

Eileen rocked back and forth to groaning protests from the chair. 'Did yez both pass the medical?'

'With flying colours,' Bill answered. 'Both one hundred per cent fit.'

Eileen's eyes met her mother's. 'Isn't that great, Mam?'

'Best news I've had in years.' Maggie smiled. She was as happy for her daughter as she was for Bill. Perhaps when she packed in work the colour would come back to those chubby cheeks, and the laughter that had been missing of late would ring through the house once again.

'I'm made up for both of yez,' Eileen said, then burst out laughing. 'But I'm the one who's gonna be best off! While you two are sloggin' yer guts out, I'll be a lady of leisure! When can I 'and me notice in, Bill?'

'We have to work a week in hand, but you could give it in next Monday if you like. It won't hurt us to do without your wages for one week.'

Arthur looked so proud and happy, Eileen said another prayer. Please God, I know I've been asking for a lot lately, but could you do me just one more favour and I'll not ask for anything else for a long time? Could you make things right for Arthur, please?

Chapter Twenty-Three

'I don't 'alf look forward to Wednesday afternoons now, don't youse?' Eileen glanced from Mary sitting opposite across the dining table, to Vera seated on her left. Since Eileen had packed in work they'd taken it in turns to host a couple of hours of tea and gossip. Today was Eileen's turn and her face was beaming with pride. She'd spent hours blackleading the grate, cleaning the brass and polishing the furniture with Mansion polish and plenty of elbow grease. 'I don't know what to do with meself half the time, now I'm a lady of leisure.'

'You wouldn't want to go back to work, though, would you?' Mary asked, her eyes sparkling. 'You moaned about it for long enough.'

'Nah, I wouldn't go back to work for a big clock.' Eileen cocked her head to one side. 'What yer lookin' so 'appy about, kid? Lost a tanner an' found 'alf a crown, 'ave yer?'

Mary couldn't contain herself any longer. 'Harry's getting a car!'

'What?' Eileen's mouth gaped in surprise. 'Go on, yer pullin' our legs!'

Mary's long blonde hair swung across her face. 'I am not!

One of the men he works with is selling his car and Harry's going to see it tonight.'

'Well, I'll be blowed! Yer were swankin' when yer got the telephone put in, but a car! There'll be no stoppin' 'er now, will there, Vera?' Eileen glanced briefly at Vera. 'The Sedgemoors are goin' up in the world.'

'Yeah, she won't know us, soon.' Vera's voice was low and lacking in enthusiasm, but Eileen was already rattling on to Mary and neither of them noticed.

'I can't wait to see the look on Cissie Maddox's face when she sees yez drivin' up 'ere in a posh car.'

'It isn't a posh car.' Mary laughed. 'It's an old banger by the sounds of it, but it'll get Harry to work when he can get the petrol. I think the ration is only a gallon a week.'

Eileen fingered the dimples in her elbows. 'Here's me, all made up 'cos Bill's savin' up to buy me one of them vacuum cleaner things, an' you sit there like a cat that's got the canary, an' tell us yez are gettin' a car!' Out of the corner of her eye, Eileen saw Vera shiver. 'Are yer cold, Vera?' She pushed her chair back and looked at the miserable fire. 'It's this bloody coal! I can't get a proper fire goin' with it . . . it's all that flippin' slate stuff.' Eileen lifted a cushion on the couch and produced a sheet of newspaper. Holding it across the front of the grate, she muttered through clenched teeth, 'Come on, yer bugger, burn!'

'You're very quiet, Vera.' Mary noticed the pale face and dull eyes. 'Are you feeling all right?'

'I think I've got a cold coming on.' Vera wrapped her cardi tightly around herself. 'I've got the shivers.'

Eileen took her eyes off the paper she was holding. 'Yer do look lousy, Vera. Perhaps yer should 'ave stayed in 'cos there's a cold wind out.' Then Eileen's eyes narrowed. 'Have yer 'eard anythin' from that 'usband of yours?'

Vera's eyes went to Mary before sending Eileen a silent warning. 'He's coming home next week.'

'Eileen, the paper!' Mary cried as she saw the newspaper turning brown in the middle.

'Oh, shit!' Eileen grabbed the paper which was now burning and rolled it into a ball before throwing it into the fire. Sucking her fingers, she moaned, 'I've burnt me bloody fingers now!'

'Run them under the cold water for a few minutes,' Mary said. 'That usually stops them from blistering.'

Eileen tucked her hand under her armpit and sat down. 'They'll be all right. I'm not leavin' 'ere in case I miss anythin'.'

'Don't be daft,' Mary said. 'What is there to miss?'

But Eileen ignored her. Looking straight into Vera's eyes, she asked, 'Yer 'aven't got a cold, 'ave yer? It's Danny comin' 'ome, isn't it?'

Vera's answer was a shrug of her shoulders.

Mary looked from one to the other, bewildered. 'What's Danny got to do with Vera having a cold? She'll be made up to have Danny home, won't you, Vera?' It was to Eileen that Vera looked. And Eileen nodded. 'Yer'll 'ave to tell 'er.'

'Tell me what, for heaven's sake?' Mary's head swivelled from side to side. 'What's going on?'

'Shall I tell 'er?' Eileen's voice was soft. 'What's the good of 'avin' mates if we can't confide in each other?'

When Vera sighed, then nodded, Eileen proceeded to tell Mary what had happened on Danny's last leave. Eileen was a born story teller, but this time she didn't have to add anything to make the story more dramatic. And when she'd finished there was a look of horror on Mary's pretty face.

'I thought everything was all right between the two of you, now.' Mary was shocked and saddened. When she'd lived next door to the Jacksons she'd often heard Danny's rantings and ravings. She could remember vividly the times she'd sat with her mother listening, but unable to help. Her mother had tried talking to Danny, but had been rudely told to mind her own business. So they'd had to sit helpless, knowing that next day Vera would be sporting a black eye. And they only saw that because a black eye was one of the bruises Vera couldn't hide. 'I thought he'd changed since he went in the army.'

'We all thought that.' Eileen was the one to answer. 'D'yer remember the Christmas at your 'ouse, when Danny was 'ome on leave? We all said 'ow much he'd changed . . . remember?'

'That's what he wanted you to think,' Vera said. 'I was daft enough to believe it meself for a while, so you weren't the only ones who fell for it. But you can take it from me, Danny Jackson hasn't changed one little bit and he never will.'

'What yer gonna do, kid?' Eileen asked. 'Yer can't put up with that for the rest of yer life.' She suddenly banged on the table, making her two friends jump. 'Honest, I could strangle the bugger with me bare 'ands.'

'But he wouldn't try anything now the two boys are grown up, would he?' Mary asked. 'They wouldn't just stand by and let him push you or Carol around, surely?'

'Oh, Danny Jackson is crafty,' Eileen said. 'He wouldn't do anything when they were there. He'd take it out on Vera in the bedroom.'

'Shall I ask Harry to have a word with him?'

'No!' The word was like a pistol shot. 'I'm not getting anybody else involved in my troubles. I'll sort it out meself.'

'Some life, isn't it?' Eileen sighed. 'You an' Arthur Kennedy! Neither of yez 'ave got much to look forward to, 'ave yez? Mind you, I 'aven't seen so much of Arthur since 'e started work, so I don't know whether things 'ave changed for 'im.'

'They haven't!' Vera's hand went to her mouth as Eileen's brows shot up.

'How d'yer know?'

'He . . . er . . . he's called at ours a few times on his way home from work, to bring Carol some sweets.' Vera's face flushed a bright red. 'He's taken up with Carol, thinks the world of her.'

'Pity he isn't taken up with you,' Eileen said. 'Yer'd make a good pair.' A smile played around her lips. 'Couldn't yer fix Danny up with Sylvia? Now there's two people that are well matched, an' they deserve each other. Then you an' Arthur could get together an' everyone would be 'appy.'

'Don't be so daft!' Vera protested hotly. 'He only comes to see Carol.' Her finger making a pattern on the tablecloth, she said softly, 'She'll miss him when he stops coming.'

'Why should 'e stop comin'?' Eileen asked innocently. 'He's only a friend, an' yer allowed to 'ave a friend, aren't yer?'

'Oh, Danny would love that!' Vera laughed cynically. 'Can you imagine what he'd do to me if he came home and found a strange man in the house? He'd kill me!'

'I think it would do Danny the world of good to know yer 'ad lots of friends callin'. Might make 'im think twice about keepin' 'is 'ands to 'imself, if 'e knew there was someone around who'd give 'im one back.' Eileen was nodding her head as the idea grew in her mind. 'Me an' Bill will come round, an' I wouldn't put Arthur off if I were you. He's quite capable of lookin' after 'imself.'

'Me and Harry will come, too,' Mary said timidly. 'But I don't know whether Arthur is a good idea. It might rub Danny up the wrong way and you're the one who'll suffer.'

'We'll just wait and see.' Vera sounded resigned to a fate worse than death. 'I'll take things as they come.'

'Does that mean you won't be able to meet us every Wednesday now?' Mary asked.

'Oh, he won't stop me doing that!' There was determination in Vera's voice. 'Seeing you two is the only thing I've got to look forward to.'

'Well, it's my birthday next week, and Harry's giving me a few bob to take you both out for afternoon tea. Will you be able to come, Vera?'

'Let anyone try and stop me.' Vera pressed Mary's arm. 'It won't matter if Danny objects, because Harry's mam said she'll mind Carol every Wednesday afternoon for me. It's been great the last few months having these get-togethers to look forward to, and I'm very grateful to Mrs Sedgemoor for minding Carol for me. I love Carol more than anything in the world, but it's nice to get out on me own just once a week.'

'Then we'll paint the town red next Wednesday.' Mary smiled. 'I'll take you somewhere nice.'

'Oh, aye?' Eileen said. 'And where might that be?'

Mary tapped her nose with a finger. 'Wait and see. But put on your best bib and tucker.'

'I'll have to go.' Vera stood up. 'By the time I collect Carol it'll be time to start on the boys' tea.'

'Shall we meet in town?' Mary asked. 'It would save me the journey here.'

'I'll pick Vera up from 'ome an' we'll get the bus down together.' Eileen was looking at Mary, and her friend read the message that said I'll make sure a certain person doesn't try to stop her coming. 'How about meetin' outside Lime Street station at two?'

Mary nodded. 'Both be there, d'you hear? Don't leave me standing like one of Lewis's.'

Eileen laughed. 'Kid, anyone that looks like you do, standin' in Lime Street, wouldn't look like one of Lewis's. Yer'll 'ave all the fellers askin' yer 'ow much yer charge.'

'What would you do with her, Vera?' Mary tutted. 'She's got a one-track mind.'

'But her heart's in the right place.' Vera turned to the door. 'See you next Wednesday, Mary.'

When Eileen came back after seeing Vera out, she found Mary staring into space. 'Penny for yer thoughts, kid.'

'I was just thinking how selfish I was, bragging about Harry getting a car when Vera's got so much trouble on her mind.'

'Don't be daft, kid! Vera will still 'ave her troubles whether yer get a car or not! Besides, yer've 'ad enough troubles of yer own in the past, 'aven't yer? An' yer sorted them out. So it's up to Vera to sort 'erself out. We can do all we can to 'elp, but in the end it's up to her. She either puts up with it, or walks out.'

'Easier said than done.' Mary rose to her feet. 'You and me don't know how lucky we are, do we?'

'I do,' Eileen said, 'and unless yer want yer bumps feelin', so do you.'

Mary picked up her handbag. 'Oh, I do, Eileen, I do!'

As they were walking down the hall, Mary suddenly asked, 'Where does your mam get to every Wednesday afternoon? She seems to disappear as soon as we arrive.'

'Me mam doesn't know she's born since I stopped work. She toddles off to a matinee a couple of times a week. I think she's gone to the Broadway in Bootle today, to see Janet Gaynor.' Eileen put her arm round Mary's waist, nearly squeezing the breath out of her. 'Yer see, kid, no matter what troubles there are, life still goes on.'

'Hi, ya, Danny!' Eileen breezed into Vera's living room. She was all dressed up in her best clothes and they gave her the confidence to face anything Danny might come up with. 'How goes it?'

Danny inclined his head, a sullen look on his swarthy face. 'She's upstairs gettin' ready.'

'She?' Miserable bugger, Eileen thought. 'Oh, yer mean Vera?'

Danny glowered. 'Who else would I mean?'

'Well, yer never know! Yer could 'ave Rita Hayworth up there, or Betty Grable.' There was a smile on Eileen's face, but anger in her heart. Fancy having to spend the rest of your life with someone as mean and bad tempered as Danny. Imagine having to look at his miserable face all the time and be afraid to say anything in case he lashed out at you. But because she knew Vera would suffer if she voiced her thoughts, Eileen kept the smile on her face. 'When did yer get 'ome, Danny?'

'Yesterday.' Danny sat down, picked up a newspaper and buried his head in it, ignoring Eileen completely.

'Sod you,' Eileen muttered the words softly, but made sure they were loud enough for Danny to hear. Then she walked to the bottom of the stairs. 'Are yer ready yet, Vera? We're gonna be late.'

'Coming!' Vera ran down the stairs, her long, auburn hair bouncing on her shoulders. Eileen could see the strain on her face as she whispered, 'I'd better tell him I'm going.'

Vera stood in the doorway, and although her whole body was shaking, she managed to control her voice. 'I'll see you later, Danny.'

The only answer was the rustle of the newspaper, and as Vera backed into the hall, she bumped into Eileen. 'Come on, let's go.'

Walking down the street, Eileen looked sideways at Vera. 'He's a happy so-and-so, isn't 'e? Full of the joys of bloody spring.'

'You should have heard him when I told him I was going out.' Vera's laugh was shaky. 'It was just as well I'd taken Carol up to Mrs Sedgemoor's before I did, 'cos the way he carried on, he'd have frightened the life out of her.'

'Yer can tell us all about it over a cup of tea.' Eileen took Vera's arm and started to hurry. 'We don't want to keep Mary waitin'.'

'Where we goin', kid?' Eileen looked Mary up and down. Even though they'd been friends for six years, Eileen never saw Mary without thinking how beautiful she was. And it wasn't only in looks, 'cos Mary was beautiful in every way.

Kind, gentle, and modest. She'd go to the ends of the earth to help a friend, and it wasn't in her nature to hurt a living soul. 'Are yer takin' us to the Adelphi?'

'I thought of the Adelphi, but it's up to you and Vera. Wherever you'd like to go, we'll go.'

'I was only jokin', kid!' Eileen laughed. 'Can yez imagine me in the Adelphi?'

'Why not?' Mary demanded. 'We're as good as anyone else. Better in fact, than some. And I believe they do a lovely afternoon tea.'

'Oh, come on, kid!' Eileen looked into Mary's face to see if she was pulling their legs. 'I can't go in there lookin' like this! All the posh people go there, an' it would cost yer a fortune, anyway!'

Mary shook her head, a knowing smile on her face. 'It was Harry who suggested we go there, and he's paying. And in case you're worried, it only costs three and six for afternoon tea.'

Eileen was standing with her eyes closed. 'I can't believe yer seriously thinkin' of takin' me in the Adelphi! I'd make a holy show of yez!' Mary nodded to Vera, and they took an arm each. Ignoring Eileen's protests they marched her up the steps of the imposing hotel. And when they came to the lovely old revolving doors, Vera went in first so she would be ready to drag Eileen out in case she decided to go right round and out again.

'Oh, my God!' Eileen's eyes rolled from side to side, taking in the uniformed doorman, the rich, ornate decor, and the expensive clothes and posh accents of the men and women standing near them. Above all, Eileen was struck dumb by the marble floor, the lush green of the palm trees, and the quietness that comes with a first class hotel catering for wealthy people.

'Come on, up those steps.' Mary guided the bemused Eileen to the beautiful, large lounge where afternoon tea was being served. But when Mary chose a table near the centre of the lounge, Eileen came to life. 'Not 'ere,' she hissed, 'somewhere at the back.'

Vera and Mary looked around with interest at the people seated at the tables around them, many of the men in uniforms. They admired the beauty of the high ornate ceiling, and the plush curtains, but Eileen was speechless. It was only when the waitress brought a tray with their afternoon tea on, the big woman found her voice. Staring at the small plates, each holding a wafer-thin sandwich and a scone, Eileen spluttered, 'Is this all yer get for three and six? Bloody daylight robbery.' But although she wouldn't admit it then, Eileen was impressed. As she was to tell her family later, 'Fancy me in the Adelphi! An' yer should 'ave seen the nobs in there! Honest, it's beautiful . . . a real eye opener. We'll go there one day, when we've got a few bob to spare, an' yez can see it for yerselves. Give yez an idea of 'ow the other 'alf live.'

Mary refilled their cups from the round silver teapot and returned it to the tray, to stand beside the silver milk jug and sugar basin. 'I wouldn't like to have to clean this lot.'

'Me neither!' Eileen's bulk completely hid the small delicate chair. 'I'll stick to me old brown teapot and pour the milk from the bottle. Bein' posh is too much like hard work.' She was relaxed now, and even if people were staring at her, she couldn't have cared less. 'But I've enjoyed it, kid, an' thanks very much. Yer'd better thank Harry for us, too, seein' as 'e paid for it.'

'That goes for me, too.' Vera smiled. 'It certainly makes a change from our two-up-two-down, and it's nice to see some cheerful faces.'

'Danny came home yesterday, then?' Mary asked. 'How is he?'

Vera grimaced. 'Ask Eileen.'

'I'm not goin' to swear, 'cos this place is too posh,' Eileen said. 'But he's a miserable b . . . if I ever saw one. It took 'im all 'is time to let me over the door, an' 'e looked real bad tempered. Honest to God, if 'e was my 'usband, I'd clock 'im one.'

'I wish he was your husband,' Vera said. 'I wish he was anyone's husband but mine. I'd made up my mind to make the best of it, try and get along with him, but it's impossible. All he wants is a wife that he can order round and treat like a servant. He came home at six o'clock last night, threw his army bag in the room and went straight out to the pub. The boys weren't home from work when he went out, and they were asleep in bed when he came in at midnight.'

'Yer mean he didn't stay in to see 'is sons?' Eileen looked disgusted.

'Uh, uh! They haven't seen him yet! They leave for work at half seven, and he didn't get up till ten.' Vera let out a deep sigh. 'I don't know how he's going to be with them, but they won't put up with any nonsense from him. When Colin was only twelve, he told me that when he grew up he wouldn't let his dad hit me. And even though he's only sixteen, and Peter's fourteen, they're both big lads. Both taller than their dad.'

'How was Carol with him?' Mary asked. 'Did she know him?'

'I wasn't exaggerating when I told you he went straight out last night. He didn't say a word to her. And he's ignored her this morning, just like he always did.' Vera clasped and unclasped her hands. 'I'm at me wits' end, 'cos I know he's gone right back to what he was . . . a big, violent bully. I'm terrified of him hurting Carol. And he'd do it to get back at me unless I toe the line. He practically told me so last night when he came in, tanked up to the eye balls. I was in bed pretending to be asleep, but that didn't stop him from trying to force me to give him what he wanted. When I pushed him away, he threatened me with everything under the sun. It's always me and Carol he picks on, he never mentions the boys.' Vera was silent for a while, as she tried to control her emotions. 'All Danny Jackson wants a wife for is to make his meals, use as a punch bag when he's in a bad temper, and satisfy his sexual needs. If I'm not prepared to satisfy him, then me and Carol will suffer.'

Eileen and Mary didn't speak. They shook their heads in sympathy but let Vera talk it all out of her system.

'It's wicked of me, and may God forgive me, but I keep asking meself why he couldn't have been killed in the war. Thousands of good men were killed, but the devil looks after his own and Danny Jackson is alive and well.' Vera ran a hand across her forehead, the fingers biting deep in a bid to relieve the pressure. 'I don't know what I'm going to do, but if he ever lays a finger on Carol I'll be out of that door for good, even though I've nowhere to go. I'd walk the streets before I'd let him harm her.'

'Yer'll not walk the streets while I'm 'ere!' Eileen told

her. 'You come round to ours, an' we'll sort somethin' out.'

'Oh, what's the good?' Vera's shoulders slumped. 'It's easy to talk, but how could I walk out and leave the boys? I love them, and they're good kids.'

'In an emergency, Vera, you walk out.' It was Mary giving advice now. 'If Danny gets violent, just pick up Carol and run. The boys can look after themselves until you find somewhere to live. And we'd all help you to do that, wouldn't we, Eileen?'

'It goes without sayin',' Eileen snorted. 'But why the 'ell should you be the one to walk out? It's the queer feller that should be thrown out! An' if I 'ad my way, I'd get a couple of real men to do it.'

'I'm sorry, Mary! You brought us out to celebrate your birthday, mugged us to a lovely tea, an' you've had to sit and listen to my moans.' Vera's smile was a brave attempt, but it didn't mask the worry in her eyes. 'Let's talk about something nice. Did Harry get the car?'

'Yes! It's an old one, you know, but Harry said it's not in bad nick.'

Eileen, who knew Mary inside out, saw a spark in her friend's eyes and waited expectantly. She wasn't disappointed and smiled approvingly when Mary said, 'We're going up to Eileen's on Saturday to let her and Bill see it. Harry managed to get hold of some petrol and he's keeping it till then so he can take them for a run round the block. The car will hold six at a squeeze, so if I get Doris to mind Emma and Tony for us, there'd be room for you and Carol.' Without giving Vera time to think about it, Mary went on, 'We'll pick you up about two, so be ready.'

Chapter Twenty-Four

'Hurry up, Bill! They'll be 'ere any minute,' Eileen bawled up the stairs on her way to answer the knock on the front door.

'I can't find me stud,' Bill called back. 'It was on the tallboy, but I must have knocked it off.'

'Then get on yer flippin' knees an' look for it! Honest to God, you men want fetchin' and carryin'.'

Eileen opened the door to Arthur Kennedy who was wearing a broad smile.

'What's poor Bill done now?' he asked.

'Lost 'is stud, an' probably expects me to go up an' find it for him.'

Eileen closed the door and with a broad wink, she shouted loud enough for her voice to reach the bedroom. 'He'll be wantin' me to blow 'is nose for 'im next.'

'I must say you're looking very smart today, Mrs Gillmoss!' Arthur stood in the living room and gave a soft wolf whistle. 'Very fetching.'

'Flattery will get yer nowhere, Mr Kennedy.' Eileen screwed her face up at him, but inside she felt very pleased. It wasn't often anyone praised her appearance. 'Don't forget I'm a married woman.'

'Just my luck.' Arthur put a hand on his heart and a pained expression on his face. 'I meet the woman of my dreams, and she belongs to another. My poor heart is broken.'

'Go on with yer, yer daft ha'porth! Sounds like yer've been reading *True Confessions*, or somethin'.'

'Yeah, I hide them under me pillow and read them in bed.' Arthur chuckled as he glanced around. 'Where is everybody?'

'Me mam's at the shops, young Billy's out with 'is mates, and Bill's upstairs gettin' changed.' Eileen's excitement surfaced. 'We're expectin' Mary an' Harry. They've got a new car an' they're takin' us out for a run.'

'I know about Harry's car. The bloke he bought it off works in our department.'

'Look, sit down, Arthur, yer makin' me nervous standin' there.'

'No, I'll not stop if you're going out.'

'Don't act so soft. Yer not comin' all that way without gettin' a cup of tea.' Eileen glanced at the wrist watch she only wore for special occasions. 'It's only a quarter to two, so we've got time for a cuppa.'

While she was waiting for the kettle to boil, Eileen stood in the doorway. 'We'll only be out for 'alf an hour, so yer can stay 'ere till we get back an' 'ave a bite of tea with us.'

Arthur's hands were laced together, his thumbs circling each other. 'Did Vera's husband come home?'

Eileen's mind clicked. So that's why Arthur's here, she told herself. He's come for news of Vera. 'Yeah, he's 'ome.' She heard Bill's footsteps on the stairs and made her escape to the kitchen. It wasn't up to her to discuss Vera's private life with Arthur, so she'd better keep her mouth shut.

When Eileen carried the tea in, Bill and Arthur were deep

in conversation about their jobs. They'd both grown in stature since they'd started work. It seemed to have given them the confidence they needed to face the world. Apart from his white hair, Bill looked almost the same as he had before he went away. He talked and laughed a lot, and was more patient with the kids, who had slowly revised their opinion of him. When he'd first come home, they'd kept out of his way, but now they told him everything that happened at school and were always at him to play Happy Families with them.

He was strict, and wouldn't stand any nonsense, but he was fair, and always quick to praise when they got good marks at school. He still had nightmares, when Eileen knew he was reliving those horrific years, and her arms were always there to comfort him. But when this happened it was hard for Eileen to keep her feelings under control, because it was more like comforting one of the children, than her husband. Even while she whispered the soothing words, she knew that as soon as his fears had gone he would turn away from her and move to his side of the bed, leaving her to shed her tears in silence and wonder if he really no longer loved her.

'I was tellin' Arthur he might as well stay until we get back.' Eileen handed the cups over. 'We won't be out all that long.'

'Yes, that's a good idea.' Bill seemed pleased. 'We can go for a pint when the pubs open.'

'I've got to be home about eight, to see to the boys.' Arthur didn't bother making excuses for his wife not being there to mind them. These two were his friends and he'd kept nothing back from them. 'They get frightened in the house on their own once it gets dark.'

Eileen tutted. 'That wife of yours should try behavin' like a mother instead of flyin' 'er kite every night.'

'Now, now, chick!' Bill shot her a warning look. 'It's Arthur's business, not ours.'

'Well, it makes me blood boil. She gets away with murder.'

They could hear the excited shrieks of children, and Eileen bounced off the chair. 'This'll be them. The girls 'ave been waitin' at the bottom of the street for them.' Her round, fat face beamed. 'They've been that excited, yer'd think it was us that 'ad a car. They'll be swankin' like mad in front of their mates.'

Bill stood up. 'We'd better get out before they wreck the thing.'

'Hello, Arthur!' Mary's face showed her surprise. 'We didn't expect to see you today.'

Arthur acknowledged Harry's wave. 'It's a week or so since I saw Eileen, so I thought I'd better put in an appearance in case she thought I'd fallen out with her.'

'Hey! Get off, the lot of yez.' Eileen shooed the children away. There were dozens of them, all the kids from both ends of the street, climbing on the bonnet and bumper, and playing with the windscreen wipers. Harry was doing his best to move them, but he was too polite. It took Eileen's loud, threatening voice to silence them. 'Off! D'yez 'ear me, I said off!' One by one the children moved to stand against the walls, just waiting for the grown-ups to move indoors so they could begin again. They didn't see many cars, no one in their street had one, and it was a rare novelty.

'Joan, Edna, you keep yer eyes peeled, an' if anyone so much as lays a finger on it, give us a shout.'

Edna was shaking Harry's arm. 'Can we sit in it, Uncle

Harry? We won't touch anything, honest.'

Harry looked down into the pleading eyes, and grinned. 'You and Joan can take turns a piece. Five minutes each, okay?'

'I hope you know what you're doing, Harry.' Bill looked very doubtful. 'They can't do any harm, can they?'

'They can't drive it away, if that's what you mean.' Harry laughed. 'I've got the key, and the handbrake is on.'

Eileen stayed behind when the others went inside, and her warning to Joan and Edna left nothing to the imagination. 'Just one little thing wrong, me ladies, an' yez won't sit down for a month.'

The car stopped outside the Jacksons'. Eileen was in the front passenger seat because she took up too much room in the back, and Mary and Bill shared the back seat with enough room left for Vera. It was a big, roomy car, a 1933 Morris Oxford, and according to Harry, only went about eighteen miles to the gallon.

'Shall I go in for Vera?' Mary volunteered, but was glad when Harry shook his head and said, 'No, I'll go.'

The minutes ticked by and there was no sign of life from the Jacksons' house. Eileen looked at her watch. 'They're a long time! I thought Vera would be ready.'

'I hope everything's all right.' Mary's face wore a frown. 'There won't be any trouble, will there?'

'No, 'ere they are now.' The door had opened and Harry, his face set, came out holding Carol's hand. Then Vera followed and banged the door behind her.

Vera looked pale and nervous, but Carol's face was a joy to behold when she saw who was in the car.

241

'Come on, sweetheart, sit on my knee.' Mary held her arms wide. 'Mummy can sit next to us.'

Carol had never been in a car before and she jumped up and down with pleasure, pointing to everything they passed. Her happiness was infectious and soon everyone was laughing with her.

'D'yer know, I feel like wavin' me 'and like the King an' Queen do.' Eileen looked out of the car window, gave a limp wave with her chubby hand and bowed her head. Shaking with laughter, she turned to Harry. 'Where's yer chauffeur's 'at? Trust you to let the side down. The trouble is, yer not used to travellin' in style, like we are.' She turned her head and winked at Bill. 'It's easy to see 'e wasn't brought up proper, isn't it, love?'

Harry parked the car in Barnston Road, at the side of the Aintree Palace picture house. 'We'll take Carol in the park and she can play on the swings.'

They saw a reminder of the war when they turned in the gates of Aintree park. The huge air raid shelter that had been built in the grounds was overgrown with weeds, but the sloping concrete path leading down to it was a grim reminder of those nights when people fled their homes and took refuge in the underground shelter.

Carol was in her apple cart. First she had a go on the swings, then the slide, and finally the roundabout, with Mary beside her. It was a small park, with a bowling green behind, and there were only a few children with their mothers. But everyone stopped what they were doing when Carol's laugh rang out. Heads appeared over the hedge dividing the park from the bowling green, and there were smiles on the faces of young and old.

'D'yer know, that kid's a real treat to take out,' Eileen whispered to Mary. 'If she was mine, I'd love the bones of 'er.'

'Vera does love her.' Mary's face looked troubled. 'Harry didn't look very happy when he came out of their house, did he? I wonder what went on?'

Eileen saw Vera coming towards them, her hand on Carol's shoulder. 'We'll find out later.'

'Yer can come in for five minutes, surely?' They'd piled out of the car outside Eileen's, and she was now trying to coax Vera inside for a cuppa. She deliberately didn't mention Arthur was inside, because she knew Vera would run like a scared rabbit. Then she grinned. 'Yer've got no choice, 'cos Carol's already gone in.'

'Just for a few minutes, then.'

'We'll be in shortly,' Bill called. 'We're just having a look over the car.' Eileen pushed Vera along the hall, and Vera was laughing when she entered the room. But the smile faded when she saw Carol climbing on to Arthur's knee.

'Hello, Arthur, I didn't know you were here.'

Eileen pushed Vera forward. 'Will yer move, so we can all get in, missus?' She bustled towards the kitchen. 'Sit yerselves down while I stick the kettle on.'

'Carol, you're too big to be sitting on Uncle Arthur's knee.' Vera tried to coax her daughter down, but Carol wasn't having any. 'When she gets too heavy for you, Arthur, make her get down.'

'Will you stop worrying, Vera?' Arthur said with a smile. 'She's my girlfriend, aren't you, darling?'

'She's certainly enjoyed herself.' Mary pulled two chairs

from the table. 'Sit yourself down, Vera, and relax.'

But Vera couldn't relax. She was filled with apprehension about what would happen when she got home. Danny had been livid when she'd told him she was going out. He'd stormed out to the pub, but instead of staying there until closing time like he usually did, he was back again at half past one. If anyone else but Harry had called for her, she knew Danny would have kicked up a stink and refused to let her out. But he was crafty enough not to cause a row in front of Harry. That would come when she got home, Vera was sure of that.

When Bill and Harry came in, the conversation was centred around the car. 'You got a bargain,' Bill said. 'It's a nice-looking car, and in very good nick.'

'Yes, but it eats the petrol. The gallon a week ration would just about get me to work and back on one day.'

'Tell yer what, lover boy,' Eileen said. 'How about doin' a swap? We'll 'ave your car, an' you can 'ave our Edna's scooter? Yer wouldn't need petrol for that . . . only yer shoes soled and 'eeled every week.'

'I've got a better idea.' The dimple in Harry's chin deepened when he laughed. 'We've still got our Tony's pram. You've got nothing else to do all day, so you could come up to ours and push me to work.'

'What about getting a rickshaw?' Arthur joined in. 'Then you could take Bill and Harry to work.'

'Ha-ha-ha!' The floorboards began to creak as Eileen rocked with laughter, and Bill was smiling before she even said a word. 'I've got an idea that knocks all yours into a cocked hat! I could give yez a piggy back, an' yer could use our Edna's whip to gee me up. A crack on the backside would set me off at a gallop, an' I'd 'ave yez at work before yer knew yer'd left the 'ouse.'

Vera's laugh was forced, her eyes continually going to the clock. She was afraid of leaving, but more afraid not to. She let a half hour slip by, then said she'd really have to get home to get the tea on.

'I'll have to be on my way, too,' Arthur said, easing himself off the couch. 'I'll walk down the road with you.'

Bill looked surprised. 'But I thought we were going for a pint?'

'It's not worth it, Bill! It takes me an hour, on two buses, to get home. By the time the pubs open, it would be time for me to leave.'

'I'll run you home, Vera.' Harry felt in his pocket for the car keys. 'Then I can drop Arthur off at the bus stop.'

Carol's face was radiant, sitting on Arthur's knee on the front seat. But when the car stopped outside their house, and Vera tried to lift her out, she clung to Arthur's neck and screamed.

'Move back, Vera, and I'll get her.' Harry had walked round the car and stood behind her. 'She'll come for me, won't you, sweetheart?'

With a bit of coaxing, and a promise to go in the house with her, Carol kissed Arthur goodbye. 'Open the door, Vera, and I'll bring her in.'

'There's no need.' Vera tried to take Carol's hand but Harry pushed her gently. 'I'm coming in, Vera.' He looked down at Arthur, who had wound the car window down. 'I'll only be a tick, Arthur.'

Arthur noticed Vera's hand shaking as she inserted the

key in the lock and he breathed in deeply before blowing his breath out slowly.

Harry slammed the front door and walked round to the driver's seat. He didn't say a word as he turned the engine on and pulled away from the kerb. But half way down the road he slammed on the brakes so hard Arthur just saved himself from going through the windscreen. 'What's wrong?'

Harry drummed his fingers on the steering wheel. He was silent for a while, then he turned to Arthur. 'I forgot I had a message for me mam. She only lives three doors away from Vera, and Mary asked me to call in.'

'You're a lousy liar, Harry,' Arthur said. 'It's something to do with Vera, isn't it?'

'Of course not! What would . . .'

'Harry, I know all about Vera's troubles,' Arthur interrupted. 'You see I often call there on me way home from work to take Carol some sweets.' Seeing Harry's eyes widen in surprise, Arthur went on quickly, 'There's nothing in it, Harry, I swear to God. It's just that we're alike, me and Vera. Two lonely, lost souls, without much to look forward to. So we can sympathise with each other, and it's nice to have someone to talk to who understands.'

Harry's eyes searched Arthur's face for several seconds before he spoke. 'I don't know what to say, Arthur. I've known Vera a long time, nearly all me life, and I'm very fond of her and the kids. It doesn't seem right to talk about her.' There was another short silence, then Harry said, 'Damn and blast Danny Jackson. He's not fit to wipe Vera's shoes.'

'What did he have to say?'

'He didn't say anything, that's what's worrying me. Didn't

say hello, goodbye, or kiss me backside.' Harry's knuckles on the steering wheel were white. 'He stalked the room like a tiger after its prey, and you could see the anger raging inside him. He wouldn't say anything while I was there, he knows better, but I had a feeling he would start on Vera the minute I walked out of the house.'

'I'm going back.' Arthur had his hand on the door handle when Harry grabbed his arm. 'Hang on a minute, Arthur. If you rush back there you'll make things ten times worse for Vera and Carol. Just let's think things over carefully.'

'Sit here while she's getting a hammering?' Arthur shook his head. 'No chance! I'm going back.'

This time Harry's grip was like iron. 'If you go there, a strange man, what d'you think Danny would make of that? He'd kill Vera, and Carol as well. And don't think I'm exaggerating, Arthur, 'cos I'm not. You don't know what Danny Jackson's like . . . I do.'

Arthur closed the door. Harry was right. It would look bad for Vera if he went knocking on the door. 'What shall we do?'

Harry was rubbing his forehead, seeking a solution. 'Look, I told you my mam and dad live near them, so I'll drive round the block and stop outside our house. That way I won't have to pass their window, and Danny will think we're miles away. I'll sort something out when we get that far.'

They drove round the block and came to a stop outside the house Harry was born in. Making a motion with his hand to tell Arthur to stay where he was, Harry rapped on his mother's window. When Lizzie Sedgemoor opened the door, Arthur saw her face light up at the sight of her son. He couldn't hear what was being said, but as Harry's finger pointed down the street, Arthur saw the smile leave Lizzie's face. Then, as Harry went to walk away, she held his arm, as if to physically stop him from doing something she thought was dangerous. But Harry freed his arm, smiled to assure her there was nothing to worry about, then walked the few yards to the third door down.

Arthur left the car to stand beside Mrs Sedgemoor. He didn't introduce himself, merely smiled. Time enough for pleasantries later. They saw Harry stop outside the door, his head cocked. In a matter of seconds he was hurrying back to them, his face pale and angry. 'He's having a go at them, I can hear him. In fact it's a wonder the whole street can't hear him. What's wrong with the neighbours, Mam?'

'The people in Mary's old house, it's their wall that's next to the Jacksons', they don't know Danny. He's been away all the time they've lived there.' Lizzie looked worried to death. 'They don't know Vera that well, either, because you know she doesn't bother with anyone. They probably don't like to interfere.' Lizzie straightened her pinny, and her face was an angry red now. 'If he touches Carol, I'll take the brush to him meself.'

'We're not just going to stand here, are we?' Arthur demanded. 'If you're not going, I am!'

'And how are you going to get in?' Harry's chest was heaving. 'If we knock at the door, d'you think he's going to answer it? Not bloody likely, he's not!' Harry scratched his head. 'Mam, d'you know if they leave their back yard door unlocked?'

'They haven't got a lock on it,' Lizzie said. 'It's only on a latch.'

'I'll go through yours and down the entry.' Standing on

the top step, Harry looked over his shoulder at Arthur. 'You stay here, and don't move.'

'I'm coming with you,' Arthur said. 'You might need some help.'

'Stand in the entry with me mam, if you must, but don't come near the house,' Harry warned. 'If I need you, I'll yell.'

Harry lifted the latch, and keeping close to the wall, out of sight of the window, he crept stealthily to the kitchen door. The noise from inside was enough to urge him forward. As he tried the door, his shoulder was ready to burst it open if necessary, but the handle turned in his hands.

The scene that met his eyes sent him into a rage. Vera was cowering in the corner, next to the fireplace, and Carol was behind her, screaming in terror. One of Danny's hands was gripping Vera's neck while the other one was raised to strike. Harry moved quickly, but wasn't in time to prevent the blow from landing on the side of Vera's face, sending her reeling.

'You bastard!' Harry grabbed Danny by the back of the neck and threw him to the other side of the room. 'I warned you once before what would happen if you ever raised your hand to Vera or Carol, or have you forgotten? If you have, let me remind you.'

Danny straightened himself up, his face purple with anger. 'An' I told you not to interfere between man and wife. This is my 'ouse, so get the hell out of 'ere, quick, before I throw yer out.'

Without taking his eyes off Danny, Harry said to Vera, 'Take Carol and go up to me mam's. Go out the back way.'

The sight of Vera leading Carol out of the room incensed Danny further. Roaring like a bull, he charged. 'I'll teach yer not to meddle in my affairs.' Head down, arms waving madly, and eyes bulging, he lunged with full force. But when he threw his fist, Harry sidestepped and the blow landed in the air before Danny hit the floor. Expecting Harry to take advantage while he was down, Danny lifted an arm to shield his face. When the blows he was expecting didn't rain down on him, he peeped under his elbow to see Harry standing before him, his arms folded. Fooled by Harry's calm, Danny tried to bluff. 'Go on, get out if yer too frightened to fight.'

'Not frightened, Danny, I just don't like hitting a man when he's down. So do us both a favour and stand up and fight like a man. Of course you're not used to fighting with men, are you? Women are more in your line.'

Still Danny didn't stir. So Harry resorted to more insults. 'You are a coward, Danny Jackson. A cruel, mean coward. And if you don't get up off that floor, I'll drag you out into the street so all the neighbours can see you for what you are. A wife beater.'

And Danny knew by Harry's tone of voice he meant what he said. So he tried to talk his way out of it. 'How would you like it if yer wife started goin' out and leavin' yer, eh? Wouldn't like it, would yer? And yer wouldn't put up with her turnin' 'er back on yer in bed, either, would yer? Oh, yer don't know the half of it. She's a real bitch, is my wife.'

Danny's whining voice was the last straw. Harry grabbed him by the scruff of the neck and yanked him up. 'You can either put up a fight, or stand there and be beaten to a pulp, it's up to you. But either way, I'm going to give you what Vera can't . . . a bloody good hiding.' Harry drew his arm back and threw it forward with his full strength behind it. When he heard it land, he said through clenched teeth, 'That's for Vera.'

Chapter Twenty-Five

'Oh, thank goodness for that!' Mary sighed with relief as Eileen hurried to answer the knock on the door. 'Harry's been gone so long I thought he must have had an accident.'

'Oh, my God!' Eileen's words sent Mary scurrying down the hall to peer over her shoulder. When she saw Harry with Carol in his arms and Vera by his side, her first thought was that her fears had been right, and there had been an accident with the car. Pushing Eileen's arm aside, she asked, 'What's wrong?'

'Can we talk inside, please?' Harry waited till Vera was in the hall then followed, closing the door behind him with his foot. He lowered Carol to the floor, saying, 'Run in and see Uncle Bill, there's a sweetheart.'

'What's up?' Eileen asked, her eyes going from Vera to Harry.

Harry put a finger to his lips. 'Keep your voice down or you'll upset Carol. She's had enough frights in the last hour.' He explained briefly what had happened, then said, 'Let's go inside and we'll tell you the whole story. But for heaven's sake don't raise your voices or you'll scare the wits out of the poor kid. It's taken us all our time to calm her down.'

Eileen walked straight to the window in the living room

and lifted the net curtain. 'Our Joan and Edna are in the yard making a tent out of an old blanket, Carol can play with them.'

Bill's eyes flicked from one to the other, questioning, but Eileen shook her head. 'Later, love.'

She knocked on the window to attract the girls' attention, then when they came running in, she told them they could take some of the things out of the cupboard to play shop with. 'An' take Carol out with yez.'

With Carol safely out of the way, Eileen sat down. 'Now, out with it.' Then she noticed the angry red mark on Vera's cheek and her eyes rolled upwards. 'Oh, Danny's left 'is trademark again, eh?'

Vera lowered her head in shame. 'I'm sorry to be such a nuisance to all of you, but I couldn't go back in there the way he was. Not with Carol, anyway.'

'Tell them what happened, Vera, then I'll carry on from where I came into it.' Harry urged her on. 'You've got nothing to be ashamed of, just tell them the truth.'

Vera started slowly, then as the anger in her built up, her words poured out. As soon as Harry had left, she told them, Danny had started shouting and swearing. When she didn't answer, he started pushing her around. Her one thought was to protect Carol, so she carried the child into the corner and stood in front of her. Her action inflamed Danny more, and he started lashing out at her with his fists. All the time he was hitting her he was shouting obscenities and blaming her for making him a laughing stock by giving him a daughter who was a gormless imbecile.

Vera picked at a speck on her coat, and was silent for a while. Then she said, 'My whole body must be black and blue all over with the belts he gave me. And all I could think of was that I mustn't black out, because then he would have a go at Carol. I was never so glad to see anyone as I was to see Harry walk through that door, because I couldn't have taken much more.' She turned her eyes to Harry. 'You can tell them the rest.'

Harry told in detail what he had seen when he walked in, and what had happened when Vera left. He ended by saying, 'He was sitting in a chair with his head in his hands when I came away, nursing his bruises.'

'I hope yer gave 'im what he deserved.' Eileen was the first to speak, her voice thick with disgust. 'He's an evil man.' She looked across at her husband. 'What do you say, Bill?'

'He's not a fit husband or father, that's for sure.' Bill looked at Vera's bowed head, and there was sympathy in his voice when he asked, 'Has he hurt you badly, Vera? D'you think you should see a doctor?'

Vera shook her head. 'I'm all right. My body is sore and stiff, but I know from experience it'll ease off in a few days.'

'She can't go back home . . . not today anyway.' Harry looked at his wife who was standing by Vera's side. 'I asked her to come home with us, Mary, but she's worried about the boys and doesn't want to go too far away. Me mam tried to persuade her to stay in their house, they've got a spare bedroom, but as Vera said, if Danny found out she was there, me mam would get the height of abuse from him.'

'She'll stay 'ere,' Eileen said promptly, having already worked it out in her head. 'Our Billy can sleep on the couch, and Vera and Carol can 'ave 'is room.'

Vera's whole body slumped. 'I can't put Billy out of his bed, it wouldn't be fair.'

'He won't mind, lass,' Bill said. 'It'll only be till you can get yourself sorted out.'

'Me mam's going to watch out for the boys coming home,' Harry said. 'And she'll tell them not to worry, that Vera will get in touch with them tomorrow. She's going to warn them not to say anything, just to keep quiet and pretend they don't know anything.'

'What a bloody life!' Eileen exploded. 'We've just got one war over an' Danny Jackson 'as to start one of 'is own! The man's a ravin' bloody lunatic.'

'What will you do, Vera?' Mary's voice was soft. 'No matter whose house you stay in, it's only a temporary measure. You've got your whole future to think about.'

'I know that, Mary, but what can I do?' Vera cried. 'I've got Carol and the boys to think about. Even if I could get a house, away from Danny, where do I get the money from to keep us?' She threw her arms wide. 'I've been over it a dozen times in me head, but there's no answer. I can't get a job because of Carol, the boys don't earn enough to keep us, so what do I do? The only thing I can do is stay with Danny.'

'Where was Arthur while all this was goin' on?' Eileen asked. 'Had yer dropped 'im at the bus stop before yer went back to Vera's?'

'No, I left him with me mam.' For the first time a smile crossed Harry's face. 'He was straining at the leash, wanting to come with me to "sort the bastard out", as he put it. But I didn't think it was advisable. Mind you,' Harry chuckled, 'if the army had turned Danny into a Tarzan, and I'd been in trouble, I'd have yelled me head off for him.'

'If I'd known what was going on, I'd have been there with you as well,' Bill said. The thought of anyone harming a hair on Carol's head was enough to put the normally mild man in a fighting mood. 'I've a good mind to go round there now and tell him what I think about him.'

'I'm gettin' jealous now, Vera.' Eileen kept her face straight. 'All these men wantin' to fight over yer . . . yer'll 'ave to tell me yer secret.'

'I think Vera could do with a cup of tea, Eileen.' Harry stood up. 'We better be going, love, or your mam will think we've left home.'

'I'll come up tomorrow and see if there's anything I can do.' Mary stroked Vera's hair. 'Try not to worry, Danny won't find you here.'

'If 'e tried, he'd 'ave to get through me first.' Eileen pretended to roll her sleeves up. 'There's nothin' I'd like better than to knock Danny Jackson into the middle of next week.'

Bill's slow smile accompanied his knowing nod. 'She could too, you know. Mr Jackson would be well advised to steer clear of my wife. She's got a left hook like Joe Louis.'

'I've changed our Billy's bed, so why don't you take Carol up and 'ave a lie down?' Eileen asked. 'I'll give yer a shout when the tea's ready.'

'I think I will, if you don't mind.' Vera's whole body ached, and her head was splitting. 'But I feel terrible putting Billy out of his bed.'

'That's one worry yer can forget about,' Eileen assured her. 'He won't mind in the least.'

Eileen showed them into the small box room, kissed Carol,

then made her way downstairs shaking her head. 'I know yer don't like me swearing, Bill, but that Danny would make a saint swear. He's a rotten swine, an' the sooner Vera can get away from 'im, the better.'

'I agree with you, but that's easier said than done.' Bill tore a strip off the *Echo* and folded it into a taper. Pushing it between the bars of the grate he waited till it caught fire, then lit his cigarette. 'She hasn't got much of a future to look forward to.'

'That's the understatement of the year, that is! She's got no bloody . . .'

'Ssssh!' Bill put a warning finger to his lips just as Edna dashed in.

'Mam, Mrs Maddox wants yer.'

'Oh, no!' Eileen groaned. 'What does she want?'

'I dunno.' Edna was bobbing up and down, her spindly legs crossing and uncrossing. 'She just said to ask yer to go down 'cos she wanted a word with yer.' Message delivered, Edna turned on her heels eager to return to the game of skipping, when her mother's thunderous voice halted her in her tracks.

'Where d'yer think you're goin'?' Eileen stood in the middle of the room, hands on her wide hips. 'Down the yard to the lavvy, if yer don't mind.'

'Ah, ay, Mam! It's my turn to jump in!' Edna protested, her legs clamped firmly together. 'They're waitin' for me.'

'Then let them wait.' Eileen raised an arm and pointed to the kitchen door. 'Down the yard before yer wet yer knickers.' As Edna dashed past, huffing and puffing at the injustice, Eileen added, 'That's if yer 'aven't wet them already, yer lazy faggot.'

'It's a wonder Cissie didn't come up herself.' Bill blew a smoke ring in the air. 'Wonder what she wants?'

'Give me two guesses, Bill, an' I bet I'll get it right. She's either seen all the comin' and goin', an' her nose is twitchin' to find out what's happenin', or she's on the cadge to borrow somethin'.'

'You're being bad minded, chick,' Bill chuckled.

'I'll bet yer two bob I'm right.' Eileen gazed at her reflection in the mirror and grimaced. 'I look as though I've been dragged through a hedge, backwards.'

'You look all right to me, chick.'

Eileen's eyes slid across the mirror till she had Bill in her sight. I look all right, she thought. Not nice, or attractive, just all right. Would it kill yer to pay me a compliment now and again, Bill Gillmoss, or am I not even worth that?

'I'd better get down and see what nose fever wants.' Eileen walked slowly towards the door, her feelings down in the dumps. 'If it's a loan she's after, she's out of luck.'

Cissie was waiting on the front step, her arms folded across her tummy. She'd been like a cat on hot bricks for hours, watching through the net curtains the flurry of activity at Eileen's. She was dying to know what was going on but couldn't think of an excuse to talk to Eileen. Then she happened to look in the back entry to see where her daughter was, and she witnessed a scene that gave her the excuse she needed.

'Yer wanted to see me, Cissie?'

'Well, yer know I'm not one to carry tales,' Cissie's expression was as innocent as a baby's, 'but I thought yer should know.'

Eileen almost laughed in Cissie's face. Not one to carry

tales? The woman thrived on gossip! 'What should I know, Cissie?'

'Well,' Cissie's mouth formed a straight line, 'I saw your Billy smokin' in the entry.'

Eileen stepped back a pace, flabbergasted. All the troubles she had on her mind, what with Vera, and her own problems with Bill, and here was gabby Annie tryin' to pile more on her! Oh, Eileen had Cissie's measure all right. She thought Eileen would be so grateful for putting her wise about young Billy she'd get all matey and tell her why Harry Sedgemoor's car had been back and forth so much. But she was out of luck because Eileen wasn't falling for it. She'd kill young Billy when she got her hands on him, but she wasn't going to give Cissie Maddox the satisfaction of telling her that.

All of these thoughts flitted through Eileen's head in the few seconds it took her to put a smile on her face. 'Is that what yer wanted me for, Cissie? All this cloak an' dagger stuff, just to tell me somethin' I already know?'

The smirk disappeared from Cissie's chubby face. 'Yer mean yer knew he was smokin', an' him only fourteen?'

'Yeah, I knew,' Eileen lied, a silent prayer winging its way to heaven to remind God that a little white lie was necessary now and then. 'I've caught him at it meself, in our lavvy. But boys will be boys, Cissie, an' I'm not goin' to lose any sleep over it. An' I don't think you should worry about your Leslie smokin', either.' Eileen was beginning to enjoy this exchange, and a laugh was building up inside of her. Leslie was Cissie's eldest son, and the same age as Billy. 'As I said, Cissie, boys will be boys!'

Cissie had been leaning against the wall, all matey like, but now she straightened up, her eyes showing the anger she felt at having had the tables turned on her. 'Are you insinuating that our Leslie smokes?'

Eileen spread her hands out, her face a mask of innocence. 'I'm sayin' nothin', Cissie, 'cos like yerself, I'm the last person in the world to carry tales.' With this Eileen turned on her heels, leaving Cissie fuming and vowing to clout their Leslie when he came in.

Eileen waited till she was back home to relieve her feelings, and her laugh rang through the house. 'She certainly got her eye wiped,' she told Bill. 'I wasn't goin' to let Cissie Maddox get the better of me.'

'What happened?'

Eileen acted out the whole scene, playing the roles of both characters. When playing Cissie, she moved to one side, mimicking to perfection the voice and facial expressions of their neighbour. Her arms waved, her eyes widened then formed slits, and her mouth did contortions. The whole thing was so hilarious, Bill rocked back and forth with laughter. Then when Eileen sat down, he asked through his tears, 'And does our Billy smoke?'

'How the 'ell do I know? He could be smokin' like a bloody chimney, but he's not goin' to tell me, is 'e?'

Bill was holding the stitch in his side. 'And what do you intend doing about it?'

'Break 'is bloody neck for 'im, that's what I'm goin' to do.'

'Bit drastic, isn't it?' Bill waited till he got his breath back before saying, 'Before you do anything, can I tell you a little tale?'

'I think I've 'ad enough tales today to last me a life time,' Eileen said. 'But go 'ed, another won't kill me.'

'I remember when I was fourteen and had me first smoke.' Bill smiled across at her. 'I'd been working for a few weeks, and all the men I worked with smoked. I thought it was the grown-up thing to do, so one night I bought a packet of five Woodbines. Me and me mate, Sammy Dickinson, went down an entry in Grace Road, off Walton Vale, and we smoked two and a half cigarettes each.' Grinning at the memory, Bill went on, 'We staggered out of that entry, green about the gills. We felt so ill, we swore we'd never smoke another cigarette. But the feeling soon wore off, and the next week it was Sammy's turn to buy the Woodies.'

'Yer mean yer've been smokin' since yer were fourteen?' Eileen looked bewildered. 'Yer've never told our Billy that tale, 'ave yer?'

'No, and I never will,' Bill answered. 'I'm only telling you so you'll understand that even though he may only be fourteen, our Billy is working with men, and he wants to feel like a man himself.'

'What am I supposed to do, then? Say nowt?'

'Leave it to me,' Bill said. 'I'll have a word with his Lordship.'

'If it's not one thing, it's another,' Eileen sighed. 'Anyway, I'd better go an' wake our lodgers.'

'Just a minute, chick.' Bill pulled at her skirt. 'There's something I want to talk to you about.'

'What is it now, Bill? I think I've 'ad enough for one day.'

'It's Ma. She's been having a go at me about you not eating properly and losing weight.'

'Take no notice of me mam, she's imaginin' things,' Eileen said. 'She's always naggin' me about it, but there's nothin' wrong with me. The trouble with me mam is, if she's got nothing to worry about, she'll find somethin'.'

'She's not imagining things, chick, and you know it. You have lost weight, and you've lost the colour in your cheeks. It's not only your mam that thinks that, either, because I do.'

'Well yer both wrong, so yez can stop yer worryin'. There's nowt the matter with me, an' that's all there is to it. And now I'm goin' to wake Vera.'

As she reached the door, Bill said, 'You know, chick, you should be on the stage. Your impressions are spot on.'

Eileen didn't answer, but as she climbed the stairs, she muttered under her breath. 'Bloody marvellous when all yer 'usband can find to say about yer is that yer look all right, an' yer good at impersonations. Makes me wonder why I bother.'

Eileen looked down on the sleeping forms, her face sad. Vera was cradling Carol in her arms, and the little girl whose mind would always be that of a child, was sucking peacefully on her thumb. It was beyond Eileen's comprehension how anyone could be cruel to such an innocent, trusting human being. Aye, there were some wicked people in the world.

'Wakey, wakey!' Eileen drew back the curtains. 'Tea's up, Vera.'

Vera looked around the strange room, confused for a minute. Then she slipped her arm from beneath Carol and sat up, rubbing the sleep from her eyes. 'I was dead to the world.'

Eileen's hand flew to her mouth, her eyes wide with disbelief. Vera had slipped her dress off before she got into bed, and the ugly red and blue bruises stood out against the white of the sheets. Both arms were covered with them, and her shoulders and chest. 'Oh, my God, Vera, he certainly 'ad a go at yer, didn't he?'

'No more than usual, Eileen.' Vera held her arms out. 'If I had a pound for every time I looked like this, I'd be a rich woman.'

Carol began to stir, and Vera put a finger to her lips. 'Don't say anything in front of her.'

'I'll take Carol down,' Eileen said. 'Our Billy's in now, an' he can look after 'er for a few minutes. You cover yerself with the sheet to make yerself decent, but don't put yer dress on. I want Bill to see what Danny's done to yer.'

'Oh, no!' Vera cried. 'I couldn't do that!'

'Please, Vera? He's sensible, is my Bill, an' he'll know what to do. Tellin' him what Danny's done, an' him seein' for 'imself, are two different things. Yer can't carry on like this, an' Bill is the best person I know to give advice.' Eileen was smiling as she spoke because Carol was now sitting up in bed taking notice. 'Come on, sunshine, Auntie Eileen will take yer down for some tea.'

Unaware that anything was amiss, Carol held her arms out. 'Uncle Bill.'

'Yes, Uncle Bill's downstairs waitin' for yer. But I'm not carryin' yer down, 'cos yer a big girl now.'

Her hand holding Carol's, Eileen reached the door. Then she turned her head to look at Vera. 'Make yerself respectable an' I'll be back in a minute.' A few minutes later Eileen and Bill stood at the foot of the bed. 'What d'yer make of that?'

Bill searched for the right words to describe his feelings, but could find none. None that were suitable to say in front of women, anyway. He'd often heard of men beating their wives, but had never seen for himself the result of such beatings. Not until now.

Vera was clutching the sheet around her, her face as red as the angry bruises. 'I'm sorry, Bill, but Eileen insisted.'

'Quite right, too!' Bill could feel a rage building up inside of him. He was not a violent man, but if Danny Jackson had walked in then, he'd have throttled him. 'If you want my advice, you'll see a doctor.'

'But I'll be all right!' Vera said. 'Honest, I will! These,' she threw out an arm, 'will be gone in a week or so.' But the pain of the movement showed on her face and wasn't lost on Bill.

'I can't, and won't, interfere in your life, Vera. You must decide for yourself what you want to do. But if you see a doctor, you'll have all the evidence you need should you decide to leave Danny.'

'That makes sense, Vera.' Eileen looked at the stricken face. 'Yer know Doctor Greenfield's a smashin' bloke, an' very understandin'. He'll help yer, I know he will.'

Vera's gaze went from one to the other. These were her friends, and they were trying to help. But she was afraid. If she saw Doctor Greenfield she could be opening the way for a lot of trouble. Then she thought, I haven't done any wrong, so why should I worry? And Eileen's right! I can't go on like this, something has to be done. Not only for my sake, but for the children.

'Okay, I'll go and see Doctor Greenfield on Monday.'

'By Monday, yer'll 'ave thought of an excuse not to see him,' Eileen said. 'I'll nip up to Milly Knight's now and ring 'is surgery from there. If he's in, he'll come out tonight an' see yer.' When Vera went to object, Eileen lifted her hand.

'Don't argue, Vera, I'm on me way.'

John Greenfield held one of Vera's arms in his hand, his eyes running over the ugly bruises. 'Has your husband always been a violent man, Mrs Jackson?'

'When we were first married he wasn't. He's always been a loud man, especially when he's had a few drinks down him, but he never raised his hand to me or the boys.' Vera winced with pain when the doctor tilted her head to examine the bruises on her neck. 'It's only since Carol was born he's thrown his weight around. He can't stand the sight of her. I'd never leave him alone with her, 'cos I'd be too frightened of him hitting her.'

The doctor straightened up and looked across the bed to where Eileen was standing, raised his eyebrows, then gazed down at Vera. 'Does he ever hit the children?'

'No, I wouldn't stand for that.' Vera shivered as she pulled her dress over her head. 'He's not what you'd call a good father to the boys, but he doesn't pick on them, like he does Carol.'

'How often have you had injuries like these?'

'Too many times to count. I usually keep them to meself because I feel ashamed, but me friends know about it now.'

'Well, your husband's a very lucky man.' Pointing to a bruise on Vera's throat, the doctor went on, 'That blow, so close to the windpipe, could have killed you, and he'd have been up on a murder charge.'

'He wants hangin',' Eileen muttered, 'for what he's done to 'er.'

'I'll have to report this to the police.' When he saw Vera's eyes widen in fear, the doctor touched her gently on the shoulder. He'd known her since Carol was a baby, but this was the first time he'd seen her since he came back from the army. 'I have no choice, I'm afraid. The police won't interfere in a domestic argument between man and wife, but they have to be notified where there's a chance of a child being in danger. And as I have reason to believe that Carol is in danger, it's my duty to report the matter.'

'Oh, Eileen, what am I going to do?' Vera twisted round to face her friend. 'You know what Danny's like . . . he'll kill me if the police call to the house.'

Through Eileen's mind flashed snatches of a conversation she'd had with Mary many years ago. According to Mary, Vera had once been an attractive, outgoing woman, always well made-up and dressed in the height of fashion. One line of the conversation stood out in Eileen's mind now. 'When I was young,' Mary had said, 'I wanted to grow up to be like Vera, 'cos she was beautiful.'

Looking now at the cowed woman, Eileen had to fight hard to keep her anger at bay. 'He will kill yer one of these days, anyway, if yer don't get 'im sorted out. So let the doctor do what he's got to do, an' if the high an' mighty Danny Jackson doesn't like it, then it's just tough luck on 'im.' Under her breath, she added, 'I won't lose any sleep if 'e gets 'is comeuppance. In fact, I'd be bloody delighted.'

John Greenfield suppressed a grin. Since he'd come back from the army he'd found many things changed. But there were some things that even the war couldn't change, and one of them was Eileen Gillmoss's sense of humour. She was big and bawdy, but her heart was pure gold. He'd have her on his side, any day.

Chapter Twenty-Six

Eileen spooned the hot fat over the lightly browned potatoes, while her tummy rumbled and saliva formed at the corners of her mouth. Using an old towel to protect her hands, she slid the roasting tin back into the oven, careful not to spill any fat on to the rice pudding cooking slowly on the bottom shelf. The smell of the dinner cooking made her feel more hungry and she sighed as she threw the towel on to the draining board. What the hell I'm starvin' meself for, God only knows, she thought. It certainly doesn't seem to be getting me anywhere.

Wiping her hands on the corner of her pinny, Eileen waddled through to the living room and flopped on the couch. She stretched out her legs, and her dress rode up her thighs to reveal the deep dimples in her knees. The house was as quiet as a graveyard, with the ticking of the clock the only sound to break the silence. Her mam and the girls had gone to eleven o'clock Mass, Bill had taken Vera and Carol home, and young Billy was still in bed. Eileen's eyes went to the ceiling and she spoke to the empty room. 'Just wait till you get up, young feller-me-lad, I'll wipe the floor with yer! Comin' in at eleven o'clock at night, an' yer not even fifteen yet!' She shook her fist at the ceiling. 'If yer think yer got away with it 'cos Vera was 'ere, then yer've got another think comin'. I'll put a halt to your bloody gallop, mark my words.'

Eileen rubbed the back of her hand across her forehead to ease the headache she could feel coming on. What with Vera's troubles on top of her own, she felt physically and mentally worn out. It was all too much for her. She hadn't slept much last night, worrying about one thing and another, and the events of this morning had just about put the top hat on things.

Eileen breathed in deeply, held her breath for a few seconds, then exhaled slowly. If she and Bill were getting along all right, she'd think nothing of running to the ends of the earth to help Vera. But things were far from all right . . . for her anyway, and she wondered how much more she could take. Putting a brave face on all the time, and trying to laugh and joke, was taxing her endurance to the limit, and she knew the time was coming when she'd just blow up.

The sound of the key turning in the lock brought Eileen forward to the edge of the couch. She was hoping it was Bill, but the light footsteps told her it was her mother.

Maggie dropped her keys on the sideboard, her brows drawn together in a frown. 'Where is everyone?'

Eileen's ears were cocked. 'Are the girls with yer?'

'No. They were dawdling, so I hurried ahead of them.' Maggie drew out the silver pin from the navy velour hat and placed it next to the keys. 'They're probably playing in the street.'

'If they get their best coats dirty, I'll flog the livin' daylights out of them. They're the only decent things they've got!' Eileen saw the impatience in Maggie's eyes. 'Okay, Mam, I know yer dyin' to 'ear what's gone on. But you take yer coat off while I stick the kettle on for a cuppa.' Counting up to three, Eileen heaved herself from the couch. 'Me tummy thinks me throat's cut, an' I'll 'ave to 'ave a drink before I start gabbin'.'

'Yer'd only been gone about five minutes when two policemen called. One was a sergeant, an' he was smashin' with Vera an' Carol. He even let Carol play with 'is helmet while he talked to Vera. The other one was a young feller, barely out of 'is teens. They stayed for about twenty minutes, then the sergeant told Vera to give them half an hour, then go 'ome. He said 'e thought she wouldn't 'ave any more trouble with Danny, once they'd cautioned 'im.' Eileen sipped her tea, pulling a face. 'I can't stand tea without sugar, an' I 'ate those bloody saccharin things.' She heard her mother's impatient tut, and went on. 'I offered to go round with Vera 'cos she was terrified, but Bill insisted on taking her.' She leaned forward and put her cup on the table. 'So there yer 'ave it, Mam! There's more 'appened in the last twenty-four hours, than in a flamin' month o' Sundays.' Eileen flopped back heavily on the couch. 'I never thought the day would come when I'd 'ave the police knockin' on me door . . . Sunday mornin', an' all! God only knows what the neighbours are thinkin'.'

'I wouldn't be worrying about the neighbours,' Maggie said. 'I'd be more worried about Bill. You know the temper Danny Jackson's got. I hope he doesn't start anything with Bill.'

'Just let 'im try, an' he won't know what's 'it 'im when I've finished with 'im. He'll rue the day 'e was born.'

'The police were all right with Vera, then?'

'The young bobby didn't 'ave much to say for 'imself, but the Sergeant was great. He said 'e 'ad three children of 'is own, an' yer could see 'e was a family man the way 'e was with Carol. Yer should 'ave seen 'er face when she 'ad the helmet on, she was over the moon.'

Maggie put her fingers to her lips. 'Here's someone now.'

'If it's the kids, say nowt,' Eileen whispered. 'If they get to know, it'll be all over the neighbourhood before yer can say Jack Robinson.'

But it was a very stern-faced Bill who entered the room. He dropped into his favourite chair by the fire, and took a deep breath. 'Someone should take a whip to that man.'

'Why, what happened?' Eileen swivelled round to face him. 'He didn't say anythin' to yer, did 'e?'

'He didn't say a word to anyone! When we walked in, he looked up from his paper, sneered, then went back to reading the *News of the World*.'

'The ignorant, bloody sod!' Eileen roared. 'Yer'd think he'd 'ang 'is 'ead in shame, after what he's done.'

'There's no shame in the man,' Bill said sadly. 'In fact he doesn't seem to have any feelings at all. I don't know what the police said to him, but it doesn't seem to have had any effect. Of course it might make him think twice about laying a hand on the children, but he's crafty enough to get his own back on Vera in other ways.' Bill reached into his pocket for his cigarettes. 'I know I wouldn't like to be in Vera's shoes. You can cut the tension in that house with a knife.'

'Didn't 'e say anythin' at all to yer?'

'Not an hello, goodbye, or kiss me backside.' Bill drew in deeply on his cigarette. 'I was so angry I was willing him to say something so I could belt him one. But as I said, Danny's very crafty. He'll make Vera suffer without laying a finger on her, an' no one will be able to do anything about it.'

'Well, you've both done your best, there's nothing more you could have done,' Maggie said. 'Danny Jackson's got the laugh on everyone, even the police.'

'Yer should 'ave let me go with Vera,' Eileen said. 'Danny's too much of a coward to tackle a man, but 'e might 'ave said somethin' to me, an' there's nothin' I'd like better than to give 'im a fourpenny one. Not only for what he's done to Vera, but for the way 'e treats young Carol. Instead of 'elping the poor mite, 'e calls 'er names, like imbecile an' gormless.'

Bill raised his eyes to the ceiling. 'Who's upstairs?'

'It's our Billy, just gettin' up, the lazy beggar. With everythin' goin' on, he got away with missing Church this mornin'. I was goin' to give 'im the length of me tongue when 'e got up, about comin' in so late last night, but I'll leave it to you, Bill. Yer can kill two birds with one stone, an' tell 'im off about smokin'.'

'I'll go up now and get it over with.' A smile crossed Bill's face. 'A man to man talk.'

Maggie sniffed up. 'Is that our dinner I can smell? If it is, we'll be eating burnt offerings.'

'Oh, my gawd!' Eileen was off the couch and out of the door like a shot. 'I forgot about the flamin' potatoes!'

Maggie pressed her lips together when she saw the small portion of dinner on Eileen's plate. Her eyes went to Bill, and she opened her mouth to say something, but he shook his head. He sensed Eileen's tension, and knew she would lose her temper if he or Maggie criticised her.

'Ah, ray, Mam!' Edna had been taking stock. 'Our Billy's got six roasties, an' I've only got two little tidgy ones.'

Young Billy held his knife and fork upwards, a look of disgust on his face. 'I'm a workin' man, an' I need feedin' up.'

'Yeah, but you've got big ones,' Joan squeaked, 'an' ours are fiddlin' little things.'

'Will you all behave yourselves at the table, please?' Bill spoke quietly but firmly. Pointing his fork at Edna, he said, 'Sit up straight and eat your dinner in a proper manner. And don't speak with your mouth half full.' His fork moved to Joan. 'Keep your mouth closed when you eat and you won't make so much noise.'

Silence reigned, and Eileen was thankful. It was bad enough having a plateful of dinner that wasn't enough to feed a child, without having to listen to the children squabbling.

Joan and Edna finished their dinner and scrambled from the table, only to be stopped at the door by their mother's voice. 'Get back 'ere, you two! Unless, of course, yez don't want any rice puddin'.'

With a swish, the girls were back on their chairs. 'Ooh, goody!'

On her way to the kitchen, Eileen turned. 'Will you dish the puddin' out for us, Mam, while I go down the yard? An' don't save any for me, I don't feel like any.'

Maggie met Bill's eyes, and her nostrils flared. 'It's getting to be ridiculous with her. She's not eating enough to keep a sparrow alive.'

'I know,' Bill sighed. Then he rapped his knuckles on the table to quieten the children. 'If you don't behave yourselves, it'll be bed for you, not pudding.'

When Eileen came back in, the table had been cleared and Maggie was washing the dishes. 'You'll be sorry, my girl. And don't come to me for sympathy when you're sick, because you'll have brought it on yourself.'

Eileen picked up the tea towel and started to dry the dishes. 'Okay, missus, don't start on me, 'cos I'm not in the mood.'

'Ooh, now for 'alf an hour's rest.' Eileen swung her legs on to the couch and stretched out. 'I'm sure fate meant me to be a rich lady, with servants at me beck an' call to pander to me every wish.' She let out an exaggerated sigh. 'Somethin' must 'ave gone wrong somewhere along the line.'

'Joe Loss is on the wireless,' Maggie said, 'if you feel like some music.'

'No, thanks, Mam, I'm not in the mood for In The Mood.' Eileen craned her neck to look at Bill. 'I wonder 'ow Vera's gettin' on with the queer fellow?'

'Oh, no! There's a knock on the door, lass.' Maggie clicked her tongue in sympathy. 'No rest for the wicked.'

Sliding her legs over the edge of the couch, Eileen wheedled, 'Be a pal an' answer the door for us, Mam, while I make meself presentable.'

When she heard the sound of several voices greeting Maggie, Eileen closed her eyes and grimaced. 'We've got visitors, an' I look like the wreck of the Hesperus.'

Eileen forced a smile to her face when Mary came in with the two children, followed by Harry and then Arthur. 'Yez'll 'ave to excuse the place, we've just finished dinner, an' I was 'avin' a rest before tidyin' up.' She pulled her dress down over her knees. 'If it's not too nosey a question, 'ow

275

come yez all arrived at the same time?'

'We passed Arthur on the way, and gave him a lift,' Harry answered. 'Does that satisfy your curiosity?'

'That answers one question, yes!' Eileen squinted. 'Now I'd like to know where yer gettin' all the petrol from to run back an' forth. I thought it was rationed?'

Harry tapped his nose. 'For someone who got through the war buying things that fell off the back of a lorry, I'm surprised you ask.'

Eileen licked a finger and made a sign in the air. 'Okay, clever clogs, that's one to you.'

Arthur was getting impatient. 'How did Vera get on?'

Eileen glanced down at Emma and Tony, who were standing between her legs, their arms round her neck. She gathered them close, while her eyes sought Arthur's. 'Little pigs 'ave big ears.' She held the children away from her, thinking with pride, these two little beauties are my god-children. They were always clean and tidy, in clothes Mary made herself, and always well mannered. Not like her own children, who never seemed to be clean, and were anything but well mannered. Still, a smile crossed Eileen's face, I can't blame the kids. With me looking like a tramp most of the time, and swearing like a trooper, what can I expect?

'How would you two like some sweeties?' Eileen turned her gaze to Bill. 'Go an' bring the girls in, will yer? They can take Emma and Tony to the corner shop.'

The girls didn't need much persuading.

With a penny in each of their hands, they hopped from one foot to the other as they listened to their mother's warning. 'They look like two little angels now. If yez bring them back lookin' like the Bisto kids, I'll throttle yez.'

Maggie stood up and offered her chair to Mary, who was looking very pretty in a coat she'd made herself. She was very handy with the sewing machine now, and you'd never dream her clothes were home-made.

But with her looks, Maggie thought, she'd look good in a coal sack.

'I'll put the kettle on, shall I?' Maggie's smile swept over their visitors. 'But we've no sugar, I'm afraid.'

'Chick, you go and give Ma a hand with the tea.' Bill didn't want Eileen getting excited again over Vera's troubles. He was pretty sure it was that that was making her bad tempered and edgy. 'I'll tell them all there is to know, so poppy off.'

Without a word, Eileen made her way to the kitchen, where Maggie was setting a tray. 'I've 'ad orders from Bill to give yer a 'and.' She held her hands out, palms upwards. 'Which one would yer like?'

'I'm lost for words,' Harry said. 'After getting the doctor, and the police, Vera is no better off than she was before.'

'I'd leave him,' Mary said. 'I couldn't stay with a man who hit me, never mind the way he treats Carol.'

'We've been all through this before, love.' Harry sighed. 'We can talk till we're blue in the face, but Vera can't leave Danny, 'cos she's got nowhere to go and no money.'

Eileen pushed the kitchen door open with her hip, carrying the tray very carefully. On it stood her new china cups and saucers, being used for the first time since she'd bought them. Her face wore a proud smile as she placed the tray on the table. 'I hope it doesn't escape yer attention that I've actually got cups and saucers to match, that they've all got 'andles on, an' there's not a chip or a crack in sight.' She handed the first cup to Mary. 'Your tea, Madam! An' if yer break me cup, I'll break yer flamin' neck.'

'I wish I knew 'ow Vera's gettin' on.' Eileen was standing in front of the mirror putting a few dinkie curlers in the front of her hair. The family were all in bed and Bill was enjoying his last cigarette before they too climbed the stairs. 'I 'ope she's all right.'

'Chick, will you stop worrying about her! Unless Danny Jackson's got a screw loose, he'll behave himself from now on. He's too big headed to show it, but I bet the police put the fear of God into him.' Bill didn't believe this himself, but he'd have said anything to calm Eileen's fears.

'Well, I'm callin' round there tomorrow to see 'ow she is.' Eileen pulled the stray hairs from the comb and threw them in the grate. 'I want to see for meself.'

'Keep out of it, chick,' Bill warned. 'You've done all you can.'

'I'm goin' round there temorrer, so yer can save yer breath,' Eileen said, defiantly. 'Some friend I'd be, if I just left 'er to it.'

Bill knew it was no good arguing, not with Eileen in this mood. He took a long draw on his cigarette then threw the stub in the fire. Keeping his voice as casual as he could, he said, 'I'll be a bit late getting home tomorrow night, chick, I'm going to see the doctor.'

Eileen swung round. 'What's the matter? Yer not ill, are yer?'

'No, of course not! It's just that I get a bit tired at times, and I thought he might be able to give me a tonic to pick me up.'

Eileen's eyes narrowed. 'I've never noticed yer lookin' tired.'

'It's nothing to worry about, chick. It's just that sometimes at work me bones feel weary. All I need is a tonic.'

'I'll keep the tea back for half an hour, then.' Eileen pulled the cord of her blue dressing gown tighter round her waist, and yawned. 'I'm off to bed. I don't know about your bones feelin' tired, my whole body's tired . . . even my blinkin' eyelashes!'

Bill followed her up the stairs. 'Don't forget what I said about Danny Jackson,' he whispered. 'You rub him up the wrong way and he'll go for you.'

'Oh, aye! Him an' whose army?' Eileen turned to face him. 'Danny Jackson thinks he's the whole cheese, but he's only the maggot.'

Bill was shaking his head as he followed her into the bedroom. The sayings she came out with! She had an answer for everything!

Bill sighed softly as he closed the bedroom door behind them. He wished he had an answer for everything. In fact, he'd be more than happy if he had the answer to his main worry. Perhaps he'd have it after he'd seen the doctor tomorrow night.

Chapter Twenty-Seven

'I hate Mondays.' Eileen draped the folded wet sheet over one arm while pressing the ends between the wooden rollers of the old mangle. 'Why we 'ave to do our flamin' washin' religiously every Monday I'll never know.' A small turn of the large wooden handle secured the sheet, and letting a yard of it fall from her arm, she said, 'Catch it as it comes through, Mam, 'cos if it touches this floor it'll be dirtier than it was before.'

It was hard work turning the heavy, creaking handle, and sweat poured down Eileen's face. 'We'd be better off splittin' the big wash into two days instead of killin' ourselves doin' it in one go.'

Maggie folded the sheet in layers on her arm as it came through the rollers. The back kitchen was very small at the best of times, but with the big mangle pulled into the middle it was almost impossible to move.

'When you and our Rene were young, I used to go to the wash-house every Monday, and it was a damn sight easier than doing it at home. They had big machines for the washing, and a huge drying room to hang the clothes in to dry. It used to take all morning, but I came home with all me washing dry, ready for ironing.'

Eileen stopped turning the handle, a look of surprise on her face. 'D'yer know, I can remember that! I can remember sittin' in me pram with the washin' piled up in front of me. We lived down Lodge Lane then, didn't we?'

Maggie nodded. 'You were five when we left there, and our Rene was just a baby. We had a neighbour called Mrs Halford, and when you got to the stage where you were running around, and into everything, she used to mind you while I went to the wash-house.'

'I remember her! She 'ad a big nose, an' a squint in one eye,' Eileen said triumphantly. 'An' I used to call her Hally?'

'That's right!' Maggie laughed at the memory. 'She used to spoil you soft. I missed her when we moved to Walton, 'cos she was a good neighbour.'

Eileen was leaning back against the wall, glad of a small break away from the heavy mangle. 'I started school then, didn't I?'

'Don't remind me of that!' Maggie clicked her tongue. 'I used to have to drag you through those school gates, kicking and screaming. You made a holy show of me.'

Eileen's chubby cheeks, wet with sweat, moved upwards into a smile. 'I 'aven't changed much, 'ave I?'

'Except that you're cheekier and louder,' Maggie said. 'Anyway, come and take this sheet off me. Me arm's dropping off with the weight.'

Eileen stuck three wooden pegs in her mouth and relieved Maggie of the sheet. Waddling to the door, she muttered, 'I wish some bright spark would invent paper clothes an' sheets. It would do away with all this runnin' round on a Monday like blue-arsed flies.'

'Why not go the whole hog,' Maggie asked, 'and have

paper cups and plates? Then we'd have nothing to do all day but sit on our backsides.'

Eileen was smiling when she went to hang the sheet out, but seconds later she returned with a scowl on her face. 'Wouldn't yer bloody know it! It's startin' to flamin' spit!'

Maggie sighed. 'D'you want to bring the clothes in now, before it starts to throw it down?'

'Nah! Sod it! If it rains they can stay out all night. Right now I'm goin' to make a drink an' get a warm by the fire.'

Maggie looked through the window into the yard, where the wet clothes were hanging limp. There didn't seem to be the slightest breeze out, and the sky was very overcast. She hoped the rain would stay off long enough to get some of the wet out of the clothes, so they could be brought in. Mr Williamson up the street let his pigeons out at six every morning, and they weren't fussy where their droppings landed.

Maggie sat at the table, her hands curled round a cup of hot tea. 'I can't make out why Bill's going to see the doctor. He hasn't complained of not feeling well, and he looks fine to me.'

'Don't be worryin', missus, there's nothin' wrong with 'im!' Eileen's legs were stretched out to catch the warmth from the fire. 'It's just that 'e gets tired quickly, an' he wants a tonic.'

'Please God, that's all it is,' Maggie said. 'There's enough trouble and woe without Bill getting sick.'

'Thinkin' about Vera, are yer? I've just been doin' the same.' Eileen stared into the flames. 'When I get enough energy back to move me backside, I'll empty the dolly tub, make us a bite to eat, then walk round there.' With a half smile on her face, she asked, 'Fancy comin' round there with me? I thought, if Danny does take off, you could 'old 'im while I belt 'im one.'

'If that's what you think, then you've got another think coming.' Maggie's lips formed a straight line. 'I wouldn't go within a mile of that man.'

Eileen roused herself. 'Well, sittin' here isn't goin' to get the tub emptied, so I'd better get crackin'.'

'You shouldn't sit so near the fire, anyway,' Maggie warned. 'You'll end up with burn marks all over the front of your legs, and there's nothing worse on a woman. Shows she's lazy and sits in front of the fire all day.'

Eileen's bust swelled as she stood to attention and saluted. 'Aye, aye, Captain.' She did a swift turn, 'To the left, q-ui-ck march!'

Maggie pushed her chair back, tutting. What could you do with someone like her daughter? 'I'm nipping down the yard for a sweet one.'

'Say one for me while yer down there,' Eileen called.

Maggie came back from the yard shivering. Wrapping her cardi closely around her body, she said, 'It's starting to rain.'

'Yer a barrel of laughs, you are, missus!' Eileen heaved the heavy bucket of water from the tub and tipped it down the sink. 'Any more good news, while yer at it?'

'Yes, there is, clever clogs,' Maggie said. 'There's no paper in the lavvy.'

'Milly's got no toilet paper in, so it'll 'ave to be newspaper.' Eileen turned to the tub to refill the bucket. 'I'll see to it when I've emptied this flamin' thing.'

Eileen and Maggie were having their lunch when Vera arrived

with Carol. Forever thinking she was a nuisance, Vera eyed the plates of sandwiches and began to apologise. 'I'm sorry, I wouldn't have come if I'd known you were having your lunch. I'll only stay a minute.'

'For cryin' out loud, will yer stop worryin'!' Eileen said. 'Yer've saved me a journey, 'cos I was comin' round to yours, after.'

Vera had her long auburn hair brushed back off her face and tied with a dark blue ribbon. She looked pale and nervous, her tongue darting out to wet her lips every few seconds. 'Danny went out early so I took the chance to come while the coast was clear. I knew you'd be on pins wondering how things were.'

'D'yer want a Spam buttie, sunshine?' As Eileen smiled down at Carol, it flashed through her mind that no matter how troubled Vera was, she always kept her daughter nice. The round, moon-like face was shining with health, her hair was neatly brushed, and Eileen could smell the fragrance of the scented soap she'd been washing with.

Vera pulled Carol to her. 'Let Auntie Eileen have her dinner in peace. You had something to eat before we came out.'

Speaking with her mouth full, Eileen said, 'Park yer carcass, Vera, an' let's 'ave yer news.'

'Well, he didn't tell me, but I heard Danny telling the boys he was going down to the docks today, to see his mates. He's probably gone to see about getting his old job back.'

Eileen picked a crumb from the table and popped it in her mouth. 'Has 'e been up to any shinanigans?'

Vera shrugged her shoulders. 'He never opened his mouth at all yesterday after Bill had left. The boys stayed in all day and I think that put a halt to his gallop.' She ran a hand over Carol's hair before dropping a kiss on her cheek. 'He went to the pub as usual, and when he came back I was in Carol's bed pretending to be asleep. I heard him open the door and look in, but I kept me eyes closed and Carol was away to the world.'

Eileen pushed her plate away and lifted Carol on to her lap, smothering her with kisses. 'Who's a clever little girl? An' who's got a clever mummy?' Looking over her head, Eileen winked. 'Yer want to sleep in Carol's bed every night. Might bring 'im to 'is senses.'

'A letter came for him this morning, from Holland.' Vera pinched her lips, nervously. 'I took it up and threw it on the bed. When he came down an hour later, he was humming to himself and had a smile on his face.'

Eileen's face did contortions. 'Ooh, fancy that! Who was it from?'

'I haven't a clue,' Vera said. 'But whoever it was from he seemed very pleased with himself.' She lowered her head. 'When he'd gone out, I went up to the bedroom to look for the letter, but there was no sign. He must have taken it out with him.'

'It was probably from one of his army mates.' Eileen tickled Carol's tummy, bringing forth gales of laughter. 'Some of our soldiers are still over there.'

'No, it wasn't,' Vera said quietly. 'The handwriting didn't look English to me.'

Maggie stood up and collected the plates. 'I'll rinse these through, then start on the potatoes. You sit and talk to Vera.'

In the kitchen, Maggie put the dishes in the sink and gazed out of the window at the white-washed yard wall. Life was changing, she thought, and I'm too old to keep up with it. When her husband had been alive, their whole lives were centred around each other and the children. They wouldn't have dreamt of looking at anyone else. But it wasn't like that now. Men were coming home from the war to find their wives had been cheating on them . . . some even had babies to other men.

Maggie sighed. Life had been hard all those years ago, when many men couldn't find work and wives were hard put to make ends meet. But at least families pulled together, and stayed together. People said they were the bad old days, but Maggie looked back on them with nostalgia. They might not have had much in material things, and, yes, there were many days when the only way to put a meal on the table was by a visit to the pawn shop. But the one thing she had always been sure of was her husband's love for her and the children.

Maggie put the plug in the sink and turned the tap on. No woman could ask for more than that.

Eileen folded a newspaper in half and ran a knife between the folds. 'It didn't rain much, after all, Mam.' She folded and cut the paper twice more, then passed the squares to her mother. 'I'm glad I didn't bring the clothes in, 'cos there's a good dry out, now.'

Maggie punched a hole in the corner of the squares with a screw driver, then threaded a piece of string through. 'I'll iron a few things tonight, then we can do the rest tomorrow.'

Eileen kept a key on a length of string inside the letter box in case of emergency, and she now heard the key rattling against the door as it was pulled upwards. She glanced at the clock. 'The kids are 'ome early.'

Joan stood framed in the doorway, puffing and panting. 'D'yer know that Joey Wilson? Well, 'e's just chased me down the street, an' when he grabbed me coat I felt me blouse tear.'

'What was 'e chasin' yer for?'

'I dunno.' Joan blushed bright red as she scraped the lino with the toe of her shoe. 'He said 'e was goin' to kiss me.'

'Did yer clock 'im one?' Eileen asked, indignantly.

'I kicked 'im on the shin.' Joan hunched her shoulders up and giggled. 'I didn't 'alf hurt 'im too, 'cos he hobbled down the street an' his face was all screwed up.'

'Good for you, sunshine!' Eileen laughed. 'Never let a feller get the better of yer.'

Joan dropped her coat on the floor and lifted her arm. 'Just look what the daft begger did.'

Eileen was silent as she eyed the rip in the side of the blouse. My God, she was only just thirteen, and she had a bust! For the first time, Eileen realised her daughter was filling out. The spindly legs were becoming shapely, her face had lost that thin, peaked look, and the school uniform which had once hung loosely, was now stretched tight across her chest. The skinny ugly duckling was changing into a swan.

'Put these squares on the nail in the lavvy for us, then change into an old dress to play out in. I'll sew yer blouse later, ready for school temorrer.'

When Joan dashed down the yard, Eileen made a face at her mother. 'Kids grow up quick these days, don't they, Mam? She's only 'ad that blouse an' gymslip a few months, an' she's grown out of them already. The gymslip's up to 'er backside, an' the blouse fits where it touches.'

'She's as tall as you now.' Maggie nodded. 'She left me behind ages ago.'

'Aye, but you're only a midget, Mam.' Eileen laughed. 'Even our Edna's taller than you.'

Maggie huffed. 'You know the old saying, that good stuff comes in little parcels.'

'So does poison.' Eileen lifted an arm as though fending off a blow. 'So put that in yer pipe an' smoke it, missus.' She peeked cheekily under her raised arm. 'That was a joke, missus, an' yer supposed to laugh.'

'Oh, I'm laughing me head off,' Maggie said huffily. 'In fact, I'm splitting me sides, it was so funny.'

Bill was very late getting in and Eileen had got herself so het up with worry, she jumped on him. 'Where the 'ell 'ave yer been? I've been out of me mind, thinkin' all sorts of things 'ad 'appened to yer.'

Bill's smile was forced. 'There were a few before me in the surgery so I had to wait.'

Eileen watched him take his coat off, and when he didn't volunteer any further information, she asked, 'Well? Are yer goin' to tell us, or do we 'ave to drag it out of yer?'

Maggie tutted. 'Give the man a chance to get in the door, for heaven's sake.'

'There's nothing much to tell you, chick.' Bill didn't meet Eileen's eyes. 'It's just as I said, I need a tonic.'

'Bill Gillmoss, are you tellin' me the truth?' Eileen stood in the middle of the room, her feet spaced apart, her hands on her hips. 'If yer keepin' anythin' from me, so 'elp me, I'll flatten yer.'

'Eileen, if you don't believe me, go and see Doctor

Greenfield.' Bill's face was pale, his voice weary. 'He said there's nothing wrong with me that iron tablets, and cod liver oil and malt, wouldn't put right.'

Eileen's eyes became slits. She wanted to believe him, but something about the set of his face convinced her he wasn't being perfectly honest with her. But she could feel her mother's eyes on her and decided she'd get the truth out of him later. 'I'll get yer some from the chemist's temorrer. An' if yer not swingin' from the lamp-posts like Tarzan in a few weeks, I'll be round to that surgery meself.'

'I can't promise that, chick, but I'll do me best.' Bill fell back into his chair and fished in his pocket for his packet of Capstan. 'The neighbours might think it funny though, if I start swinging from lamp-posts.'

'Yer needn't light up that fag,' Eileen said. 'Yer dinner is boiled dry as it is. I expected yer 'ome an hour ago.'

'Just a couple of puffs, chick, I'm not really hungry, anyway, I've gone past it.'

'Yer'll eat yer dinner an' like it, Bill Gillmoss! I've made some broth with pigs trotters, carrots, split peas, and barley. It's lovely an' thick, an' it'll put a linin' on yer tummy.'

Bill returned the unlit cigarette to the packet. 'I may as well give in, 'cos you'll have your own way no matter what I say.'

Eileen marched to the kitchen, missing the wink exchanged between Bill and her mother. But she heard Maggie saying, 'I don't know who she takes after. I still think they got the babies mixed up in Oxford Street, an' I got the wrong one.'

Eileen's head appeared round the door. 'Ay, don't be talkin' about me be'ind me back. I 'aven't got cloth ears, yer know.' Her head disappeared for a second, and when it reappeared her brows were drawn together in a frown. 'Yer know, Mam, I think yer may be right about me bein' someone else's baby. 'Cos I must 'ave got me good looks from someone.'

Eileen ducked when her mother sent a cushion hurtling through the air.

'Now, now, temper!' Eileen wagged a finger. 'Yer see, Bill, there's another sign that I don't belong 'ere. How could anyone with a sweet nature like mine, come from a mother who throws things?'

While Bill grinned, Maggie clicked her teeth. 'I give up. She's beyond redemption.'

'I expected Arthur to come tonight to see 'ow Vera 'ad got on.' Eileen was sewing the tear in Joan's blouse and wasn't making a very good job of it. Her hands were too fat to hold the needle properly, and the stitches were like tacking stitches. 'He seems to be very interested in 'er affairs.' Eileen broke off the cotton with her teeth and looked with disgust at her handiwork. 'I'd never make any money as a seamstress, that's for sure.' She folded the blouse neatly over the back of her chair. 'It's a pity he's not married to Vera. They'd make a nice couple.'

Bill looked at her sharply. 'Don't go matchmaking, chick. They're both married and that's the end of that.'

Eileen leaned forward, her chubby hands resting on her chubby knees. 'Now we've talked about everything under the sun, except the price of fish, let's get down to brass tacks. What really 'appened at the doctor's?'

'I've told you, chick, I just went . . .'

Eileen broke in. 'Come off it, Bill Gillmoss! D'yer think

I'm daft? Yer came in 'ere lookin' like death warmed up, an' yer expect me to believe yer only went for a tonic? I might have been the last in the queue when they were dishin' beauty out, but I did manage to get a few brains. I wasn't born yesterday, yer know.'

Bill looked down at his hands. He hadn't gone to the doctor's for a tonic, and Eileen was entitled to know the truth. But he couldn't bear to see the look he knew he'd see on her face if he told her what the doctor had said. That his impotence was due to the deprivation and degradation he'd suffered in the prison camp. It was something that could last a year or two, or even longer. It could even last forever.

Bill's conscience was in conflict. He knew he should be honest with Eileen, but he lacked the courage to tell her now. He would have to eventually, but not now . . . not tonight.

'Chick, if I don't feel any better in a couple of weeks, you can come to the doctor's with me, and hear for yourself what he's got to say. Now, does that satisfy you?'

'It'll 'ave to, I suppose.' Eileen screwed her face up and rubbed her nose. 'I'll get yer them things from the chemist temorrer, an' we'll see 'ow yer go on.' Wearily she rose from the chair. Why hadn't he asked the doctor about something else, something more important than tired bones? Something that affected them both and was driving them further away from each other. Because they were drifting apart, even though she didn't want to admit it. The way they were living now, they were more like brother and sister than man and wife.

Chapter Twenty-Eight

'I wonder what's up with our Rene, she 'asn't been for weeks.' Eileen stood back to inspect herself in the mirror. She licked a finger and thumb and tried to coax a strand of hair into a kiss curl. But the second she removed her fingers the hair flopped down on her forehead. 'It's not like 'er to leave it so long.' With a look of disgust at the lank, thin hair, she turned from the mirror and reached for her coat. Thank God for small mercies, she thought, at least I've got a decent coat to me name. 'If we 'ad a phone, I'd ring our Rene, to make sure there's nothing wrong.'

Maggie eyed her daughter suspiciously. 'Very concerned about our Rene all of a sudden, aren't you? It would do you no harm to go down and see her, instead of expecting her to come here all the time. After all, you've got no excuse now 'cos you've got plenty of time on your hands.'

'You've no need to talk, Mam, 'cos you don't visit 'er either!'

'There's an excuse for me, at my age.' Maggie straightened the lace runner on the sideboard with one hand while patting her white hair with the other. 'I can't be hopping on and off buses.'

'I didn't hear yer complainin' about yer legs last week,

when yer went into town to the Forum. Yer ran down this street like a two year old when yer knew Cary Grant was on.'

Eileen checked her bag to make sure her purse was there. 'I'll nip into Milly's on me way past, an' give our Rene a ring from there. Just to make sure they're all right.'

'Where are you and Mary off to?'

'Paddy's market. Our Joan needs a new blouse an' gymslip, an' our Edna's shoes look like a pair of Charlie Chaplin's cast offs. I want to see what they've got down at the market before trying the shops.'

'You'll be home in time for dinner, won't you?' Maggie followed Eileen down the hall, fussing. 'Don't forget it's Saturday, and Bill only works half day.'

'Keep yer hair on, missus, I'll be home in time. An' I'll bring somethin' in for our dinner, so don't start gettin' all het up an' get yer knickers in a twist.'

Eileen's hips swayed from side to side as she walked down the street. A fresh breeze fanned her cheeks and she gulped in the fresh air. She felt better now she was out, away from the house that was beginning to stifle her. The little house she'd always loved, that had always been filled with love, warmth and humour. Even in the dark days of the war, when Bill had been away so long, she'd tried to keep it the same for the sake of her mam and the kids. They never knew then what it cost her to keep a smile on her face and a joke on her lips, and they didn't know what it was costing her now.

'Hi, ya, Milly! Still rakin' the money in?'

'My, my, aren't we posh today!' Milly's smile was the one she wore for her favourite customers. 'Got a heavy date, have yer?'

'Huh! I should be so lucky!' Eileen rolled her eyes. 'I'm

meetin' Mary down in Scottie Road, an' we're goin' to look round Paddy's market. Yer never know yer luck in a big city, do yer, Milly? Anyway, would yer let me use yer phone to ring our kid?'

Milly lifted the hinged counter top. 'Help yourself, you know where it is.'

Eileen wasn't used to a telephone and it frightened the life out of her. But this was an emergency. She dialled the number and listened to the ringing tone. Then Rene's voice came down the line. 'Hello.'

'It's me, our kid!' Eileen's voice was loud with nerves. 'Me mam was wonderin' if there was anythin' wrong, with yer not coming for a few weeks.'

'Victoria's had a sore throat and a temperature for the last week or so, and she's been really poorly. But she seems a lot brighter today, so I might slip up with her tomorrow. A bit of fresh air will do her good.'

'Try an' come, our kid, 'cos yer know 'ow me mam worries.' Another lie, Eileen thought. But I need to see our Rene. She's the only one I can talk to. And I've got to talk to someone soon, or I'll go off me rocker.

'All right, Eileen, you can tell me mam I'll be there.'

'Thanks, kid! Ta-ra for now.'

Milly was busy serving when Eileen emerged from the back of the shop, so she slapped two pennies on the counter and made for the door. 'Thanks, Milly! Yer'll never see what I'll buy yer for yer birthday.'

Eileen stared out of the window as the bus swayed to and fro on its way to the Pier Head. They passed the burned-out houses and shops with their boarded-up windows and doors,

295

and the empty spaces where buildings had been so badly damaged during the blitz that they were a danger to the public and had to be pulled down. But Eileen didn't see them, her mind was miles away, worrying about the state of her marriage.

The bus lurched to a halt at a stop opposite Sturla's, and Eileen's mind was momentarily diverted as her bag slipped from her knee. Holding it in a firm grip, she returned once more to her thoughts. She'd done everything she could in the last few weeks to please and attract Bill. She made sure she was neat and tidy when he came home from work, with her face lightly made-up and wearing a smile. She'd even treated herself to a new, pretty nightdress, a bottle of African Violets, and a tin of perfumed talcum powder. But she might as well not have bothered for all the notice Bill took. He never had been one for dishing out compliments, or flattery, but she didn't need them before because he proved his love for her in the privacy of their bedroom. But the passion had gone out of their lives now, and although Eileen kept telling herself she should be more understanding, that it wasn't Bill's fault, she needed some show of love from him to keep her going. Even if it was only in words.

'Scotland Road.' At the sound of the clippie's voice, Eileen shook her head to clear her mind. It was time to don the mask again, and pretend that big, fat Eileen didn't have a care in the world.

Eileen sighed as she moved to the platform of the bus. She was probably clutching at straws, but their Rene was her last hope.

As she stepped from the bus, Eileen saw Mary hurrying towards her. 'Hi, ya, kid! Been waitin' long?'

'Only five minutes.' Mary linked her arm through Eileen's. 'You look very smart, today.'

'Well now, begorrah, tank yer very much.' Eileen's Irish accent was very convincing. 'An' if I may make so bold, me darlin', 'tis foine yer lookin' yer dear self.'

Mary's laugh rang out. Oh, it was good to be with Eileen again. Just the two of them, like old times. No one could cheer her up, or make her laugh, like her old mate. 'Are you going to treat yourself?'

'By the time I've sorted the kids out, I'll be lucky if I've got the bus fare 'ome.' Eileen squeezed Mary's arm. 'Still, it's nice to be out together, even if we get nowt, eh, kid?'

The market was a hive of activity. The second-hand stalls were doing a thriving business as women searched through the piles of clothes and bedding, hoping to find a bargain. There was many a fight between two women who both grabbed for something at the same time. With clothing rationed and coupons scarce, no one was prepared to give way.

Mary stood back smiling, as Eileen thrust her way into the crowd around a busy stall. And with her size, no one was going to complain if her elbow landed in their tummy. After twenty minutes, she emerged, grinning from ear to ear. 'Success, kid! An almost new blouse an' gymslip for our Joan, an' a smashin' pair of shoes for Edna that look as though they've only been worn once.'

Mary grinned, happy for her friend. 'What now?'

'We'll just 'ave a nose around, eh? Might see somethin' that takes our fancy.'

Arm in arm they walked to where the black-shawled barrow women were shouting out the value of their wares. 'Carrots tuppence a pound, spuds thruppence for five pounds. Come on now, ladies, get yer spuds in for temorrer's dinner for the ol' feller. Fresh cabbage, thruppence each. Yer won't get 'em cheaper anywhere in Liverpool.'

One of the Mary Ellens caught Eileen's eye. 'Get yer spuds and veg, missus, an' I'll let yer have a couple of oranges.'

'Ye gods, I 'aven't 'ad an orange since Adam was a lad.' Eileen hurried to the cart before someone else took up the offer. She was followed closely by Mary who offered the use of her large shopping bag as Eileen's list of purchases grew.

'Don't get too much,' Mary said, 'you've got to walk all the way from the bus stop with it.'

While Eileen filled the bag, Mary spotted an unsavoury-looking character standing near. He had a large case open at his feet and was inviting a potential customer to feel the quality of a towel. Mary nudged Eileen. 'Look at the things he's got in that case. Nightdresses, knickers . . . everything you can mention.'

'He's a spiv, an' he'll charge yer through the nose, kid,' Eileen warned.

'Oh, blow it,' Mary laughed. 'Let's go mad for a change. If he's got anything you like, I'll treat you.'

'I'm not skint yet, kid,' Eileen said, lugging the heavy bag towards the spiv whose eyes were everywhere, on the look out for a policeman. One sight of a blue uniform and the case would be snapped shut and the offender would disappear into the crowds until the danger had passed.

While Mary was looking at a tea towel, Eileen spotted the straps of a white cotton bra in the case. 'What size is that, mister?'

The man smirked. 'Not yours, lady. You need to go to a

factory where they make parachutes.'

'Oh, very funny.' Eileen bridled. 'But yer'll pardon me if I don't laugh, won't yer, 'cos I've 'eard it before.'

'Come on.' Mary was pulling at Eileen's arm, angry that her friend had been insulted. 'I'm not buying anything off him, the cheeky beggar.'

'Just 'ang on a minute, kid.' Eileen pulled her arm free and glared at the man who was already regretting his words. 'I've eaten bigger men than you for breakfast, sonny boy, so I'd watch me mouth if I was you, or yer'll be missin' a few teeth.' Several people had stopped at the sound of Eileen's voice and were listening intently. 'I'm askin' yer again what size that bra is, an' I want none of yer lip.'

The man's eyes were scanning the crowd that had now gathered. This fat piece had a mouth on her like a fog horn. If she kept this up, the rozzers would be swarming round in no time. 'It's a size thirty-two.' He shifted uneasily on his feet. 'I didn't mean no 'arm, missus, it was only a joke.'

'Aye, well, I'd advise yer to keep yer jokes to yerself in future if yer want to live to be an old man.'

'Come on.' Mary tugged at Eileen's arm. She was sorry now she'd spotted the horrible man.

But Eileen stood her ground. 'How much is it?'

The man's head was telling him to give her the bloody thing for nothing to get rid of her. But the look on Eileen's face told him it wouldn't be a wise move. 'Yer can have it for one and eleven.'

Eileen bent down and picked up the white cotton bra. She inspected it closely, then looked into eyes that were willing her to take it and clear off. 'I'll take it.'

Mary watched in amazement as Eileen slowly counted out

the right money. What on earth did she want a bra that size for?

'Wrap it up.' Eileen heard a titter from the watching crowd. 'I don't want to get it dirty, 'cos I'll be wearin' it tonight to go dancin'.'

An angry retort was on the man's lips, but he bit it back. 'I'm sorry but I 'aven't got any bags.' He was about to hand over the bra when he saw the set of Eileen's face. Vainly he searched in the case for a piece of paper, then he heard Eileen's voice. 'Yer can wrap it in one of them elevenpence ha'penny towels. That would keep it clean.'

The man's eyes swivelled. If this crowd didn't move soon, ten to one the rozzers would be round to see what was happening. The towel in question was one shilling and elevenpence halfpenny, and he knew Eileen was well aware of the price. But he also knew she had him over a barrel. His anger showing in his movements, he grabbed the towel, wrapped it around the bra, and handed it over.

Eileen smiled sweetly, and kept her voice low. 'That was a very expensive joke, wasn't it, sonny boy?'

'You're a case, you are,' Mary said, as they pushed through the crowd. 'All that for a bra that's no use to you.'

'It's not for me, yer daft nit!' Eileen said. 'It's for our Joan.'

'Go way!' Mary stared in disbelief. 'Pull the other one, Eileen, it's got bells on.'

'Kid, our Joan's got a bust on her nearly as big as yours.' They were outside the market now, and Eileen put the heavy bag on the ground. 'You were right, kid, it is bloody 'eavy.' She rubbed the hand where the handles of the bag had dug deeply into the flesh. 'I've got to get somethin' for our dinner, or me mam'll 'ave kittens if Bill comes 'ome an' there's nothin' in.' Her eyes travelled along the block of shops opposite, stopped half way, then travelled back. 'My God, there's Arthur's wife.'

Mary followed Eileen's eyes to see a slim woman leaning against the wall. 'Go way, that's never Arthur's wife, is it?'

When Eileen nodded, Mary took a closer look. Dyed blonde hair framed a face thick with make-up, and a cigarette dangled from heavily painted lips. The woman's painfully thin body was clad in a dress that was skin tight and very short.

'She looks awful common,' Mary said.

'Well, she's no angel, that's for sure.' Eileen was silent for a while, a thoughtful expression on her face. Then she turned to Mary. 'I think I'll go an' 'ave a word with 'er, kid. You stay 'ere an' keep yer eye on me bag.'

Eileen stood in front of Sylvia, a half smile on her face. 'Remember me, Sylvia?'

Recognition dawned. Sylvia took the cigarette from her lips, threw it on the ground and stubbed it out with her foot, before meeting Eileen's eyes. 'Yeh, I remember yer.'

'I've just been round the market with me mate an' when I saw yer, I thought I'd nip across an' ask 'ow yer are.' A few weeks ago, Arthur had told Eileen he'd had it out with his wife. Either she stayed home and looked after the children and the house properly, or he was leaving and taking the boys with him. Only last week he'd said his words seemed to have had an effect, because the house was now being cleaned properly, the kids looked better, and there was a dinner on the table when he came home from work. And, she'd taken to staying in at night. Arthur said he didn't know whether it was a flash in the pan, but he was prepared to give her a chance because of the children. He'd lost all love and respect for her, but the welfare of his children came first. When they were older, then he'd decide where his future lay.

Knowing all this, Eileen kept a smile on her face. 'Keepin' all right, are yer, Sylvia?'

'Bearing up, you know.' Sylvia was weighing the big woman up. She didn't like her, and never would. But she was afraid of showing it in case it got back to Arthur. Being stuck in the house every night was miserable enough, without having him on her back again. 'How's yerself?'

'Can't complain, yer know. D'yer come 'ere to do yer shoppin'?'

'Now and again.' Sylvia turned her head, offering no further information.

Eileen could feel the hostility. They had nothing in common and could never be friends in a month of Sundays. 'I'd better get back to me mate. It's been nice seein' yer again, Sylvia. Look after yerself, an' give my love to the boys, won't yer?'

Sylvia's thin lips curled. 'Oh, yeh, I will! Ta-ra, now!'

As Eileen turned, Sylvia couldn't resist the temptation. 'An' I won't forget to tell me 'usband I bumped into his fat friend.'

With as much dignity as she could muster, Eileen crossed the road to Mary.

Eileen sat on the end of the seat, her two arms around the big, heavy bag. 'She didn't want to know, but at least I tried.' She shifted uncomfortably on the seat, the cheek of her backside numb. 'They say marriages are made in 'eaven, but someone,

somewhere, didn't 'alf slip up when they matched Arthur with Sylvia, and Vera with Danny. It should 'ave been the other way round.'

'It should be Vera's turn for our Wednesday afternoon get-together,' Mary said. 'D'you think I should offer to have it at ours, again?'

'No, it'll be all right 'cos Danny's back at work. Anyway 'e seems to 'ave quietened down. He still doesn't speak to Vera, an' she's still sleepin' in Carol's room, but she said she can put up with that as long as 'e doesn't raise 'is 'and or 'is voice.'

'Is he still getting letters from Holland?' Mary waited for Eileen's nod, then said, 'If it was me, I'd be dying of curiosity to know who they were from.'

'He's a dark horse, is Danny,' Eileen said. 'Vera's searched the 'ouse for those letters and can't find a trace of them.' She leaned across Mary to peer out of the window. 'The next stop's mine.' She cursed the heavy bag as she struggled to her feet. 'I'll see yer on Wednesday at Vera's, kid. Ta-ra for now.'

'Ta-ra, Eileen.'

Mary pressed her face against the window, her hand raised to wave as Eileen passed, but her friend walked by without a glance. She looked so dejected, Mary felt angry with herself. It was that horrible man insulting her that had upset Eileen, and if Mary hadn't been so insistent on seeing what he was selling, it would never have happened.

Mary, shy and timid, would normally walk away from trouble. But right now she would willing have strangled the spiv who had upset her dearest friend.

* * *

'Ah, ray, Mam!' At first Joan thought her mother was pulling her leg, but when she realised it wasn't a joke, she was horrified. 'I'm not wearing that! All the girls in our class would make fun of me . . . and what about our Billy? He'd laugh 'is 'ead off.'

Eileen held the bra out. 'Unless yer intend takin' yer clothes off halfway through an 'istory lesson, or sittin' down to dinner in yer undies, 'ow the 'ell will anyone know yer've got it on?'

Joan turned to her nan for support, but to her surprise Maggie backed Eileen. 'You don't know how lucky you are, lass! When I was your age there was no such things as nice brassieres, like that. My mum had to wrap a binding around my chest to keep it flat.'

'I don't care what yez say, I'm not wearin' it!' Joan was near to tears, thinking of the taunts and sneers of her school mates. 'No one else in our class 'as one.'

'How d'yer know, sunshine?' Eileen had waited till young Billy had gone off with his friends, Edna was playing in the street, and Bill, having been let into the secret, had suddenly discovered he was out of ciggies. 'They might all be wearin' them for all you know.'

'If they're not, they won't half be jealous of you,' Maggie said. 'They're the latest thing, you know, and not everyone's mam is as thoughtful as yours.'

Maggie's words did the trick, and Joan started to view the wearing of a bra in a different light. She'd be the envy of all her mates. 'How d'yer put it on? Does it go over yer vest?'

'We'll go upstairs an' try it while there's no one in.' Eileen winked at her mother. 'Yer can try it with yer new gymslip an' blouse.'

Maggie watched them leave the room, Eileen with her arm around Joan's shoulder, and the older woman sighed deeply. Eileen might be able to fool everyone else, but not the woman who had given birth to her. And when Eileen was unhappy, then Maggie too was unhappy.

'You're not eating, chick.' Bill watched Eileen push a chip around her plate. 'Aren't you hungry?'

'We 'ad some chocolate while we were out, an' it's taken me appetite away,' Eileen lied. She was too miserable and upset to eat. All she could think of was the sneer on Sylvia's lips, and her words, 'my husband's fat friend'. Then the face of the spiv would appear, like a ghost to haunt her, telling her she needed to go to a parachute factory to buy a bra to fit her. If that was how strangers saw her, then that must be how Bill saw her, too.

Eileen was brought out of her reverie by Vera dashing into the room like a whirlwind. ''Ow the 'ell did you get in?'

'Your front door was open,' Vera said, breathlessly. 'Danny's gone!'

Eileen put her fork down and stared. 'How d'yer mean, gone?'

'He's left home.' Vera's hair was untidy, her face white, and her eyes red-rimmed. 'He just packed his bags and went.'

There was a stunned silence for a while, then Eileen said, 'Sit down, Vera, and calm down.'

'How can I calm down?' cried the distraught Vera. 'He's left me and the kids, and I don't know what we're going to do.'

'I'll make a cup of tea.' Maggie left the table to put the kettle on. A cup of tea was always Maggie's first thought in times of trouble.

'The first thing yer can do is pull yerself together.' Eileen groaned inwardly. Didn't she have enough troubles of her own right now, without falling over herself to help someone else? Then she felt ashamed. After all, Vera was a good friend. So in a softer voice, she said, 'Sit down an' tell us what brought this on?'

'Nothing brought it on! He just came down the stairs with his case packed, put some money on the table, and said he'd send more when he could. He told the boys he was going to Holland, and he'd write to them. Then he picked up his case and went.'

Bill was too surprised to speak, so he looked to Eileen to sympathise with Vera. But Eileen, sad as she was for her friend, couldn't summon her usual reserves of strength. 'I'd say good riddance to bad rubbish, if I were you, Vera. You an' the kids might get a bit of happiness out of life, now.'

Bill was stunned. He hadn't expected words like those from Eileen. They certainly were no comfort to Vera.

'I'm not worried about him going,' Vera said. 'I'm glad to see the back of him, and the boys are, too. But how am I going to manage?'

'By standin' on yer own two feet, that's 'ow,' Eileen said, briskly. 'Lots of women lost their 'usbands in the war, an' they've got to get on with it. You'll get by, don't worry.'

Vera started to cry. 'I don't see how I can get by without any money. What I get from the boys barely pays the rent.' She rubbed at her tears with the back of her hand. 'I can't see Danny sending me anything, 'cos he must have someone in Holland.'

Eileen folded her arms on the table and stared at Vera. She felt like crying for her friend, and herself. There was more than one way of losing a husband. But tears right now weren't going to solve anything. 'You could get yerself a little job.' When Vera shook her head, Eileen went on, 'Milly Knight was sayin' the other day that she needed a cleaner for a few hours a day. That would suit yer fine, 'cos Milly wouldn't mind yer takin' Carol with yer. The wage wouldn't be much, but at least it'd 'elp yer get by.'

Vera sniffed loudly. 'D'you think she'd have me?'

'I'm sure she would,' Eileen said. 'But the only way to find out is to go an' ask. Do it now . . . strike while the iron's hot.'

'Will you come with me?'

'No, Vera, you go by yerself. You're not a child, yer don't need me to 'old yer 'and.'

Bill listened in silence, while Maggie stood inside the kitchen door, the teapot in her hand, wondering what had got into her daughter. It wouldn't hurt her to go with Vera to see Milly.

Vera stood up, a look of uncertainty on her face. She patted her hair, wiped her eyes, and straightened her back. 'I'll go up now, then, and I'll let you know how I get on.'

'Tell Milly I sent yer, an' yer'll be all right,' Eileen called after her. 'She's a good scout, is Milly.'

'That wasn't very nice, chick,' Bill said. 'The least you could have done was to go up to Milly's with her.'

Maggie chipped in with her piece. 'What's got into you? Got a bee in your bonnet, have you?'

Eileen stared at her hands, flexing her fingers. 'I can't live Vera's life for 'er. She's got to learn to stand on 'er own two feet sometime, so she may as well start now.'

Bill shook his head. He'd never known Eileen like this before. She was usually the first to run to help someone. 'The poor woman was distraught, and you could have done more to help.'

That did it! The chair went crashing to the floor as Eileen jumped to her feet. The bottled-up pain and frustration of the last year, fuelled by the hurtful insults that day, broke to the surface. 'What the bloody 'ell d'yez think I am? A bloody miracle worker who sorts everyone's troubles out for them? Oh, yeah, good old Eileen! Always there when yer need help, or a shoulder to cry on.' Her face red with the injustice of it all, she placed her hands on the table, leaned forward, and let her eyes travel from her mother to Bill. 'But what about me? Who the 'ell can I run to for help? Shall I tell yez . . . no one! But then, I'm not supposed to 'ave any worries, am I? I'm supposed to be too busy sortin' other people out. Well, let me tell yez, I've had it up to 'ere.' Eileen patted the top of her head. 'I'm through . . . I've 'ad enough.' With that she fled from the room, leaving Bill and Maggie with their eyes wide and their mouths gaping.

'Go after her, Bill,' Maggie said. 'I've never seen our Eileen like this, she's in a right state.'

Bill took the stairs two at a time. He entered the bedroom to find Eileen struggling into her coat. 'Where d'you think you're going?'

'What do you care? You're too busy thinkin' of other people to worry about me. But as I said, I've 'ad enough, an' I'm off.'

'What d'you mean, you're off? Off where?'

'What does it matter? You don't need me!' Tears weren't far away, but by sheer willpower, Eileen kept them at bay.

'Any woman would do for what you need . . . just someone to keep yer 'ouse clean, look after the kids, and cook yer meals.'

Bill's surprise turned to anger, and within seconds they were hurling insults at each other across the room. Both saying things that shouldn't be said, hurting each other in the temper of the moment. As their shouting grew louder, it flashed through Eileen's mind that her mother would be able to hear every word, but she was past caring. 'You don't love me,' she screamed, 'but you 'aven't got the guts to be honest and tell me. I know I'm too fat, but that doesn't mean I don't have any feelings, that I don't hurt.'

Bill's anger exploded. 'What the hell are you talking about? Have you gone crazy?'

'I'm crazy for puttin' up with the way you treat me, yes! 'Cos it's not a wife you want, it's a mother, or a sister. As long as yer kept nice an' comfortable, you couldn't care less! But I'll tell yer this for nothin', Bill Gillmoss, it's not a brother I want, it's a husband . . . a man!'

Bill caught his breath. The insult had cut him like a knife. Then suddenly he realised his whole body was growing taut. 'So I'm not a man, is that what you're saying?'

Eileen hung her head. She should never have said what she did, she could have bitten her tongue out. She wouldn't hurt him for the world, but it had come out in anger.

Bill mistook Eileen's silence for confirmation. 'So, I'm not a man, eh?' With a strength he didn't know he possessed, Bill picked Eileen up and threw her, without ceremony, on the bed. Then he strode to the door and banged it so hard it nearly came off its hinges. As the room vibrated with the sound, Bill stood for a few seconds to savour the feeling of excitement coursing through his body, and control the smile threatening to light up his face. He turned and walked to the bed, undoing the buttons on his trousers.

'I'll show you whether I'm a man or not, Eileen Gillmoss!'

Try a Little Tenderness

Joan Jonker

Jenny and Laura Nightingale are as different as chalk and cheese. Jenny's pretty face and lively sense of humour make her everyone's favourite girl, whereas Laura is spoilt and moody and never out of trouble. Their mother, Mary, loves them both but she's more worried about her father's new wife, Celia, who is about to bring shame on the family . . .

Then Jenny attracts the attention of two young lads in the street who both want to court her. Mick and John have been mates since they were kids but now war is declared and it's every man for himself! Meanwhile, Laura's resentment begins to build and it's only a matter of time before things come to a head. Who will learn that a little tenderness goes a long way?

'A hilarious but touching story of life in Liverpool' *Woman's Realm*

'You can rely on Joan to give her readers hilarity and pathos in equal measure and she's achieved it again in this tale' *Liverpool Echo*

'Packed with lively, sympathetic characters and a wealth of emotions' *Bolton Evening News*

0 7472 6110 5

headline

Stay as Sweet as You Are

Joan Jonker

With the face of an angel and a sunny nature, Lucy Mellor is a daughter who'd make any parents proud. But her ever ready smile masks a dark secret. For while her friends are kissed and hugged by their mothers, Lucy only knows cruelty from the woman who brought her into the world. Her father, Bob, tries to protect her, but he is no match for a wife who has no love for him or his beloved daughter.

The Walls of their two-up two-down house are thin and Ruby Mellor's angry outbursts can be heard by their neighbours. One day, Irene Pollard, from next door, decides she can no longer stand back, so she and her friends take Lucy under their wing. But sadness remains in Lucy's heart because, despite everything, she still craves a mother's love . . .

'Hilarious but touching' *Woman's Realm*

'You can rely on Joan to give her readers hilarity and pathos in equal measure and she's achieved it again in this tale' *Liverpool Echo*

'Packed with lively, sympathetic characters and a wealth of emotions' *Bolton Evening News*

0 7472 6111 3

headline